The Octopus
A Story Of California
Book I

by

Frank Norris

Double9
BOOKS

The octopus
A story of california
Book I
by Frank Norris

ISBN: 978-93-64288-18-7

Published by

DOUBLE 9 BOOKS

2/13-B, Ansari Road
Daryaganj, New Delhi – 110002
info@double9books.com
www.double9books.com
Tel. 011-40042856

This book is under public domain

ABOUT THE AUTHOR

Frank Norris (1870-1902) was an American novelist and journalist known for his realistic and naturalistic writing style. He was born in Chicago, Illinois, and raised in a family with a strong literary background. Norris studied at the University of California, Berkeley, and later attended Harvard University. Norris is best remembered for his novels that depicted the social issues and struggles of his time. His most notable work is "The Octopus: A Story of California" (1901), a sprawling epic that explores the conflicts between wheat farmers and the powerful railroad monopolies in California. The novel is considered a classic of American literature and is often associated with the naturalist literary movement. Tragically, Norris's writing career was cut short when he died at the age of 32 due to complications from appendicitis. Despite his short life, he left a lasting impact on American literature, influencing later writers such as Upton Sinclair and Theodore Dreiser. His works continue to be celebrated for their realism, vivid portrayals of the human condition, and insightful social commentary.

CONTENTS

CHAPTER I

Just after passing Caraher's saloon, on the County Road that ran south from Bonneville, and that divided the Broderson ranch from that of Los Muertos, Presley was suddenly aware of the faint and prolonged blowing of a steam whistle that he knew must come from the railroad shops near the depot at Bonneville. In starting out from the ranch house that morning, he had forgotten his watch, and was now perplexed to know whether the whistle was blowing for twelve or for one o'clock. He hoped the former. Early that morning he had decided to make a long excursion through the neighbouring country, partly on foot and partly on his bicycle, and now noon was come already, and as yet he had hardly started. As he was leaving the house after breakfast, Mrs. Derrick had asked him to go for the mail at Bonneville, and he had not been able to refuse.

He took a firmer hold of the cork grips of his handlebars—the road being in a wretched condition after the recent hauling of the crop—and quickened his pace. He told himself that, no matter what the time was, he would not stop for luncheon at the ranch house, but would push on to Guadalajara and have a Spanish dinner at Solotari's, as he had originally planned.

There had not been much of a crop to haul that year. Half of the wheat on the Broderson ranch had failed entirely, and Derrick himself had hardly raised more than enough to supply seed for the winter's sowing. But such little hauling as there had been had reduced the roads thereabouts to a lamentable condition, and, during the dry season of the past few months, the layer of dust had deepened and thickened to such an extent that more than once Presley was obliged to dismount and trudge along on foot, pushing his bicycle in front of him.

It was the last half of September, the very end of the dry season, and all Tulare County, all the vast reaches of the San Joaquin Valley—in fact all South Central California, was bone dry, parched, and baked and crisped after four months of cloudless weather, when the day seemed always at noon, and the sun blazed white hot over the valley from the Coast Range in the west to the foothills of the Sierras in the east.

As Presley drew near to the point where what was known as the Lower Road struck off through the Rancho de Los Muertos, leading on to Guadalajara, he came upon one of the county watering-tanks, a great, iron-hooped tower of wood, straddling clumsily on its four uprights by the roadside. Since the day of its completion, the storekeepers and retailers of Bonneville had painted their advertisements upon it. It was a landmark. In that reach of level fields, the white letters upon it could be read for miles. A watering-trough stood near by, and, as he was very thirsty, Presley resolved to stop for a moment to get a drink.

He drew abreast of the tank and halted there, leaning his bicycle against the fence. A couple of men in white overalls were repainting the surface of the tank, seated on swinging platforms that hung by hooks from the roof. They were painting a sign—an advertisement. It was all but finished and read, "S. Behrman, Real Estate, Mortgages, Main Street, Bonneville, Opposite the Post Office." On the horse-trough that stood in the shadow of the tank was another freshly painted inscription: "S. Behrman Has Something To Say To You."

As Presley straightened up after drinking from the faucet at one end of the horse-trough, the watering-cart itself laboured into view around the turn of the Lower Road. Two mules and two horses, white with dust, strained leisurely in the traces, moving at a snail's pace, their limp ears marking the time; while perched high upon the seat, under a yellow cotton wagon umbrella, Presley recognised Hooven, one of Derrick's tenants, a German, whom every one called "Bismarck," an excitable little man with a perpetual grievance and an endless flow of broken English.

"Hello, Bismarck," said Presley, as Hooven brought his team to a standstill by the tank, preparatory to refilling.

"Yoost der men I look for, Mist'r Praicely," cried the other, twisting the reins around the brake. "Yoost one minute, you wait, hey? I wanta talk mit you."

Presley was impatient to be on his way again. A little more time wasted, and the day would be lost. He had nothing to do with the management of the ranch, and if Hooven wanted any advice from him, it was so much breath wasted. These uncouth brutes of farmhands and petty ranchers, grimed with the soil they worked upon, were odious to him beyond words. Never could he feel in sympathy with them, nor with their lives, their ways, their marriages, deaths, bickerings, and all the monotonous round of their sordid existence.

"Well, you must be quick about it, Bismarck," he answered sharply. "I'm late for dinner, as it is."

"Soh, now. Two minuten, und I be mit you." He drew down the overhanging spout of the tank to the vent in the circumference of the cart and pulled the chain that let out the water. Then he climbed down from the seat, jumping from the tire of the wheel, and taking Presley by the arm led him a few steps down the road.

"Say," he began. "Say, I want to hef some converzations mit you. Yoost der men I want to see. Say, Caraher, he tole me dis morgen—say, he tole me Mist'r Derrick gowun to farm der whole demn rench hisseluf der next yahr. No more tenants. Say, Caraher, he tole me all der tenants get der sach; Mist'r Derrick gowun to work der whole demn rench hisseluf, hey? ME, I get der sach alzoh, hey? You hef hear about dose ting? Say, me, I hef on der ranch been sieben yahr—seven yahr. Do I alzoh——"

"You'll have to see Derrick himself or Harran about that, Bismarck," interrupted Presley, trying to draw away. "That's something outside of me entirely."

But Hooven was not to be put off. No doubt he had been meditating his speech all the morning, formulating his words, preparing his phrases.

"Say, no, no," he continued. "Me, I wanta stay bei der place; seven yahr I hef stay. Mist'r Derrick, he doand want dot I should be ge-sacked. Who, den, will der ditch ge-tend? Say, you tell 'um Bismarck hef gotta sure stay bei der place. Say, you hef der pull mit der Governor. You speak der gut word for me."

"Harran is the man that has the pull with his father, Bismarck," answered Presley. "You get Harran to speak for you, and you're all right."

"Sieben yahr I hef stay," protested Hooven, "and who will der ditch ge-tend, und alle dem cettles drive?"

"Well, Harran's your man," answered Presley, preparing to mount his bicycle.

"Say, you hef hear about dose ting?"

"I don't hear about anything, Bismarck. I don't know the first thing about how the ranch is run."

"UND DER PIPE-LINE GE-MEND," Hooven burst out, suddenly remembering a forgotten argument. He waved an arm. "Ach, der pipe-line bei der Mission Greek, und der waater-hole for dose cettles. Say, he doand doo ut HIMSELLUF, berhaps, I doand tink."

"Well, talk to Harran about it."

"Say, he doand farm der whole demn rench bei hisseluf. Me, I gotta stay."

But on a sudden the water in the cart gushed over the sides from the vent in the top with a smart sound of splashing. Hooven was forced to turn his attention to it. Presley got his wheel under way.

"I hef some converzations mit Herran," Hooven called after him. "He doand doo ut bei hisseluf, den, Mist'r Derrick; ach, no. I stay bei der rench to drive dose cettles."

He climbed back to his seat under the wagon umbrella, and, as he started his team again with great cracks of his long whip, turned to the painters still at work upon the sign and declared with some defiance:

"Sieben yahr; yais, sir, seiben yahr I hef been on dis rench. Git oop, you mule you, hoop!"

Meanwhile Presley had turned into the Lower Road. He was now on Derrick's land, division No. I, or, as it was called, the Home ranch, of the great Los Muertos Rancho. The road was better here, the dust laid after the passage of Hooven's watering-cart, and, in a few minutes, he had come to the ranch house itself, with its white picket fence, its few flower beds, and grove of eucalyptus trees. On the lawn at the side of the house, he saw Harran in the act of setting out the automatic sprinkler. In the shade of the house, by the porch, were two or three of the greyhounds, part of the pack that were used to hunt down jack-rabbits, and Godfrey, Harran's prize deerhound.

Presley wheeled up the driveway and met Harran by the horse-block. Harran was Magnus Derrick's youngest son, a very well-looking young fellow of twenty-three or twenty-five. He had the fine carriage that marked his father, and still further resembled him in that he had the Derrick nose— hawk-like and prominent, such as one sees in the later portraits of the Duke of Wellington. He was blond, and incessant exposure to the sun had, instead of tanning him brown, merely heightened the colour of his cheeks. His yellow hair had a tendency to curl in a forward direction, just in front of the ears.

Beside him, Presley made the sharpest of contrasts. Presley seemed to have come of a mixed origin; appeared to have a nature more composite, a temperament more complex. Unlike Harran Derrick, he seemed more of a character than a type. The sun had browned his face till it was almost swarthy. His eyes were a dark brown, and his forehead was the forehead of the intellectual, wide and high, with a certain unmistakable lift about it that argued education, not only of himself, but of his people before him. The impression conveyed by his mouth and chin was that of a delicate and highly sensitive nature, the lips thin and loosely shut together, the chin small and rather receding. One guessed that Presley's refinement had been gained only by a certain loss of strength. One expected to find him nervous, introspective, to discover that his mental life was not at all the result of impressions and sensations that came to him from without, but rather of thoughts and reflections germinating from within. Though morbidly sensitive to changes in his physical surroundings, he would be slow to act upon such sensations, would not prove impulsive, not because he was sluggish, but because he was merely irresolute. It could be foreseen that morally he was of that sort who avoid evil through good taste, lack of decision, and want of opportunity. His temperament was that of the poet; when he told himself he had been thinking, he deceived himself. He had, on such occasions, been only brooding.

Some eighteen months before this time, he had been threatened with consumption, and, taking advantage of a standing invitation on the part of Magnus Derrick, had come to stay in the dry, even climate of the San Joaquin for an indefinite length of time. He was thirty years old, and had graduated and post-graduated with high honours from an Eastern college, where he had devoted himself to a passionate study of literature, and, more especially, of poetry.

It was his insatiable ambition to write verse. But up to this time, his work had been fugitive, ephemeral, a note here and there, heard, appreciated, and forgotten. He was in search of a subject; something magnificent, he did not know exactly what; some vast, tremendous theme, heroic, terrible, to be unrolled in all the thundering progression of hexameters.

But whatever he wrote, and in whatever fashion, Presley was determined that his poem should be of the West, that world's frontier of Romance, where a new race, a new people—hardy, brave, and passionate— were building an empire; where the tumultuous life ran like fire from dawn to dark, and from dark to dawn again, primitive, brutal, honest, and without fear. Something (to his idea not much) had been done to catch at that life in passing, but its poet had not yet arisen. The few sporadic attempts, thus he told himself, had only touched the keynote. He strove for the diapason, the great song that should embrace in itself a whole epoch, a complete era, the voice of an entire people, wherein all people should be included—they and their legends, their folk lore, their fightings, their loves and their lusts, their blunt, grim humour, their stoicism under stress, their adventures, their treasures found in a day and gambled in a night, their direct, crude speech, their generosity and cruelty, their heroism and bestiality, their religion and profanity, their self-sacrifice and obscenity—a true and fearless setting forth of a passing phase of history, un-compromising, sincere; each group in its proper environment; the valley, the plain, and the mountain; the ranch, the range, and the mine—all this, all the traits and types of every community from the Dakotas to the Mexicos, from Winnipeg to Guadalupe, gathered together, swept together, welded and riven together in one single, mighty song, the Song of the West. That was what he dreamed, while things without names—thoughts for which no man had yet invented words, terrible formless shapes, vague figures, colossal, monstrous, distorted—whirled at a gallop through his imagination.

As Harran came up, Presley reached down into the pouches of the sun-bleached shooting coat he wore and drew out and handed him the packet of letters and papers.

"Here's the mail. I think I shall go on."

"But dinner is ready," said Harran; "we are just sitting down."

Presley shook his head. "No, I'm in a hurry. Perhaps I shall have something to eat at Guadalajara. I shall be gone all day."

He delayed a few moments longer, tightening a loose nut on his forward wheel, while Harran, recognising his father's handwriting on one of the envelopes, slit it open and cast his eye rapidly over its pages.

"The Governor is coming home," he exclaimed, "to-morrow morning on the early train; wants me to meet him with the team at Guadalajara; AND," he cried between his clenched teeth, as he continued to read, "we've lost the case."

"What case? Oh, in the matter of rates?"

Harran nodded, his eyes flashing, his face growing suddenly scarlet.

"Ulsteen gave his decision yesterday," he continued, reading from his father's letter. "He holds, Ulsteen does, that 'grain rates as low as the new figure would amount to confiscation of property, and that, on such a basis, the railroad could not be operated at a legitimate profit. As he is powerless to legislate in the matter, he can only put the rates back at what they originally were before the commissioners made the cut, and it is so ordered.' That's our friend S. Behrman again," added Harran, grinding his teeth. "He was up in the city the whole of the time the new schedule was being drawn, and he and Ulsteen and the Railroad Commission were as thick as thieves. He has been up there all this last week, too, doing the railroad's dirty work, and backing Ulsteen up. 'Legitimate profit, legitimate profit,'" he broke out. "Can we raise wheat at a legitimate profit with a tariff of four dollars a ton for moving it two hundred miles to tide-water, with wheat at eighty-seven cents? Why not hold us up with a gun in our faces, and say, 'hands up,' and be done with it?"

He dug his boot-heel into the ground and turned away to the house abruptly, cursing beneath his breath.

"By the way," Presley called after him, "Hooven wants to see you. He asked me about this idea of the Governor's of getting along without the tenants this year. Hooven wants to stay to tend the ditch and look after the stock. I told him to see you."

Harran, his mind full of other things, nodded to say he understood. Presley only waited till he had disappeared indoors, so that he might not seem too indifferent to his trouble; then, remounting, struck at once into a brisk pace, and, turning out from the carriage gate, held on swiftly down the Lower Road, going in the direction of Guadalajara. These matters, these eternal fierce bickerings between the farmers of the San Joaquin and the Pacific and Southwestern Railroad irritated him and wearied him. He cared for none of these things. They did not belong to his world. In the picture of that huge romantic West that he saw in his imagination, these dissensions made the one note of harsh colour that refused to enter into the great scheme of harmony. It was material, sordid, deadly commonplace. But, however he strove to shut his eyes to it or his ears to it, the thing persisted and persisted. The romance seemed complete up to that point. There it broke, there it failed, there it became realism, grim, unlovely, unyielding. To be true— and it was the first article of his creed to be unflinchingly true—he could not ignore it. All the noble poetry of the ranch—the valley—seemed in his mind to be marred and disfigured by the presence of certain immovable facts. Just what he wanted, Presley hardly knew. On one hand, it was his ambition to portray life as he saw it—directly, frankly, and through no medium of personality or temperament. But, on the other hand, as well, he wished to see everything through a rose-coloured mist—a mist that dulled all harsh outlines, all crude and violent colours. He told himself that, as a part of the people, he loved the people and sympathised with their hopes and fears, and joys and griefs; and yet Hooven, grimy and perspiring, with his perpetual grievance and his contracted horizon, only revolted him. He had set himself the task of giving true, absolutely true, poetical expression to the life of the ranch, and yet, again and again, he brought up against the railroad, that stubborn iron barrier against which his romance shattered itself to froth and disintegrated, flying spume. His heart went out to the people, and his groping hand met that of a slovenly little Dutchman, whom it was impossible to consider seriously. He searched for the True Romance, and, in the end, found grain rates and unjust freight tariffs.

"But the stuff is HERE," he muttered, as he sent his wheel rumbling across the bridge over Broderson Creek. "The romance, the real romance, is here somewhere. I'll get hold of it yet."

He shot a glance about him as if in search of the inspiration. By now he was not quite half way across the northern and narrowest corner of Los Muertos, at this point some eight miles wide. He was still on the Home ranch. A few miles to the south he could just make out the line of wire fence that separated it from the third division; and to the north, seen faint and blue through the haze and shimmer of the noon sun, a long file of telegraph poles showed the line of the railroad and marked Derrick's northeast boundary. The road over which Presley was travelling ran almost diametrically straight. In front of him, but at a great distance, he could make out the giant live-oak and the red roof of Hooven's barn that stood near it.

All about him the country was flat. In all directions he could see for miles. The harvest was just over. Nothing but stubble remained on the ground. With the one exception of the live-oak by Hooven's place, there was nothing green in sight. The wheat stubble was of a dirty yellow; the ground, parched, cracked, and dry, of a cheerless brown. By the roadside the dust lay thick and grey, and, on either hand, stretching on toward the horizon, losing itself in a mere smudge in the distance, ran the illimitable parallels of the wire fence. And that was all; that and the burnt-out blue of the sky and the steady shimmer of the heat.

The silence was infinite. After the harvest, small though that harvest had been, the ranches seemed asleep. It was as though the earth, after its period of reproduction, its pains of labour, had been delivered of the fruit of its loins, and now slept the sleep of exhaustion.

It was the period between seasons, when nothing was being done, when the natural forces seemed to hang suspended. There was no rain, there was no wind, there was no growth, no life; the very stubble had no force even to rot. The sun alone moved.

Toward two o'clock, Presley reached Hooven's place, two or three grimy frame buildings, infested with a swarm of dogs. A hog or two wandered aimlessly about. Under a shed by the barn, a broken-down seeder lay rusting to its ruin. But overhead, a mammoth live-oak, the largest tree in all the country-side, towered superb and magnificent. Grey bunches of mistletoe and festoons of trailing moss hung from its bark. From its lowest branch hung Hooven's meat-safe, a square box, faced with wire screens.

What gave a special interest to Hooven's was the fact that here was the intersection of the Lower Road and Derrick's main irrigating ditch, a vast trench not yet completed, which he and Annixter, who worked the Quien Sabe ranch, were jointly constructing. It ran directly across the road and at right angles to it, and lay a deep groove in the field between Hooven's and the town of Guadalajara, some three miles farther on. Besides this, the ditch was a natural boundary between two divisions of the Los Muertos ranch, the first and fourth.

Presley now had the choice of two routes. His objective point was the spring at the headwaters of Broderson Creek, in the hills on the eastern side of the Quien Sabe ranch. The trail afforded him a short cut thitherward. As he passed the house, Mrs. Hooven came to the door, her little daughter Hilda, dressed in a boy's overalls and clumsy boots, at her skirts. Minna, her oldest daughter, a very pretty girl, whose love affairs were continually the talk of all Los Muertos, was visible through a window of the house, busy at the week's washing. Mrs. Hooven was a faded, colourless woman, middle-aged and commonplace, and offering not the least characteristic that would distinguish her from a thousand other women of her class and kind. She nodded to Presley, watching him with a stolid gaze from under her arm, which she held across her forehead to shade her eyes.

But now Presley exerted himself in good earnest. His bicycle flew. He resolved that after all he would go to Guadalajara. He crossed the bridge over the irrigating ditch with a brusque spurt of hollow sound, and shot forward down the last stretch of the Lower Road that yet intervened between Hooven's and the town. He was on the fourth division of the ranch now, the only one whereon the wheat had been successful, no doubt because of the Little Mission Creek that ran through it. But he no longer occupied himself with the landscape. His only concern was to get on as fast as possible. He had looked forward to spending nearly the whole day on the crest of the wooded hills in the northern corner of the Quien Sabe ranch, reading, idling, smoking his pipe. But now he would do well if he arrived there by the middle of the afternoon. In a few moments he had reached the line fence that marked the limits of the ranch. Here were the railroad tracks, and just beyond—a huddled mass of roofs, with here and there an adobe house on its outskirts—the little town of Guadalajara. Nearer at hand, and directly in front of Presley, were the freight and passenger depots of the P. and S. W., painted in the grey and white, which seemed to be the official colours of all the buildings owned by the corporation. The station was deserted. No trains passed at this hour. From the direction of the ticket window, Presley heard the unsteady chittering of the telegraph key. In the shadow of one of the baggage trucks upon the platform, the great yellow cat that belonged to the agent dozed complacently, her paws tucked under her body. Three flat cars, loaded with bright-painted farming machines, were on the siding above the station, while, on the switch below, a huge freight engine that lacked its cow-catcher sat back upon its monstrous driving-wheels, motionless, solid, drawing long breaths that were punctuated by the subdued sound of its steam-pump clicking at exact intervals.

But evidently it had been decreed that Presley should be stopped at every point of his ride that day, for, as he was pushing his bicycle across the tracks, he was surprised to hear his name called. "Hello, there, Mr. Presley. What's the good word?"

Presley looked up quickly, and saw Dyke, the engineer, leaning on his folded arms from the cab window of the freight engine. But at the prospect of this further delay, Presley was less troubled. Dyke and he were well acquainted and the best of friends. The picturesqueness of the engineer's life was always attractive to Presley, and more than once he had ridden on Dyke's engine between Guadalajara and Bonneville. Once, even, he had made the entire run between the latter town and San Francisco in the cab.

Dyke's home was in Guadalajara. He lived in one of the remodelled 'dobe cottages, where his mother kept house for him. His wife had died some five years before this time, leaving him a little daughter, Sidney, to bring up as best he could. Dyke himself was a heavy built, well-looking fellow, nearly twice the weight of Presley, with great shoulders and massive, hairy arms, and a tremendous, rumbling voice.

"Hello, old man," answered Presley, coming up to the engine. "What are you doing about here at this time of day? I thought you were on the night service this month."

"We've changed about a bit," answered the other. "Come up here and sit down, and get out of the sun. They've held us here to wait orders," he explained, as Presley, after leaning his bicycle against the tender, climbed to the fireman's seat of worn green leather. "They are changing the run of one of the crack passenger engines down below, and are sending her up to Fresno. There was a smash of some kind on the Bakersfield division, and she's to hell and gone behind her time. I suppose when she comes, she'll come a-humming. It will be stand clear and an open track all the way to Fresno. They have held me here to let her go by."

He took his pipe, an old T. D. clay, but coloured to a beautiful shiny black, from the pocket of his jumper and filled and lit it.

"Well, I don't suppose you object to being held here," observed Presley. "Gives you a chance to visit your mother and the little girl."

"And precisely they choose this day to go up to Sacramento," answered Dyke. "Just my luck. Went up to visit my brother's people. By the way, my brother may come down here—locate here, I mean—and go into the hop-raising business. He's got an option on five hundred acres just back of the town here. He says there is going to be money in hops. I don't know; may be I'll go in with him."

"Why, what's the matter with railroading?"

Dyke drew a couple of puffs on his pipe, and fixed Presley with a glance.

"There's this the matter with it," he said; "I'm fired."

"Fired! You!" exclaimed Presley, turning abruptly toward him. "That's what I'm telling you," returned Dyke grimly.

"You don't mean it. Why, what for, Dyke?"

"Now, YOU tell me what for," growled the other savagely. "Boy and man, I've worked for the P. and S. W. for over ten years, and never one yelp of a complaint did I ever hear from them. They know damn well they've not got a steadier man on the road. And more than that, more than that, I don't belong to the Brotherhood. And when the strike came along, I stood by them—stood by the company. You know that. And you know, and they know, that at Sacramento that time, I ran my train according to schedule, with a gun in each hand, never knowing when I was going over a mined culvert, and there was talk of giving me a gold watch at the time. To hell with their gold watches! I want ordinary justice and fair treatment. And now, when hard times come along, and they are cutting wages, what do they do? Do they make any discrimination in my case? Do they remember the man that stood by them and risked his life in their service? No. They cut my pay down just as off-hand as they do the pay of any dirty little wiper in the yard. Cut me along with—listen to this—cut me along with men that they had BLACK-LISTED; strikers that they took back because they were short of hands." He drew fiercely on his pipe. "I went to them, yes, I did; I went to the General Office, and ate dirt. I told them I was a family man, and that I didn't see how I was going to get along on the new scale, and I reminded them of my service during the strike. The swine told me that it wouldn't be fair to discriminate in favour of one man, and that the cut must apply to all their employees alike. Fair!" he shouted with laughter. "Fair! Hear the P. and S. W. talking about fairness and discrimination. That's good, that is. Well, I got furious. I was a fool, I suppose. I told them that, in justice to myself, I wouldn't do first-class work for third-class pay. And they said, 'Well, Mr. Dyke, you know what you can do.' Well, I did know. I said, 'I'll ask for my time, if you please,' and they gave it to me just as if they were glad to be shut of me. So there you are, Presley. That's the P. & S. W. Railroad Company of California. I am on my last run now."

"Shameful," declared Presley, his sympathies all aroused, now that the trouble concerned a friend of his. "It's shameful, Dyke. But," he added, an idea occurring to him, "that don't shut you out from work. There are other railroads in the State that are not controlled by the P. and S. W."

Dyke smote his knee with his clenched fist.

"NAME ONE."

Presley was silent. Dyke's challenge was unanswerable. There was a lapse in their talk, Presley drumming on the arm of the seat, meditating on this injustice; Dyke looking off over the fields beyond the town, his frown lowering, his teeth rasping upon his pipestem. The station agent came to the door of the depot, stretching and yawning. On ahead of the engine, the empty rails of the track, reaching out toward the horizon, threw off visible layers of heat. The telegraph key clicked incessantly.

"So I'm going to quit," Dyke remarked after a while, his anger somewhat subsided. "My brother and I will take up this hop ranch. I've saved a good deal in the last ten years, and there ought to be money in hops."

Presley went on, remounting his bicycle, wheeling silently through the deserted streets of the decayed and dying Mexican town. It was the hour of the siesta. Nobody was about. There was no business in the town. It was too close to Bonneville for that. Before the railroad came, and in the days when the raising of cattle was the great industry of the country, it had enjoyed a fierce and brilliant life. Now it was moribund. The drug store, the two bar-rooms, the hotel at the corner of the old Plaza, and the shops where Mexican "curios" were sold to those occasional Eastern tourists who came to visit the Mission of San Juan, sufficed for the town's activity.

At Solotari's, the restaurant on the Plaza, diagonally across from the hotel, Presley ate his long-deferred Mexican dinner—an omelette in Spanish-Mexican style, frijoles and tortillas, a salad, and a glass of white wine. In a corner of the room, during the whole course of his dinner, two young Mexicans (one of whom was astonishingly handsome, after the melodramatic fashion of his race) and an old fellow! the centenarian of the town, decrepit beyond belief, sang an interminable love-song to the accompaniment of a guitar and an accordion.

These Spanish-Mexicans, decayed, picturesque, vicious, and romantic, never failed to interest Presley. A few of them still remained in Guadalajara, drifting from the saloon to the restaurant, and from the restaurant to the Plaza, relics of a former generation, standing for a different order of things, absolutely idle, living God knew how, happy with their cigarette, their guitar, their glass of mescal, and their siesta. The centenarian remembered Fremont and Governor Alvarado, and the bandit Jesus Tejeda, and the days when Los Muertos was a Spanish grant, a veritable principality, leagues in extent, and when there was never a fence from Visalia to Fresno. Upon this occasion, Presley offered the old man a drink of mescal, and excited him to talk of the things he remembered. Their talk was in Spanish, a language with which Presley was familiar.

"De La Cuesta held the grant of Los Muertos in those days," the centenarian said; "a grand man. He had the power of life and death over his people, and there was no law but his word. There was no thought of wheat then, you may believe. It was all cattle in those days, sheep, horses—steers, not so many—and if money was scarce, there was always plenty to eat, and clothes enough for all, and wine, ah, yes, by the vat, and oil too; the Mission Fathers had that. Yes, and there was wheat as well, now that I come to think; but a very little—in the field north of the Mission where now it is the Seed ranch; wheat fields were there, and also a vineyard, all on Mission grounds. Wheat, olives, and the vine; the Fathers planted those, to provide the elements of the Holy Sacrament—bread, oil, and wine, you understand. It was like that, those industries began in California—from the Church; and now," he put his chin in the air, "what would Father Ullivari have said to such a crop as Senor Derrick plants these days? Ten thousand acres of wheat! Nothing but wheat from the Sierra to the Coast Range. I remember when De La Cuesta was married. He had never seen the young lady, only her miniature portrait, painted"—he raised a shoulder—"I do not know by whom, small, a little thing to be held in the palm. But he fell in love with that, and marry her he would. The affair was arranged between him and the girl's parents. But when the time came that De La Cuesta was to go to Monterey to meet and marry the girl, behold, Jesus Tejeda broke in upon the small rancheros near Terrabella. It was no time for De La Cuesta to be away, so he sent his brother Esteban to Monterey to marry the girl by proxy for him. I went with Esteban. We were a company, nearly a hundred men. And De La Cuesta sent a horse for the girl to ride, white, pure white; and the saddle was of red leather; the head-stall, the bit, and buckles, all the metal work, of virgin silver. Well, there was a ceremony in the Monterey Mission, and Esteban, in the name of his brother, was married to the girl. On our way back, De La Cuesta rode out to meet us. His company met ours at Agatha dos Palos. Never will I forget De La Cuesta's face as his eyes fell upon the girl. It was a look, a glance, come and gone like THAT," he snapped his fingers. "No one but I saw it, but I was close by. There was no mistaking that look. De La Cuesta was disappointed."

"And the girl?" demanded Presley.

"She never knew. Ah, he was a grand gentleman, De La Cuesta. Always he treated her as a queen. Never was husband more devoted, more respectful, more chivalrous. But love?" The old fellow put his chin in the air, shutting his eyes in a knowing fashion. "It was not there. I could tell. They were married over again at the Mission San Juan de Guadalajara—OUR Mission—and for a week all the town of Guadalajara was in fete. There were bull-fights in the Plaza—this very one—for five days, and to each of his tenants-in-chief, De La Cuesta gave a horse, a barrel of tallow, an ounce of silver, and half an ounce of gold dust. Ah, those were days. That was a gay life. This"—he made a comprehensive gesture with his left hand—"this is stupid."

"You may well say that," observed Presley moodily, discouraged by the other's talk. All his doubts and uncertainty had returned to him. Never would he grasp the subject of his great poem. To-day, the life was colourless. Romance was dead. He had lived too late. To write of the past was not what he desired. Reality was what he longed for, things that he had seen. Yet how to make this compatible with romance. He rose, putting on his hat, offering the old man a cigarette. The centenarian accepted with the air of a grandee, and extended his horn snuff-box. Presley shook his head.

"I was born too late for that," he declared, "for that, and for many other things. Adios."

"You are travelling to-day, senor?"

"A little turn through the country, to get the kinks out of the muscles," Presley answered. "I go up into the Quien Sabe, into the high country beyond the Mission."

"Ah, the Quien Sabe rancho. The sheep are grazing there this week."

Solotari, the keeper of the restaurant, explained:

"Young Annixter sold his wheat stubble on the ground to the sheep raisers off yonder;" he motioned eastward toward the Sierra foothills. "Since Sunday the herd has been down. Very clever, that young Annixter. He gets a price for his stubble, which else he would have to burn, and also manures his land as the sheep move from place to place. A true Yankee, that Annixter, a good gringo."

After his meal, Presley once more mounted his bicycle, and leaving the restaurant and the Plaza behind him, held on through the main street of the drowsing town—the street that farther on developed into the road which turned abruptly northward and led onward through the hop-fields and the Quien Sabe ranch toward the Mission of San Juan.

The Home ranch of the Quien Sabe was in the little triangle bounded on the south by the railroad, on the northwest by Broderson Creek, and on the east by the hop fields and the Mission lands. It was traversed in all directions, now by the trail from Hooven's, now by the irrigating ditch— the same which Presley had crossed earlier in the day—and again by the road upon which Presley then found himself. In its centre were Annixter's ranch house and barns, topped by the skeleton-like tower of the artesian well that was to feed the irrigating ditch. Farther on, the course of Broderson Creek was marked by a curved line of grey-green willows, while on the low hills to the north, as Presley advanced, the ancient Mission of San Juan de Guadalajara, with its belfry tower and red-tiled roof, began to show itself over the crests of the venerable pear trees that clustered in its garden.

When Presley reached Annixter's ranch house, he found young Annixter himself stretched in his hammock behind the mosquito-bar on the front porch, reading "David Copperfield," and gorging himself with dried prunes.

Annixter—after the two had exchanged greetings—complained of terrific colics all the preceding night. His stomach was out of whack, but you bet he knew how to take care of himself; the last spell, he had consulted a doctor at Bonneville, a gibbering busy-face who had filled him up to the neck with a dose of some hogwash stuff that had made him worse—a healthy lot the doctors knew, anyhow. HIS case was peculiar. HE knew; prunes were what he needed, and by the pound.

Annixter, who worked the Quien Sabe ranch—some four thousand acres of rich clay and heavy loams—was a very young man, younger even than Presley, like him a college graduate. He looked never a year older than he was. He was smooth-shaven and lean built. But his youthful appearance was offset by a certain male cast of countenance, the lower lip thrust out, the chin large and deeply cleft. His university course had hardened rather than polished him. He still remained one of the people, rough almost to insolence, direct in speech, intolerant in his opinions, relying upon absolutely no one but himself; yet, with all this, of an astonishing degree of intelligence, and possessed of an executive ability little short of positive genius. He was a ferocious worker, allowing himself no pleasures, and exacting the same degree of energy from all his subordinates. He was widely hated, and as widely trusted. Every one spoke of his crusty temper and bullying disposition, invariably qualifying the statement with a commendation of his resources and capabilities. The devil of a driver, a hard man to get along with, obstinate, contrary, cantankerous; but brains! No doubt of that; brains to his boots. One would like to see the man who could get ahead of him on a deal. Twice he had been shot at, once from ambush on Osterman's ranch, and once by one of his own men whom he had kicked from the sacking platform of his harvester for gross negligence. At college, he had specialised on finance, political economy, and scientific agriculture. After his graduation (he stood almost at the very top of his class) he had returned and obtained the degree of civil engineer. Then suddenly he had taken a notion that a practical knowledge of law was indispensable to a modern farmer. In eight months he did the work of three years, studying for his bar examinations. His method of study was characteristic. He reduced all the material of his text-books to notes. Tearing out the leaves of these note-books, he pasted them upon the walls of his room; then, in his shirt-sleeves, a cheap cigar in his teeth, his hands in his pockets, he walked around and around the room, scowling fiercely at his notes, memorising, devouring, digesting. At intervals, he drank great cupfuls of unsweetened, black coffee. When the bar examinations were held, he was admitted at the very head of all the applicants, and was complimented by the judge. Immediately afterwards, he collapsed with nervous prostration; his stomach "got out of whack," and he all but died in a Sacramento boarding-house, obstinately refusing to have anything to do with doctors, whom he vituperated as a rabble of quacks, dosing himself with a patent medicine and stuffing himself almost to bursting with liver pills and dried prunes.

He had taken a trip to Europe after this sickness to put himself completely to rights. He intended to be gone a year, but returned at the end of six weeks, fulminating abuse of European cooking. Nearly his entire time had been spent in Paris; but of this sojourn he had brought back but two souvenirs, an electro-plated bill-hook and an empty bird cage which had tickled his fancy immensely.

He was wealthy. Only a year previous to this his father—a widower, who had amassed a fortune in land speculation—had died, and Annixter, the only son, had come into the inheritance.

For Presley, Annixter professed a great admiration, holding in deep respect the man who could rhyme words, deferring to him whenever there was question of literature or works of fiction. No doubt, there was not much use in poetry, and as for novels, to his mind, there were only Dickens's works. Everything else was a lot of lies. But just the same, it took brains to grind out a poem. It wasn't every one who could rhyme "brave" and "glaive," and make sense out of it. Sure not.

But Presley's case was a notable exception. On no occasion was Annixter prepared to accept another man's opinion without reserve. In conversation with him, it was almost impossible to make any direct statement, however trivial, that he would accept without either modification or open contradiction. He had a passion for violent discussion. He would argue upon every subject in the range of human knowledge, from astronomy to the tariff, from the doctrine of predestination to the height of a horse. Never would he admit himself to be mistaken; when cornered, he would intrench himself behind the remark, "Yes, that's all very well. In some ways, it is, and then, again, in some ways, it ISN'T."

Singularly enough, he and Presley were the best of friends. More than once, Presley marvelled at this state of affairs, telling himself that he and Annixter had nothing in common. In all his circle of acquaintances, Presley was the one man with whom Annixter had never quarrelled. The two men were diametrically opposed in temperament. Presley was easy-going; Annixter, alert. Presley was a confirmed dreamer, irresolute, inactive, with a strong tendency to melancholy; the young farmer was a man of affairs, decisive, combative, whose only reflection upon his interior economy was a morbid concern in the vagaries of his stomach. Yet the two never met without a mutual pleasure, taking a genuine interest in each other's affairs, and often putting themselves to great inconvenience to be of trifling service to help one another.

As a last characteristic, Annixter pretended to be a woman-hater, for no other reason than that he was a very bull-calf of awkwardness in feminine surroundings. Feemales! Rot! There was a fine way for a man to waste his time and his good money, lally gagging with a lot of feemales. No, thank you; none of it in HIS, if you please. Once only he had an affair—a timid, little creature in a glove-cleaning establishment in Sacramento, whom he had picked up, Heaven knew how. After his return to his ranch, a correspondence had been maintained between the two, Annixter taking the precaution to typewrite his letters, and never affixing his signature, in an excess of prudence. He furthermore made carbon copies of all his letters, filing them away in a compartment of his safe. Ah, it would be a clever feemale who would get him into a mess. Then, suddenly smitten with a panic terror that he had committed himself, that he was involving himself too deeply, he had abruptly sent the little woman about her business. It was his only love affair. After that, he kept himself free. No petticoats should ever have a hold on him. Sure not.

As Presley came up to the edge of the porch, pushing his bicycle in front of him, Annixter excused himself for not getting up, alleging that the cramps returned the moment he was off his back.

"What are you doing up this way?" he demanded.

"Oh, just having a look around," answered Presley. "How's the ranch?"

"Say," observed the other, ignoring his question, "what's this I hear about Derrick giving his tenants the bounce, and working Los Muertos himself—working ALL his land?"

Presley made a sharp movement of impatience with his free hand. "I've heard nothing else myself since morning. I suppose it must be so."

"Huh!" grunted Annixter, spitting out a prune stone. "You give Magnus Derrick my compliments and tell him he's a fool." "What do you mean?"

"I suppose Derrick thinks he's still running his mine, and that the same principles will apply to getting grain out of the earth as to getting gold. Oh, let him go on and see where he brings up. That's right, there's your Western farmer," he exclaimed contemptuously. "Get the guts out of your land; work it to death; never give it a rest. Never alternate your crop, and then when your soil is exhausted, sit down and roar about hard times."

"I suppose Magnus thinks the land has had rest enough these last two dry seasons," observed Presley. "He has raised no crop to speak of for two years. The land has had a good rest."

"Ah, yes, that sounds well," Annixter contradicted, unwilling to be convinced. "In a way, the land's been rested, and then, again, in a way, it hasn't."

But Presley, scenting an argument, refrained from answering, and bethought himself of moving on.

"I'm going to leave my wheel here for a while, Buck," he said, "if you don't mind. I'm going up to the spring, and the road is rough between here and there."

"Stop in for dinner on your way back," said Annixter. "There'll be a venison steak. One of the boys got a deer over in the foothills last week. Out of season, but never mind that. I can't eat it. This stomach of mine wouldn't digest sweet oil to-day. Get here about six."

"Well, maybe I will, thank you," said Presley, moving off. "By the way," he added, "I see your barn is about done."

"You bet," answered Annixter. "In about a fortnight now she'll be all ready."

"It's a big barn," murmured Presley, glancing around the angle of the house toward where the great structure stood.

"Guess we'll have to have a dance there before we move the stock in," observed Annixter. "That's the custom all around here."

Presley took himself off, but at the gate Annixter called after him, his mouth full of prunes, "Say, take a look at that herd of sheep as you go up. They are right off here to the east of the road, about half a mile from here. I guess that's the biggest lot of sheep YOU ever saw. You might write a poem about 'em. Lamb—ram; sheep graze—sunny days. Catch on?"

Beyond Broderson Creek, as Presley advanced, tramping along on foot now, the land opened out again into the same vast spaces of dull brown earth, sprinkled with stubble, such as had been characteristic of Derrick's ranch. To the east the reach seemed infinite, flat, cheerless, heat-ridden, unrolling like a gigantic scroll toward the faint shimmer of the distant horizons, with here and there an isolated live-oak to break the sombre monotony. But bordering the road to the westward, the surface roughened and raised, clambering up to the higher ground, on the crest of which the old Mission and its surrounding pear trees were now plainly visible.

Just beyond the Mission, the road bent abruptly eastward, striking off across the Seed ranch. But Presley left the road at this point, going on across the open fields. There was no longer any trail. It was toward three o'clock. The sun still spun, a silent, blazing disc, high in the heavens, and tramping through the clods of uneven, broken plough was fatiguing work. The slope of the lowest foothills begun, the surface of the country became rolling, and, suddenly, as he topped a higher ridge, Presley came upon the sheep.

Already he had passed the larger part of the herd—an intervening rise of ground having hidden it from sight. Now, as he turned half way about, looking down into the shallow hollow between him and the curve of the creek, he saw them very plainly. The fringe of the herd was some two hundred yards distant, but its farther side, in that illusive shimmer of hot surface air, seemed miles away. The sheep were spread out roughly in the shape of a figure eight, two larger herds connected by a smaller, and were headed to the southward, moving slowly, grazing on the wheat stubble as they proceeded. But the number seemed incalculable. Hundreds upon hundreds upon hundreds of grey, rounded backs, all exactly alike, huddled, close-packed, alive, hid the earth from sight. It was no longer an aggregate of individuals. It was a mass—a compact, solid, slowly moving mass, huge, without form, like a thick-pressed growth of mushrooms, spreading out in all directions over the earth. From it there arose a vague murmur, confused, inarticulate, like the sound of very distant surf, while all the air in the vicinity was heavy with the warm, ammoniacal odour of the thousands of crowding bodies.

All the colours of the scene were sombre—the brown of the earth, the faded yellow of the dead stubble, the grey of the myriad of undulating backs. Only on the far side of the herd, erect, motionless—a single note of black, a speck, a dot—the shepherd stood, leaning upon an empty water-trough, solitary, grave, impressive.

For a few moments, Presley stood, watching. Then, as he started to move on, a curious thing occurred. At first, he thought he had heard some one call his name. He paused, listening; there was no sound but the vague noise of the moving sheep. Then, as this first impression passed, it seemed to him that he had been beckoned to. Yet nothing stirred; except for the lonely figure beyond the herd there was no one in sight. He started on again, and in half a dozen steps found himself looking over his shoulder. Without knowing why, he looked toward the shepherd; then halted and looked a second time and a third. Had the shepherd called to him? Presley knew that he had heard no voice. Brusquely, all his attention seemed riveted upon this distant figure. He put one forearm over his eyes, to keep off the sun, gazing across the intervening herd. Surely, the shepherd had called him. But at the next instant he started, uttering an exclamation under his breath. The far-away speck of black became animated. Presley remarked a sweeping gesture. Though the man had not beckoned to him before, there was no doubt that he was beckoning now. Without any hesitation, and singularly interested in the incident, Presley turned sharply aside and hurried on toward the shepherd, skirting the herd, wondering all the time that he should answer the call with so little question, so little hesitation.

But the shepherd came forward to meet Presley, followed by one of his dogs. As the two men approached each other, Presley, closely studying the other, began to wonder where he had seen him before. It must have been a very long time ago, upon one of his previous visits to the ranch. Certainly, however, there was something familiar in the shepherd's face and figure. When they came closer to each other, and Presley could see him more distinctly, this sense of a previous acquaintance was increased and sharpened.

The shepherd was a man of about thirty-five. He was very lean and spare. His brown canvas overalls were thrust into laced boots. A cartridge belt without any cartridges encircled his waist. A grey flannel shirt, open at the throat, showed his breast, tanned and ruddy. He wore no hat. His hair was very black and rather long. A pointed beard covered his chin, growing straight and fine from the hollow cheeks. The absence of any covering for his head was, no doubt, habitual with him, for his face was as brown as an Indian's—a ruddy brown quite different from Presley's dark olive. To Presley's morbidly keen observation, the general impression of the shepherd's face was intensely interesting. It was uncommon to an astonishing degree. Presley's vivid imagination chose to see in it the face of an ascetic, of a recluse, almost that of a young seer. So must have appeared the half-inspired shepherds of the Hebraic legends, the younger prophets of Israel, dwellers in the wilderness, beholders of visions, having their existence in a continual dream, talkers with God, gifted with strange powers.

Suddenly, at some twenty paces distant from the approaching shepherd, Presley stopped short, his eyes riveted upon the other.

"Vanamee!" he exclaimed.

The shepherd smiled and came forward, holding out his hands, saying, "I thought it was you. When I saw you come over the hill, I called you."

"But not with your voice," returned Presley. "I knew that some one wanted me. I felt it. I should have remembered that you could do that kind of thing."

"I have never known it to fail. It helps with the sheep."

"With the sheep?"

"In a way. I can't tell exactly how. We don't understand these things yet. There are times when, if I close my eyes and dig my fists into my temples, I can hold the entire herd for perhaps a minute. Perhaps, though, it's imagination, who knows? But it's good to see you again. How long has it been since the last time? Two, three, nearly five years."

It was more than that. It was six years since Presley and Vanamee had met, and then it had been for a short time only, during one of the shepherd's periodical brief returns to that part of the country. During a week he and Presley had been much together, for the two were devoted friends. Then, as abruptly, as mysteriously as he had come, Vanamee disappeared. Presley awoke one morning to find him gone. Thus, it had been with Vanamee for a period of sixteen years. He lived his life in the unknown, one could not tell where—in the desert, in the mountains, throughout all the vast and vague South-west, solitary, strange. Three, four, five years passed. The shepherd would be almost forgotten. Never the most trivial scrap of information as to his whereabouts reached Los Muertos. He had melted off into the surface-shimmer of the desert, into the mirage; he sank below the horizons; he was swallowed up in the waste of sand and sage. Then, without warning, he would reappear, coming in from the wilderness, emerging from the unknown. No one knew him well. In all that countryside he had but three friends, Presley, Magnus Derrick, and the priest at the Mission of San Juan de Guadalajara, Father Sarria. He remained always a mystery, living a life half-real, half-legendary. In all those years he did not seem to have grown older by a single day. At this time, Presley knew him to be thirty-six years of age. But since the first day the two had met, the shepherd's face and bearing had, to his eyes, remained the same. At this moment, Presley was looking into the same face he had first seen many, many years ago. It was a face stamped with an unspeakable sadness, a deathless grief, the permanent imprint of a tragedy long past, but yet a living issue. Presley told himself that it was impossible to look long into Vanamee's eyes without knowing that here was a man whose whole being had been at one time shattered and riven to its lowest depths, whose life had suddenly stopped at a certain moment of its development.

The two friends sat down upon the ledge of the watering-trough, their eyes wandering incessantly toward the slow moving herd, grazing on the wheat stubble, moving southward as they grazed.

"Where have you come from this time?" Presley had asked. "Where have you kept yourself?"

The other swept the horizon to the south and east with a vague gesture.

"Off there, down to the south, very far off. So many places that I can't remember. I went the Long Trail this time; a long, long ways. Arizona, The Mexicos, and, then, afterwards, Utah and Nevada, following the horizon, travelling at hazard. Into Arizona first, going in by Monument Pass, and then on to the south, through the country of the Navajos, down by the Aga Thia Needle—a great blade of red rock jutting from out the desert, like a knife thrust. Then on and on through The Mexicos, all through the Southwest, then back again in a great circle by Chihuahua and Aldama to Laredo, to Torreon, and Albuquerque. From there across the Uncompahgre plateau into the Uintah country; then at last due west through Nevada to California and to the valley of the San Joaquin." His voice lapsed to a monotone, his eyes becoming fixed; he continued to speak as though half awake, his thoughts elsewhere, seeing again in the eye of his mind the reach of desert and red hill, the purple mountain, the level stretch of alkali, leper white, all the savage, gorgeous desolation of the Long Trail.

He ignored Presley for the moment, but, on the other hand, Presley himself gave him but half his attention. The return of Vanamee had stimulated the poet's memory. He recalled the incidents of Vanamee's life, reviewing again that terrible drama which had uprooted his soul, which had driven him forth a wanderer, a shunner of men, a sojourner in waste places. He was, strangely enough, a college graduate and a man of wide reading and great intelligence, but he had chosen to lead his own life, which was that of a recluse.

Of a temperament similar in many ways to Presley's, there were capabilities in Vanamee that were not ordinarily to be found in the rank and file of men. Living close to nature, a poet by instinct, where Presley was but a poet by training, there developed in him a great sensitiveness to beauty and an almost abnormal capacity for great happiness and great sorrow; he felt things intensely, deeply. He never forgot. It was when he was eighteen or nineteen, at the formative and most impressionable period of his life, that he had met Angele Varian. Presley barely remembered her as a girl of sixteen, beautiful almost beyond expression, who lived with an aged aunt on the Seed ranch back of the Mission. At this moment he was trying to recall how she looked, with her hair of gold hanging in two straight plaits on either side of her face, making three-cornered her round, white forehead; her wonderful eyes, violet blue, heavy lidded, with their astonishing upward slant toward the temples, the slant that gave a strange, oriental cast to her face, perplexing, enchanting. He remembered the Egyptian fulness of the lips, the strange balancing movement of her head upon her slender neck, the same movement that one sees in a snake at poise. Never had he seen a girl more radiantly beautiful, never a beauty so strange, so troublous, so out of all accepted standards. It was small wonder that Vanamee had loved her, and less wonder, still, that his love had been so intense, so passionate, so part of himself. Angele had loved him with a love no less than his own. It was one of those legendary passions that sometimes occur, idyllic, untouched by civilisation, spontaneous as the growth of trees, natural as dew-fall, strong as the firm-seated mountains.

At the time of his meeting with Angele, Vanamee was living on the Los Muertos ranch. It was there he had chosen to spend one of his college vacations. But he preferred to pass it in out-of-door work, sometimes herding cattle, sometimes pitching hay, sometimes working with pick and dynamite-stick on the ditches in the fourth division of the ranch, riding the range, mending breaks in the wire fences, making himself generally useful. College bred though he was, the life pleased him. He was, as he desired, close to nature, living the full measure of life, a worker among workers, taking enjoyment in simple pleasures, healthy in mind and body. He believed in an existence passed in this fashion in the country, working hard, eating full, drinking deep, sleeping dreamlessly.

But every night, after supper, he saddled his pony and rode over to the garden of the old Mission. The 'dobe dividing wall on that side, which once had separated the Mission garden and the Seed ranch, had long since crumbled away, and the boundary between the two pieces of ground was marked only by a line of venerable pear trees. Here, under these trees, he found Angele awaiting him, and there the two would sit through the hot, still evening, their arms about each other, watching the moon rise over the foothills, listening to the trickle of the water in the moss-encrusted fountain in the garden, and the steady croak of the great frogs that lived in the damp north corner of the enclosure. Through all one summer the enchantment of that new-found, wonderful love, pure and untainted, filled the lives of each of them with its sweetness. The summer passed, the harvest moon came and went. The nights were very dark. In the deep shade of the pear trees they could no longer see each other. When they met at the rendezvous, Vanamee found her only with his groping hands. They did not speak, mere words were useless between them. Silently as his reaching hands touched her warm body, he took her in his arms, searching for her lips with his. Then one night the tragedy had suddenly leaped from out the shadow with the abruptness of an explosion.

It was impossible afterwards to reconstruct the manner of its occurrence. To Angele's mind—what there was left of it—the matter always remained a hideous blur, a blot, a vague, terrible confusion. No doubt they two had been watched; the plan succeeded too well for any other supposition. One moonless night, Angele, arriving under the black shadow of the pear trees a little earlier than usual, found the apparently familiar figure waiting for her. All unsuspecting she gave herself to the embrace of a strange pair of arms, and Vanamee arriving but a score of moments later, stumbled over her prostrate body, inert and unconscious, in the shadow of the overspiring trees.

Who was the Other? Angele was carried to her home on the Seed ranch, delirious, all but raving, and Vanamee, with knife and revolver ready, ranged the country-side like a wolf. He was not alone. The whole county rose, raging, horror-struck. Posse after posse was formed, sent out, and returned, without so much as a clue. Upon no one could even the shadow of suspicion be thrown. The Other had withdrawn into an impenetrable mystery. There he remained. He never was found; he never was so much as heard of. A legend arose about him, this prowler of the night, this strange, fearful figure, with an unseen face, swooping in there from out the darkness, come and gone in an instant, but leaving behind him a track of terror and death and rage and undying grief. Within the year, in giving birth to the child, Angele had died.

The little babe was taken by Angele's parents, and Angele was buried in the Mission garden near to the aged, grey sun dial. Vanamee stood by during the ceremony, but half conscious of what was going forward. At the last moment he had stepped forward, looked long into the dead face framed in its plaits of gold hair, the hair that made three-cornered the round, white forehead; looked again at the closed eyes, with their perplexing upward slant toward the temples, oriental, bizarre; at the lips with their Egyptian fulness; at the sweet, slender neck; the long, slim hands; then abruptly turned about. The last clods were filling the grave at a time when he was already far away, his horse's head turned toward the desert.

For two years no syllable was heard of him. It was believed that he had killed himself. But Vanamee had no thought of that. For two years he wandered through Arizona, living in the desert, in the wilderness, a recluse, a nomad, an ascetic. But, doubtless, all his heart was in the little coffin in the Mission garden. Once in so often he must come back thither. One day he was seen again in the San Joaquin. The priest, Father Sarria, returning from a visit to the sick at Bonneville, met him on the Upper Road. Eighteen years had passed since Angele had died, but the thread of Vanamee's life had been snapped. Nothing remained now but the tangled ends. He had never forgotten. The long, dull ache, the poignant grief had now become a part of him. Presley knew this to be so.

While Presley had been reflecting upon all this, Vanamee had continued to speak. Presley, however, had not been wholly inattentive. While his memory was busy reconstructing the details of the drama of the shepherd's life, another part of his brain had been swiftly registering picture after picture that Vanamee's monotonous flow of words struck off, as it were, upon a steadily moving scroll. The music of the unfamiliar names that occurred in his recital was a stimulant to the poet's imagination. Presley had the poet's passion for expressive, sonorous names. As these came and went in Vanamee's monotonous undertones, like little notes of harmony in a musical progression, he listened, delighted with their resonance.— Navajo, Quijotoa, Uintah, Sonora, Laredo, Uncompahgre—to him they were so many symbols. It was his West that passed, unrolling there before the eye of his mind: the open, heat-scourged round of desert; the mesa, like a vast altar, shimmering purple in the royal sunset; the still, gigantic mountains, heaving into the sky from out the canyons; the strenuous, fierce life of isolated towns, lost and forgotten, down there, far off, below the horizon. Abruptly his great poem, his Song of the West, leaped up again in his imagination. For the moment, he all but held it. It was there, close at hand. In another instant he would grasp it.

"Yes, yes," he exclaimed, "I can see it all. The desert, the mountains, all wild, primordial, untamed. How I should have loved to have been with you. Then, perhaps, I should have got hold of my idea."

"Your idea?"

"The great poem of the West. It's that which I want to write. Oh, to put it all into hexameters; strike the great iron note; sing the vast, terrible song; the song of the People; the forerunners of empire!"

Vanamee understood him perfectly. He nodded gravely.

"Yes, it is there. It is Life, the primitive, simple, direct Life, passionate, tumultuous. Yes, there is an epic there."

Presley caught at the word. It had never before occurred to him.

"Epic, yes, that's it. It is the epic I'm searching for. And HOW I search for it. You don't know. It is sometimes almost an agony. Often and often I can feel it right there, there, at my finger-tips, but I never quite catch it. It always eludes me. I was born too late. Ah, to get back to that first clear-eyed view of things, to see as Homer saw, as Beowulf saw, as the Nibelungen poets saw. The life is here, the same as then; the Poem is here; my West is here; the primeval, epic life is here, here under our hands, in the desert, in the mountain, on the ranch, all over here, from Winnipeg to Guadalupe. It is the man who is lacking, the poet; we have been educated away from it all. We are out of touch. We are out of tune."

Vanamee heard him to the end, his grave, sad face thoughtful and attentive. Then he rose.

"I am going over to the Mission," he said, "to see Father Sarria. I have not seen him yet."

"How about the sheep?"

"The dogs will keep them in hand, and I shall not be gone long. Besides that, I have a boy here to help. He is over yonder on the other side of the herd. We can't see him from here."

Presley wondered at the heedlessness of leaving the sheep so slightly guarded, but made no comment, and the two started off across the field in the direction of the Mission church.

"Well, yes, it is there—your epic," observed Vanamee, as they went along. "But why write? Why not LIVE in it? Steep oneself in the heat of the desert, the glory of the sunset, the blue haze of the mesa and the canyon."

"As you have done, for instance?"

Vanamee nodded.

"No, I could not do that," declared Presley; "I want to go back, but not so far as you. I feel that I must compromise. I must find expression. I could not lose myself like that in your desert. When its vastness overwhelmed me, or its beauty dazzled me, or its loneliness weighed down upon me, I should have to record my impressions. Otherwise, I should suffocate."

"Each to his own life," observed Vanamee.

The Mission of San Juan, built of brown 'dobe blocks, covered with yellow plaster, that at many points had dropped away from the walls, stood on the crest of a low rise of the ground, facing to the south. A covered colonnade, paved with round, worn bricks, from whence opened the doors of the abandoned cells, once used by the monks, adjoined it on the left. The roof was of tiled half-cylinders, split longitudinally, and laid in alternate rows, now concave, now convex. The main body of the church itself was at right angles to the colonnade, and at the point of intersection rose the belfry tower, an ancient campanile, where swung the three cracked bells, the gift of the King of Spain. Beyond the church was the Mission garden and the graveyard that overlooked the Seed ranch in a little hollow beyond.

Presley and Vanamee went down the long colonnade to the last door next the belfry tower, and Vanamee pulled the leather thong that hung from a hole in the door, setting a little bell jangling somewhere in the interior. The place, but for this noise, was shrouded in a Sunday stillness, an absolute repose. Only at intervals, one heard the trickle of the unseen fountain, and the liquid cooing of doves in the garden.

Father Sarria opened the door. He was a small man, somewhat stout, with a smooth and shiny face. He wore a frock coat that was rather dirty, slippers, and an old yachting cap of blue cloth, with a broken leather vizor. He was smoking a cheap cigar, very fat and black.

But instantly he recognised Vanamee. His face went all alight with pleasure and astonishment. It seemed as if he would never have finished shaking both his hands; and, as it was, he released but one of them, patting him affectionately on the shoulder with the other. He was voluble in his welcome, talking partly in Spanish, partly in English. So he had come back again, this great fellow, tanned as an Indian, lean as an Indian, with an Indian's long, black hair. But he had not changed, not in the very least. His beard had not grown an inch. Aha! The rascal, never to give warning, to drop down, as it were, from out the sky. Such a hermit! To live in the desert! A veritable Saint Jerome. Did a lion feed him down there in Arizona, or was it a raven, like Elijah? The good God had not fattened him, at any rate, and, apropos, he was just about to dine himself. He had made a salad from his own lettuce. The two would dine with him, eh? For this, my son, that was lost is found again.

But Presley excused himself. Instinctively, he felt that Sarria and Vanamee wanted to talk of things concerning which he was an outsider. It was not at all unlikely that Vanamee would spend half the night before the high altar in the church.

He took himself away, his mind still busy with Vanamee's extraordinary life and character. But, as he descended the hill, he was startled by a prolonged and raucous cry, discordant, very harsh, thrice repeated at exact intervals, and, looking up, he saw one of Father Sarria's peacocks balancing himself upon the topmost wire of the fence, his long tail trailing, his neck outstretched, filling the air with his stupid outcry, for no reason than the desire to make a noise.

About an hour later, toward four in the afternoon, Presley reached the spring at the head of the little canyon in the northeast corner of the Quien Sabe ranch, the point toward which he had been travelling since early in the forenoon. The place was not without its charm. Innumerable live-oaks overhung the canyon, and Broderson Creek—there a mere rivulet, running down from the spring—gave a certain coolness to the air. It was one of the few spots thereabouts that had survived the dry season of the last year. Nearly all the other springs had dried completely, while Mission Creek on Derrick's ranch was nothing better than a dusty cutting in the ground, filled with brittle, concave flakes of dried and sun-cracked mud.

Presley climbed to the summit of one of the hills—the highest—that rose out of the canyon, from the crest of which he could see for thirty, fifty, sixty miles down the valley, and, filling his pipe, smoked lazily for upwards of an hour, his head empty of thought, allowing himself to succumb to a pleasant, gentle inanition, a little drowsy comfortable in his place, prone upon the ground, warmed just enough by such sunlight as filtered through the live-oaks, soothed by the good tobacco and the prolonged murmur of the spring and creek. By degrees, the sense of his own personality became blunted, the little wheels and cogs of thought moved slower and slower; consciousness dwindled to a point, the animal in him stretched itself, purring. A delightful numbness invaded his mind and his body. He was not asleep, he was not awake, stupefied merely, lapsing back to the state of the faun, the satyr.

After a while, rousing himself a little, he shifted his position and, drawing from the pocket of his shooting coat his little tree-calf edition of the Odyssey, read far into the twenty-first book, where, after the failure of all the suitors to bend Ulysses's bow, it is finally put, with mockery, into his own hands. Abruptly the drama of the story roused him from all his languor. In an instant he was the poet again, his nerves tingling, alive to every sensation, responsive to every impression. The desire of creation, of composition, grew big within him. Hexameters of his own clamoured, tumultuous, in his brain. Not for a long time had he "felt his poem," as he called this sensation, so poignantly. For an instant he told himself that he actually held it.

It was, no doubt, Vanamee's talk that had stimulated him to this point. The story of the Long Trail, with its desert and mountain, its cliff-dwellers, its Aztec ruins, its colour, movement, and romance, filled his mind with picture after picture. The epic defiled before his vision like a pageant. Once more, he shot a glance about him, as if in search of the inspiration, and this time he all but found it. He rose to his feet, looking out and off below him.

As from a pinnacle, Presley, from where he now stood, dominated the entire country. The sun had begun to set, everything in the range of his vision was overlaid with a sheen of gold.

First, close at hand, it was the Seed ranch, carpeting the little hollow behind the Mission with a spread of greens, some dark, some vivid, some pale almost to yellowness. Beyond that was the Mission itself, its venerable campanile, in whose arches hung the Spanish King's bells, already glowing ruddy in the sunset. Farther on, he could make out Annixter's ranch house, marked by the skeleton-like tower of the artesian well, and, a little farther to the east, the huddled, tiled roofs of Guadalajara. Far to the west and north, he saw Bonneville very plain, and the dome of the courthouse, a purple silhouette against the glare of the sky. Other points detached themselves, swimming in a golden mist, projecting blue shadows far before them; the mammoth live-oak by Hooven's, towering superb and magnificent; the line of eucalyptus trees, behind which he knew was the Los Muertos ranch house—his home; the watering-tank, the great iron-hooped tower of wood that stood at the joining of the Lower Road and the County Road; the long wind-break of poplar trees and the white walls of Caraher's saloon on the County Road.

But all this seemed to be only foreground, a mere array of accessories—a mass of irrelevant details. Beyond Annixter's, beyond Guadalajara, beyond the Lower Road, beyond Broderson Creek, on to the south and west, infinite, illimitable, stretching out there under the sheen of the sunset forever and forever, flat, vast, unbroken, a huge scroll, unrolling between the horizons, spread the great stretches of the ranch of Los Muertos, bare of crops, shaved close in the recent harvest. Near at hand were hills, but on that far southern horizon only the curve of the great earth itself checked the view. Adjoining Los Muertos, and widening to the west, opened the Broderson ranch. The Osterman ranch to the northwest carried on the great sweep of landscape; ranch after ranch. Then, as the imagination itself expanded under the stimulus of that measureless range of vision, even those great ranches resolved themselves into mere foreground, mere accessories, irrelevant details. Beyond the fine line of the horizons, over the curve of the globe, the shoulder of the earth, were other ranches, equally vast, and beyond these, others, and beyond these, still others, the immensities multiplying, lengthening out vaster and vaster. The whole gigantic sweep of the San Joaquin expanded, Titanic, before the eye of the mind, flagellated with heat, quivering and shimmering under the sun's red eye. At long intervals, a faint breath of wind out of the south passed slowly over the levels of the baked and empty earth, accentuating the silence, marking off the stillness. It seemed to exhale from the land itself, a prolonged sigh as of deep fatigue. It was the season after the harvest, and the great earth, the mother, after its period of reproduction, its pains of labour, delivered of the fruit of its loins, slept the sleep of exhaustion, the infinite repose of the colossus, benignant, eternal, strong, the nourisher of nations, the feeder of an entire world. Ha! there it was, his epic, his inspiration, his West, his thundering progression of hexameters. A sudden uplift, a sense of exhilaration, of physical exaltation appeared abruptly to sweep Presley from his feet. As from a point high above the world, he seemed to dominate a universe, a whole order of things. He was dizzied, stunned, stupefied, his morbid supersensitive mind reeling, drunk with the intoxication of mere immensity. Stupendous ideas for which there were no names drove headlong through his brain. Terrible, formless shapes, vague figures, gigantic, monstrous, distorted, whirled at a gallop through his imagination.

He started homeward, still in his dream, descending from the hill, emerging from the canyon, and took the short cut straight across the Quien Sabe ranch, leaving Guadalajara far to his left. He tramped steadily on through the wheat stubble, walking fast, his head in a whirl.

Never had he so nearly grasped his inspiration as at that moment on the hilltop. Even now, though the sunset was fading, though the wide reach of valley was shut from sight, it still kept him company. Now the details came thronging back—the component parts of his poem, the signs and symbols of the West. It was there, close at hand, he had been in touch with it all day. It was in the centenarian's vividly coloured reminiscences—De La Cuesta, holding his grant from the Spanish crown, with his power of life and death; the romance of his marriage; the white horse with its pillion of red leather and silver bridle mountings; the bull-fights in the Plaza; the gifts of gold dust, and horses and tallow. It was in Vanamee's strange history, the tragedy of his love; Angele Varian, with her marvellous loveliness; the Egyptian fulness of her lips, the perplexing upward slant of her violet eyes, bizarre, oriental; her white forehead made three cornered by her plaits of gold hair; the mystery of the Other; her death at the moment of her child's birth. It was in Vanamee's flight into the wilderness; the story of the Long Trail, the sunsets behind the altar-like mesas, the baking desolation of the deserts; the strenuous, fierce life of forgotten towns, down there, far off, lost below the horizons of the southwest; the sonorous music of unfamiliar names— Quijotoa, Uintah, Sonora, Laredo, Uncompahgre. It was in the Mission, with its cracked bells, its decaying walls, its venerable sun dial, its fountain and old garden, and in the Mission Fathers themselves, the priests, the padres, planting the first wheat and oil and wine to produce the elements of the Sacrament—a trinity of great industries, taking their rise in a religious rite.

Abruptly, as if in confirmation, Presley heard the sound of a bell from the direction of the Mission itself. It was the de Profundis, a note of the Old World; of the ancient regime, an echo from the hillsides of mediaeval Europe, sounding there in this new land, unfamiliar and strange at this end-of-the-century time.

By now, however, it was dark. Presley hurried forward. He came to the line fence of the Quien Sabe ranch. Everything was very still. The stars were all out. There was not a sound other than the de Profundis, still sounding from very far away. At long intervals the great earth sighed dreamily in its sleep. All about, the feeling of absolute peace and quiet and security and untroubled happiness and content seemed descending from the stars like a benediction. The beauty of his poem, its idyl, came to him like a caress; that alone had been lacking. It was that, perhaps, which had left it hitherto incomplete. At last he was to grasp his song in all its entity. But suddenly there was an interruption. Presley had climbed the fence at the limit of the Quien Sabe ranch. Beyond was Los Muertos, but between the two ran the railroad. He had only time to jump back upon the embankment when, with a quivering of all the earth, a locomotive, single, unattached, shot by him with a roar, filling the air with the reek of hot oil, vomiting smoke and sparks; its enormous eye, cyclopean, red, throwing a glare far in advance, shooting by in a sudden crash of confused thunder; filling the night with the terrific clamour of its iron hoofs.

Abruptly Presley remembered. This must be the crack passenger engine of which Dyke had told him, the one delayed by the accident on the Bakersfield division and for whose passage the track had been opened all the way to Fresno.

Before Presley could recover from the shock of the irruption, while the earth was still vibrating, the rails still humming, the engine was far away, flinging the echo of its frantic gallop over all the valley. For a brief instant it roared with a hollow diapason on the Long Trestle over Broderson Creek, then plunged into a cutting farther on, the quivering glare of its fires losing itself in the night, its thunder abruptly diminishing to a subdued and distant humming. All at once this ceased. The engine was gone.

But the moment the noise of the engine lapsed, Presley—about to start forward again—was conscious of a confusion of lamentable sounds that rose into the night from out the engine's wake. Prolonged cries of agony, sobbing wails of infinite pain, heart-rending, pitiful.

The noises came from a little distance. He ran down the track, crossing the culvert, over the irrigating ditch, and at the head of the long reach of track—between the culvert and the Long Trestle—paused abruptly, held immovable at the sight of the ground and rails all about him.

In some way, the herd of sheep—Vanamee's herd—had found a breach in the wire fence by the right of way and had wandered out upon the tracks. A band had been crossing just at the moment of the engine's passage. The pathos of it was beyond expression. It was a slaughter, a massacre of innocents. The iron monster had charged full into the midst, merciless, inexorable. To the right and left, all the width of the right of way, the little bodies had been flung; backs were snapped against the fence posts; brains knocked out. Caught in the barbs of the wire, wedged in, the bodies hung suspended. Under foot it was terrible. The black blood, winking in the starlight, seeped down into the clinkers between the ties with a prolonged sucking murmur.

Presley turned away, horror-struck, sick at heart, overwhelmed with a quick burst of irresistible compassion for this brute agony he could not relieve. The sweetness was gone from the evening, the sense of peace, of security, and placid contentment was stricken from the landscape. The hideous ruin in the engine's path drove all thought of his poem from his mind. The inspiration vanished like a mist. The de Profundis had ceased to ring.

He hurried on across the Los Muertos ranch, almost running, even putting his hands over his ears till he was out of hearing distance of that all but human distress. Not until he was beyond ear-shot did he pause, looking back, listening. The night had shut down again. For a moment the silence was profound, unbroken.

Then, faint and prolonged, across the levels of the ranch, he heard the engine whistling for Bonneville. Again and again, at rapid intervals in its flying course, it whistled for road crossings, for sharp curves, for trestles; ominous notes, hoarse, bellowing, ringing with the accents of menace and defiance; and abruptly Presley saw again, in his imagination, the galloping monster, the terror of steel and steam, with its single eye, cyclopean, red, shooting from horizon to horizon; but saw it now as the symbol of a vast power, huge, terrible, flinging the echo of its thunder over all the reaches of the valley, leaving blood and destruction in its path; the leviathan, with tentacles of steel clutching into the soil, the soulless Force, the iron-hearted Power, the monster, the Colossus, the Octopus.

CHAPTER II

On the following morning, Harran Derrick was up and about by a little after six o'clock, and a quarter of an hour later had breakfast in the kitchen of the ranch house, preferring not to wait until the Chinese cook laid the table in the regular dining-room. He scented a hard day's work ahead of him, and was anxious to be at it betimes. He was practically the manager of Los Muertos, and, with the aid of his foreman and three division superintendents, carried forward nearly the entire direction of the ranch, occupying himself with the details of his father's plans, executing his orders, signing contracts, paying bills, and keeping the books.

For the last three weeks little had been done. The crop—such as it was—had been harvested and sold, and there had been a general relaxation of activity for upwards of a month. Now, however, the fall was coming on, the dry season was about at its end; any time after the twentieth of the month the first rains might be expected, softening the ground, putting it into condition for the plough. Two days before this, Harran had notified his superintendents on Three and Four to send in such grain as they had reserved for seed. On Two the wheat had not even shown itself above the ground, while on One, the Home ranch, which was under his own immediate supervision, the seed had already been graded and selected.

It was Harran's intention to commence blue-stoning his seed that day, a delicate and important process which prevented rust and smut appearing in the crop when the wheat should come up. But, furthermore, he wanted to find time to go to Guadalajara to meet the Governor on the morning train. His day promised to be busy.

But as Harran was finishing his last cup of coffee, Phelps, the foreman on the Home ranch, who also looked after the storage barns where the seed was kept, presented himself, cap in hand, on the back porch by the kitchen door.

"I thought I'd speak to you about the seed from Four, sir," he said. "That hasn't been brought in yet."

Harran nodded.

"I'll see about it. You've got all the blue-stone you want, have you, Phelps?" and without waiting for an answer he added, "Tell the stableman I shall want the team about nine o'clock to go to Guadalajara. Put them in the buggy. The bays, you understand." When the other had gone, Harran drank off the rest of his coffee, and, rising, passed through the dining-room and across a stone-paved hallway with a glass roof into the office just beyond.

The office was the nerve-centre of the entire ten thousand acres of Los Muertos, but its appearance and furnishings were not in the least suggestive of a farm. It was divided at about its middle by a wire railing, painted green and gold, and behind this railing were the high desks where the books were kept, the safe, the letter-press and letter-files, and Harran's typewriting machine. A great map of Los Muertos with every water-course, depression, and elevation, together with indications of the varying depths of the clays and loams in the soil, accurately plotted, hung against the wall between the windows, while near at hand by the safe was the telephone.

But, no doubt, the most significant object in the office was the ticker. This was an innovation in the San Joaquin, an idea of shrewd, quick-witted young Annixter, which Harran and Magnus Derrick had been quick to adopt, and after them Broderson and Osterman, and many others of the wheat growers of the county. The offices of the ranches were thus connected by wire with San Francisco, and through that city with Minneapolis, Duluth, Chicago, New York, and at last, and most important of all, with Liverpool. Fluctuations in the price of the world's crop during and after the harvest thrilled straight to the office of Los Muertos, to that of the Quien Sabe, to Osterman's, and to Broderson's. During a flurry in the Chicago wheat pits in the August of that year, which had affected even the San Francisco market, Harran and Magnus had sat up nearly half of one night watching the strip of white tape jerking unsteadily from the reel. At such moments they no longer felt their individuality. The ranch became merely the part of an enormous whole, a unit in the vast agglomeration of wheat land the whole world round, feeling the effects of causes thousands of miles distant—a drought on the prairies of Dakota, a rain on the plains of India, a frost on the Russian steppes, a hot wind on the llanos of the Argentine.

Harran crossed over to the telephone and rang six bells, the call for the division house on Four. It was the most distant, the most isolated point on all the ranch, situated at its far southeastern extremity, where few people ever went, close to the line fence, a dot, a speck, lost in the immensity of the open country. By the road it was eleven miles distant from the office, and by the trail to Hooven's and the Lower Road all of nine.

"How about that seed?" demanded Harran when he had got Cutter on the line.

The other made excuses for an unavoidable delay, and was adding that he was on the point of starting out, when Harran cut in with:

"You had better go the trail. It will save a little time and I am in a hurry. Put your sacks on the horses' backs. And, Cutter, if you see Hooven when you go by his place, tell him I want him, and, by the way, take a look at the end of the irrigating ditch when you get to it. See how they are getting along there and if Billy wants anything. Tell him we are expecting those new scoops down to-morrow or next day and to get along with what he has until then.... How's everything on Four? ... All right, then. Give your seed to Phelps when you get here if I am not about. I am going to Guadalajara to meet the Governor. He's coming down to-day. And that makes me think; we lost the case, you know. I had a letter from the Governor yesterday.... Yes, hard luck. S. Behrman did us up. Well, good-bye, and don't lose any time with that seed. I want to blue-stone to-day."

After telephoning Cutter, Harran put on his hat, went over to the barns, and found Phelps. Phelps had already cleaned out the vat which was to contain the solution of blue-stone, and was now at work regrading the seed. Against the wall behind him ranged the row of sacks. Harran cut the fastenings of these and examined the contents carefully, taking handfuls of wheat from each and allowing it to run through his fingers, or nipping the grains between his nails, testing their hardness.

The seed was all of the white varieties of wheat and of a very high grade, the berries hard and heavy, rigid and swollen with starch.

"If it was all like that, sir, hey?" observed Phelps.

Harran put his chin in the air.

"Bread would be as good as cake, then," he answered, going from sack to sack, inspecting the contents and consulting the tags affixed to the mouths.

"Hello," he remarked, "here's a red wheat. Where did this come from?"

"That's that red Clawson we sowed to the piece on Four, north the Mission Creek, just to see how it would do here. We didn't get a very good catch."

"We can't do better than to stay by White Sonora and Propo," remarked Harran. "We've got our best results with that, and European millers like it to mix with the Eastern wheats that have more gluten than ours. That is, if we have any wheat at all next year."

A feeling of discouragement for the moment bore down heavily upon him. At intervals this came to him and for the moment it was overpowering. The idea of "what's-the-use" was upon occasion a veritable oppression. Everything seemed to combine to lower the price of wheat. The extension of wheat areas always exceeded increase of population; competition was growing fiercer every year. The farmer's profits were the object of attack from a score of different quarters. It was a flock of vultures descending upon a common prey—the commission merchant, the elevator combine, the mixing-house ring, the banks, the warehouse men, the labouring man, and, above all, the railroad. Steadily the Liverpool buyers cut and cut and cut. Everything, every element of the world's markets, tended to force down the price to the lowest possible figure at which it could be profitably farmed. Now it was down to eighty-seven. It was at that figure the crop had sold that year; and to think that the Governor had seen wheat at two dollars and five cents in the year of the Turko-Russian War!

He turned back to the house after giving Phelps final directions, gloomy, disheartened, his hands deep in his pockets, wondering what was to be the outcome. So narrow had the margin of profit shrunk that a dry season meant bankruptcy to the smaller farmers throughout all the valley. He knew very well how widespread had been the distress the last two years. With their own tenants on Los Muertos, affairs had reached the stage of desperation. Derrick had practically been obliged to "carry" Hooven and some of the others. The Governor himself had made almost nothing during the last season; a third year like the last, with the price steadily sagging, meant nothing else but ruin.

But here he checked himself. Two consecutive dry seasons in California were almost unprecedented; a third would be beyond belief, and the complete rest for nearly all the land was a compensation. They had made no money, that was true; but they had lost none. Thank God, the homestead was free of mortgage; one good season would more than make up the difference.

He was in a better mood by the time he reached the driveway that led up to the ranch house, and as he raised his eyes toward the house itself, he could not but feel that the sight of his home was cheering. The ranch house was set in a great grove of eucalyptus, oak, and cypress, enormous trees growing from out a lawn that was as green, as fresh, and as well-groomed as any in a garden in the city. This lawn flanked all one side of the house, and it was on this side that the family elected to spend most of its time. The other side, looking out upon the Home ranch toward Bonneville and the railroad, was but little used. A deep porch ran the whole length of the house here, and in the lower branches of a live-oak near the steps Harran had built a little summer house for his mother. To the left of the ranch house itself, toward the County Road, was the bunk-house and kitchen for some of the hands. From the steps of the porch the view to the southward expanded to infinity. There was not so much as a twig to obstruct the view. In one leap the eye reached the fine, delicate line where earth and sky met, miles away. The flat monotony of the land, clean of fencing, was broken by one spot only, the roof of the Division Superintendent's house on Three—a mere speck, just darker than the ground. Cutter's house on Four was not even in sight. That was below the horizon.

As Harran came up he saw his mother at breakfast. The table had been set on the porch and Mrs. Derrick, stirring her coffee with one hand, held open with the other the pages of Walter Pater's "Marius." At her feet, Princess Nathalie, the white Angora cat, sleek, over-fed, self-centred, sat on her haunches, industriously licking at the white fur of her breast, while near at hand, by the railing of the porch, Presley pottered with a new bicycle lamp, filling it with oil, adjusting the wicks.

Harran kissed his mother and sat down in a wicker chair on the porch, removing his hat, running his fingers through his yellow hair.

Magnus Derrick's wife looked hardly old enough to be the mother of two such big fellows as Harran and Lyman Derrick. She was not far into the fifties, and her brown hair still retained much of its brightness. She could yet be called pretty. Her eyes were large and easily assumed a look of inquiry and innocence, such as one might expect to see in a young girl. By disposition she was retiring; she easily obliterated herself. She was not made for the harshness of the world, and yet she had known these harshnesses in her younger days. Magnus had married her when she was twenty-one years old, at a time when she was a graduate of some years' standing from the State Normal School and was teaching literature, music, and penmanship in a seminary in the town of Marysville. She overworked herself here continually, loathing the strain of teaching, yet clinging to it with a tenacity born of the knowledge that it was her only means of support. Both her parents were dead; she was dependent upon herself. Her one ambition was to see Italy and the Bay of Naples. The "Marble Faun," Raphael's "Madonnas" and "Il Trovatore" were her beau ideals of literature and art. She dreamed of Italy, Rome, Naples, and the world's great "art-centres." There was no doubt that her affair with Magnus had been a love-match, but Annie Payne would have loved any man who would have taken her out of the droning, heart-breaking routine of the class and music room. She had followed his fortunes unquestioningly. First at Sacramento, during the turmoil of his political career, later on at Placerville in El Dorado County, after Derrick had interested himself in the Corpus Christi group of mines, and finally at Los Muertos, where, after selling out his fourth interest in Corpus Christi, he had turned rancher and had "come in" on the new tracts of wheat land just thrown open by the railroad. She had lived here now for nearly ten years. But never for one moment since the time her glance first lost itself in the unbroken immensity of the ranches had she known a moment's content. Continually there came into her pretty, wide-open eyes—the eyes of a young doe—a look of uneasiness, of distrust, and aversion. Los Muertos frightened her. She remembered the days of her young girlhood passed on a farm in eastern Ohio—five hundred acres, neatly partitioned into the water lot, the cow pasture, the corn lot, the barley field, and wheat farm; cosey, comfortable, home-like; where the farmers loved their land, caressing it, coaxing it, nourishing it as though it were a thing almost conscious; where the seed was sown by hand, and a single two-horse plough was sufficient for the entire farm; where the scythe sufficed to cut the harvest and the grain was thrashed with flails.

But this new order of things—a ranch bounded only by the horizons, where, as far as one could see, to the north, to the east, to the south and to the west, was all one holding, a principality ruled with iron and steam, bullied into a yield of three hundred and fifty thousand bushels, where even when the land was resting, unploughed, unharrowed, and unsown, the wheat came up—troubled her, and even at times filled her with an undefinable terror. To her mind there was something inordinate about it all; something almost unnatural. The direct brutality of ten thousand acres of wheat, nothing but wheat as far as the eye could see, stunned her a little. The one-time writing-teacher of a young ladies' seminary, with her pretty deer-like eyes and delicate fingers, shrank from it. She did not want to look at so much wheat. There was something vaguely indecent in the sight, this food of the people, this elemental force, this basic energy, weltering here under the sun in all the unconscious nakedness of a sprawling, primordial Titan.

The monotony of the ranch ate into her heart hour by hour, year by year. And with it all, when was she to see Rome, Italy, and the Bay of Naples? It was a different prospect truly. Magnus had given her his promise that once the ranch was well established, they two should travel. But continually he had been obliged to put her off, now for one reason, now for another; the machine would not as yet run of itself, he must still feel his hand upon the lever; next year, perhaps, when wheat should go to ninety, or the rains were good. She did not insist. She obliterated herself, only allowing, from time to time, her pretty, questioning eyes to meet his. In the meantime she retired within herself. She surrounded herself with books. Her taste was of the delicacy of point lace. She knew her Austin Dobson by heart. She read poems, essays, the ideas of the seminary at Marysville persisting in her mind. "Marius the Epicurean," "The Essays of Elia," "Sesame and Lilies," "The Stones of Venice," and the little toy magazines, full of the flaccid banalities of the "Minor Poets," were continually in her hands.

When Presley had appeared on Los Muertos, she had welcomed his arrival with delight. Here at last was a congenial spirit. She looked forward to long conversations with the young man on literature, art, and ethics. But Presley had disappointed her. That he—outside of his few chosen deities— should care little for literature, shocked her beyond words. His indifference to "style," to elegant English, was a positive affront. His savage abuse and open ridicule of the neatly phrased rondeaux and sestinas and chansonettes of the little magazines was to her mind a wanton and uncalled-for cruelty. She found his Homer, with its slaughters and hecatombs and barbaric feastings and headstrong passions, violent and coarse. She could not see with him any romance, any poetry in the life around her; she looked to Italy for that. His "Song of the West," which only once, incoherent and fierce, he had tried to explain to her, its swift, tumultous life, its truth, its nobility and savagery, its heroism and obscenity had revolted her.

"But, Presley," she had murmured, "that is not literature."

"No," he had cried between his teeth, "no, thank God, it is not."

A little later, one of the stablemen brought the buggy with the team of bays up to the steps of the porch, and Harran, putting on a different coat and a black hat, took himself off to Guadalajara. The morning was fine; there was no cloud in the sky, but as Harran's buggy drew away from the grove of trees about the ranch house, emerging into the open country on either side of the Lower Road, he caught himself looking sharply at the sky and the faint line of hills beyond the Quien Sabe ranch. There was a certain indefinite cast to the landscape that to Harran's eye was not to be mistaken. Rain, the first of the season, was not far off.

"That's good," he muttered, touching the bays with the whip, "we can't get our ploughs to hand any too soon."

These ploughs Magnus Derrick had ordered from an Eastern manufacturer some months before, since he was dissatisfied with the results obtained from the ones he had used hitherto, which were of local make. However, there had been exasperating and unexpected delays in their shipment. Magnus and Harran both had counted upon having the ploughs in their implement barns that very week, but a tracer sent after them had only resulted in locating them, still en route, somewhere between The Needles and Bakersfield. Now there was likelihood of rain within the week. Ploughing could be undertaken immediately afterward, so soon as the ground was softened, but there was a fair chance that the ranch would lie idle for want of proper machinery.

It was ten minutes before train time when Harran reached the depot at Guadalajara. The San Francisco papers of the preceding day had arrived on an earlier train. He bought a couple from the station agent and looked them over till a distant and prolonged whistle announced the approach of the down train.

In one of the four passengers that alighted from the train, he recognised his father. He half rose in his seat, whistling shrilly between his teeth, waving his hand, and Magnus Derrick, catching sight of him, came forward quickly.

Magnus—the Governor—was all of six feet tall, and though now well toward his sixtieth year, was as erect as an officer of cavalry. He was broad in proportion, a fine commanding figure, imposing an immediate respect, impressing one with a sense of gravity, of dignity and a certain pride of race. He was smooth-shaven, thin-lipped, with a broad chin, and a prominent hawk-like nose—the characteristic of the family—thin, with a high bridge, such as one sees in the later portraits of the Duke of Wellington. His hair was thick and iron-grey, and had a tendency to curl in a forward direction just in front of his ears. He wore a top-hat of grey, with a wide brim, and a frock coat, and carried a cane with a yellowed ivory head.

As a young man it had been his ambition to represent his native State—North Carolina—in the United States Senate. Calhoun was his "great man," but in two successive campaigns he had been defeated. His career checked in this direction, he had come to California in the fifties. He had known and had been the intimate friend of such men as Terry, Broderick, General Baker, Lick, Alvarado, Emerich, Larkin, and, above all, of the unfortunate and misunderstood Ralston. Once he had been put forward as the Democratic candidate for governor, but failed of election. After this Magnus had definitely abandoned politics and had invested all his money in the Corpus Christi mines. Then he had sold out his interest at a small profit—just in time to miss his chance of becoming a multi-millionaire in the Comstock boom—and was looking for reinvestments in other lines when the news that "wheat had been discovered in California" was passed from mouth to mouth. Practically it amounted to a discovery. Dr. Glenn's first harvest of wheat in Colusa County, quietly undertaken but suddenly realised with dramatic abruptness, gave a new matter for reflection to the thinking men of the New West. California suddenly leaped unheralded into the world's market as a competitor in wheat production. In a few years her output of wheat exceeded the value of her out-put of gold, and when, later on, the Pacific and Southwestern Railroad threw open to settlers the rich lands of Tulare County—conceded to the corporation by the government as a bonus for the construction of the road—Magnus had been quick to seize the opportunity and had taken up the ten thousand acres of Los Muertos. Wherever he had gone, Magnus had taken his family with him. Lyman had been born at Sacramento during the turmoil and excitement of Derrick's campaign for governor, and Harran at Shingle Springs, in El Dorado County, six years later.

But Magnus was in every sense the "prominent man." In whatever circle he moved he was the chief figure. Instinctively other men looked to him as the leader. He himself was proud of this distinction; he assumed the grand manner very easily and carried it well. As a public speaker he was one of the last of the followers of the old school of orators. He even carried the diction and manner of the rostrum into private life. It was said of him that his most colloquial conversation could be taken down in shorthand and read off as an admirable specimen of pure, well-chosen English. He loved to do things upon a grand scale, to preside, to dominate. In his good humour there was something Jovian. When angry, everybody around him trembled. But he had not the genius for detail, was not patient. The certain grandiose lavishness of his disposition occupied itself more with results than with means. He was always ready to take chances, to hazard everything on the hopes of colossal returns. In the mining days at Placerville there was no more redoubtable poker player in the county. He had been as lucky in his mines as in his gambling, sinking shafts and tunnelling in violation of expert theory and finding "pay" in every case. Without knowing it, he allowed himself to work his ranch much as if he was still working his mine. The old-time spirit of '49, hap-hazard, unscientific, persisted in his mind. Everything was a gamble—who took the greatest chances was most apt to be the greatest winner. The idea of manuring Los Muertos, of husbanding his great resources, he would have scouted as niggardly, Hebraic, ungenerous.

Magnus climbed into the buggy, helping himself with Harran's outstretched hand which he still held. The two were immensely fond of each other, proud of each other. They were constantly together and Magnus kept no secrets from his favourite son.

"Well, boy."

"Well, Governor."

"I am very pleased you came yourself, Harran. I feared that you might be too busy and send Phelps. It was thoughtful."

Harran was about to reply, but at that moment Magnus caught sight of the three flat cars loaded with bright-painted farming machines which still remained on the siding above the station. He laid his hands on the reins and Harran checked the team.

"Harran," observed Magnus, fixing the machinery with a judicial frown, "Harran, those look singularly like our ploughs. Drive over, boy."

The train had by this time gone on its way and Harran brought the team up to the siding.

"Ah, I was right," said the Governor. "'Magnus Derrick, Los Muertos, Bonneville, from Ditson & Co., Rochester.' These are ours, boy."

Harran breathed a sigh of relief.

"At last," he answered, "and just in time, too. We'll have rain before the week is out. I think, now that I am here, I will telephone Phelps to send the wagon right down for these. I started blue-stoning to-day."

Magnus nodded a grave approval.

"That was shrewd, boy. As to the rain, I think you are well informed; we will have an early season. The ploughs have arrived at a happy moment."

"It means money to us, Governor," remarked Harran.

But as he turned the horses to allow his father to get into the buggy again, the two were surprised to hear a thick, throaty voice wishing them good-morning, and turning about were aware of S. Behrman, who had come up while they were examining the ploughs. Harran's eyes flashed on the instant and through his nostrils he drew a sharp, quick breath, while a certain rigour of carriage stiffened the set of Magnus Derrick's shoulders and back. Magnus had not yet got into the buggy, but stood with the team between him and S. Behrman, eyeing him calmly across the horses' backs. S. Behrman came around to the other side of the buggy and faced Magnus.

He was a large, fat man, with a great stomach; his cheek and the upper part of his thick neck ran together to form a great tremulous jowl, shaven and blue-grey in colour; a roll of fat, sprinkled with sparse hair, moist with perspiration, protruded over the back of his collar. He wore a heavy black moustache. On his head was a round-topped hat of stiff brown straw, highly varnished. A light-brown linen vest, stamped with innumerable interlocked horseshoes, covered his protuberant stomach, upon which a heavy watch chain of hollow links rose and fell with his difficult breathing, clinking against the vest buttons of imitation mother-of-pearl.

S. Behrman was the banker of Bonneville. But besides this he was many other things. He was a real estate agent. He bought grain; he dealt in mortgages. He was one of the local political bosses, but more important than all this, he was the representative of the Pacific and Southwestern Railroad in that section of Tulare County. The railroad did little business in that part of the country that S. Behrman did not supervise, from the consignment of a shipment of wheat to the management of a damage suit, or even to the repair and maintenance of the right of way. During the time when the ranchers of the county were fighting the grain-rate case, S. Behrman had been much in evidence in and about the San Francisco court rooms and the lobby of the legislature in Sacramento. He had returned to Bonneville only recently, a decision adverse to the ranchers being foreseen. The position he occupied on the salary list of the Pacific and Southwestern could not readily be defined, for he was neither freight agent, passenger agent, attorney, real-estate broker, nor political servant, though his influence in all these offices was undoubted and enormous. But for all that, the ranchers about Bonneville knew whom to look to as a source of trouble. There was no denying the fact that for Osterman, Broderson, Annixter and Derrick, S. Behrman was the railroad.

"Mr. Derrick, good-morning," he cried as he came up. "Good-morning, Harran. Glad to see you back, Mr. Derrick." He held out a thick hand.

Magnus, head and shoulders above the other, tall, thin, erect, looked down upon S. Behrman, inclining his head, failing to see his extended hand.

"Good-morning, sir," he observed, and waited for S. Behrman's further speech.

"Well, Mr. Derrick," continued S. Behrman, wiping the back of his neck with his handkerchief, "I saw in the city papers yesterday that our case had gone against you."

"I guess it wasn't any great news to YOU," commented Harran, his face scarlet. "I guess you knew which way Ulsteen was going to jump after your very first interview with him. You don't like to be surprised in this sort of thing, S. Behrman."

"Now, you know better than that, Harran," remonstrated S. Behrman blandly. "I know what you mean to imply, but I ain't going to let it make me get mad. I wanted to say to your Governor—I wanted to say to you, Mr. Derrick—as one man to another—letting alone for the minute that we were on opposite sides of the case—that I'm sorry you didn't win. Your side made a good fight, but it was in a mistaken cause. That's the whole trouble. Why, you could have figured out before you ever went into the case that such rates are confiscation of property. You must allow us—must allow the railroad—a fair interest on the investment. You don't want us to go into the receiver's hands, do you now, Mr. Derrick?"

"The Board of Railroad Commissioners was bought," remarked Magnus sharply, a keen, brisk flash glinting in his eye.

"It was part of the game," put in Harran, "for the Railroad Commission to cut rates to a ridiculous figure, far below a REASONABLE figure, just so that it WOULD be confiscation. Whether Ulsteen is a tool of yours or not, he had to put the rates back to what they were originally."

"If you enforced those rates, Mr. Harran," returned S. Behrman calmly, "we wouldn't be able to earn sufficient money to meet operating expenses or fixed charges, to say nothing of a surplus left over to pay dividends——"

"Tell me when the P. and S. W. ever paid dividends."

"The lowest rates," continued S. Behrman, "that the legislature can establish must be such as will secure us a fair interest on our investment."

"Well, what's your standard? Come, let's hear it. Who is to say what's a fair rate? The railroad has its own notions of fairness sometimes."

"The laws of the State," returned S. Behrman, "fix the rate of interest at seven per cent. That's a good enough standard for us. There is no reason, Mr. Harran, why a dollar invested in a railroad should not earn as much as a dollar represented by a promissory note—seven per cent. By applying your schedule of rates we would not earn a cent; we would be bankrupt."

"Interest on your investment!" cried Harran, furious. "It's fine to talk about fair interest. I know and you know that the total earnings of the P. and S. W.—their main, branch and leased lines for last year—was between nineteen and twenty millions of dollars. Do you mean to say that twenty million dollars is seven per cent. of the original cost of the road?"

S. Behrman spread out his hands, smiling.

"That was the gross, not the net figure—and how can you tell what was the original cost of the road?" "Ah, that's just it," shouted Harran, emphasising each word with a blow of his fist upon his knee, his eyes sparkling, "you take cursed good care that we don't know anything about the original cost of the road. But we know you are bonded for treble your value; and we know this: that the road COULD have been built for fifty-four thousand dollars per mile and that you SAY it cost you eighty-seven thousand. It makes a difference, S. Behrman, on which of these two figures you are basing your seven per cent."

"That all may show obstinacy, Harran," observed S. Behrman vaguely, "but it don't show common sense."

"We are threshing out old straw, I believe, gentlemen," remarked Magnus. "The question was thoroughly sifted in the courts."

"Quite right," assented S. Behrman. "The best way is that the railroad and the farmer understand each other and get along peaceably. We are both dependent on each other. Your ploughs, I believe, Mr. Derrick." S. Behrman nodded toward the flat cars.

"They are consigned to me," admitted Magnus.

"It looks a trifle like rain," observed S. Behrman, easing his neck and jowl in his limp collar. "I suppose you will want to begin ploughing next week."

"Possibly," said Magnus.

"I'll see that your ploughs are hurried through for you then, Mr. Derrick. We will route them by fast freight for you and it won't cost you anything extra."

"What do you mean?" demanded Harran. "The ploughs are here. We have nothing more to do with the railroad. I am going to have my wagons down here this afternoon."

"I am sorry," answered S. Behrman, "but the cars are going north, not, as you thought, coming FROM the north. They have not been to San Francisco yet."

Magnus made a slight movement of the head as one who remembers a fact hitherto forgotten. But Harran was as yet unenlightened.

"To San Francisco!" he answered, "we want them here—what are you talking about?"

"Well, you know, of course, the regulations," answered S. Behrman. "Freight of this kind coming from the Eastern points into the State must go first to one of our common points and be reshipped from there."

Harran did remember now, but never before had the matter so struck home. He leaned back in his seat in dumb amazement for the instant. Even Magnus had turned a little pale. Then, abruptly, Harran broke out violent and raging.

"What next? My God, why don't you break into our houses at night? Why don't you steal the watch out of my pocket, steal the horses out of the harness, hold us up with a shot-gun; yes, 'stand and deliver; your money or your life.' Here we bring our ploughs from the East over your lines, but you're not content with your long-haul rate between Eastern points and Bonneville. You want to get us under your ruinous short-haul rate between Bonneville and San Francisco, AND RETURN. Think of it! Here's a load of stuff for Bonneville that can't stop at Bonneville, where it is consigned, but has got to go up to San Francisco first BY WAY OF Bonneville, at forty cents per ton and then be reshipped from San Francisco back to Bonneville again at FIFTY-ONE cents per ton, the short-haul rate. And we have to pay it all or go without. Here are the ploughs right here, in sight of the land they have got to be used on, the season just ready for them, and we can't touch them. Oh," he exclaimed in deep disgust, "isn't it a pretty mess! Isn't it a farce! the whole dirty business!"

S. Behrman listened to him unmoved, his little eyes blinking under his fat forehead, the gold chain of hollow links clicking against the pearl buttons of his waistcoat as he breathed.

"It don't do any good to let loose like that, Harran," he said at length. "I am willing to do what I can for you. I'll hurry the ploughs through, but I can't change the freight regulation of the road."

"What's your blackmail for this?" vociferated Harran. "How much do you want to let us go? How much have we got to pay you to be ALLOWED to use our own ploughs—what's your figure? Come, spit it out."

"I see you are trying to make me angry, Harran," returned S. Behrman, "but you won't succeed. Better give up trying, my boy. As I said, the best way is to have the railroad and the farmer get along amicably. It is the only way we can do business. Well, s'long, Governor, I must trot along. S'long, Harran." He took himself off.

But before leaving Guadalajara Magnus dropped into the town's small grocery store to purchase a box of cigars of a certain Mexican brand, unprocurable elsewhere. Harran remained in the buggy.

While he waited, Dyke appeared at the end of the street, and, seeing Derrick's younger son, came over to shake hands with him. He explained his affair with the P. and S. W., and asked the young man what he thought of the expected rise in the price of hops.

"Hops ought to be a good thing," Harran told him. "The crop in Germany and in New York has been a dead failure for the last three years, and so many people have gone out of the business that there's likely to be a shortage and a stiff advance in the price. They ought to go to a dollar next year. Sure, hops ought to be a good thing. How's the old lady and Sidney, Dyke?"

"Why, fairly well, thank you, Harran. They're up to Sacramento just now to see my brother. I was thinking of going in with my brother into this hop business. But I had a letter from him this morning. He may not be able to meet me on this proposition. He's got other business on hand. If he pulls out—and he probably will—I'll have to go it alone, but I'll have to borrow. I had thought with his money and mine we would have enough to pull off the affair without mortgaging anything. As it is, I guess I'll have to see S. Behrman."

"I'll be cursed if I would!" exclaimed Harran.

"Well, S. Behrman is a screw," admitted the engineer, "and he is 'railroad' to his boots; but business is business, and he would have to stand by a contract in black and white, and this chance in hops is too good to let slide. I guess we'll try it on, Harran. I can get a good foreman that knows all about hops just now, and if the deal pays—well, I want to send Sid to a seminary up in San Francisco."

"Well, mortgage the crops, but don't mortgage the homestead, Dyke," said Harran. "And, by the way, have you looked up the freight rates on hops?"

"No, I haven't yet," answered Dyke, "and I had better be sure of that, hadn't I? I hear that the rate is reasonable, though."

"You be sure to have a clear understanding with the railroad first about the rate," Harran warned him.

When Magnus came out of the grocery store and once more seated himself in the buggy, he said to Harran, "Boy, drive over here to Annixter's before we start home. I want to ask him to dine with us to-night. Osterman and Broderson are to drop in, I believe, and I should like to have Annixter as well."

Magnus was lavishly hospitable. Los Muertos's doors invariably stood open to all the Derricks' neighbours, and once in so often Magnus had a few of his intimates to dinner.

As Harran and his father drove along the road toward Annixter's ranch house, Magnus asked about what had happened during his absence.

He inquired after his wife and the ranch, commenting upon the work on the irrigating ditch. Harran gave him the news of the past week, Dyke's discharge, his resolve to raise a crop of hops; Vanamee's return, the killing of the sheep, and Hooven's petition to remain upon the ranch as Magnus's tenant. It needed only Harran's recommendation that the German should remain to have Magnus consent upon the instant. "You know more about it than I, boy," he said, "and whatever you think is wise shall be done."

Harran touched the bays with the whip, urging them to their briskest pace. They were not yet at Annixter's and he was anxious to get back to the ranch house to supervise the blue-stoning of his seed.

"By the way, Governor," he demanded suddenly, "how is Lyman getting on?"

Lyman, Magnus's eldest son, had never taken kindly toward ranch life. He resembled his mother more than he did Magnus, and had inherited from her a distaste for agriculture and a tendency toward a profession. At a time when Harran was learning the rudiments of farming, Lyman was entering the State University, and, graduating thence, had spent three years in the study of law. But later on, traits that were particularly his father's developed. Politics interested him. He told himself he was a born politician, was diplomatic, approachable, had a talent for intrigue, a gift of making friends easily and, most indispensable of all, a veritable genius for putting influential men under obligations to himself. Already he had succeeded in gaining for himself two important offices in the municipal administration of San Francisco—where he had his home—sheriff's attorney, and, later on, assistant district attorney. But with these small achievements he was by no means satisfied. The largeness of his father's character, modified in Lyman by a counter-influence of selfishness, had produced in him an inordinate ambition. Where his father during his political career had considered himself only as an exponent of principles he strove to apply, Lyman saw but the office, his own personal aggrandisement. He belonged to the new school, wherein objects were attained not by orations before senates and assemblies, but by sessions of committees, caucuses, compromises and expedients. His goal was to be in fact what Magnus was only in name—governor. Lyman, with shut teeth, had resolved that some day he would sit in the gubernatorial chair in Sacramento.

"Lyman is doing well," answered Magnus. "I could wish he was more pronounced in his convictions, less willing to compromise, but I believe him to be earnest and to have a talent for government and civics. His ambition does him credit, and if he occupied himself a little more with means and a little less with ends, he would, I am sure, be the ideal servant of the people. But I am not afraid. The time will come when the State will be proud of him."

As Harran turned the team into the driveway that led up to Annixter's house, Magnus remarked:

"Harran, isn't that young Annixter himself on the porch?"

Harran nodded and remarked:

"By the way, Governor, I wouldn't seem too cordial in your invitation to Annixter. He will be glad to come, I know, but if you seem to want him too much, it is just like his confounded obstinacy to make objections."

"There is something in that," observed Magnus, as Harran drew up at the porch of the house. "He is a queer, cross-grained fellow, but in many ways sterling."

Annixter was lying in the hammock on the porch, precisely as Presley had found him the day before, reading "David Copperfield" and stuffing himself with dried prunes. When he recognised Magnus, however, he got up, though careful to give evidence of the most poignant discomfort. He explained his difficulty at great length, protesting that his stomach was no better than a spongebag. Would Magnus and Harran get down and have a drink? There was whiskey somewhere about.

Magnus, however, declined. He stated his errand, asking Annixter to come over to Los Muertos that evening for seven o'clock dinner. Osterman and Broderson would be there.

At once Annixter, even to Harran's surprise, put his chin in the air, making excuses, fearing to compromise himself if he accepted too readily. No, he did not think he could get around—was sure of it, in fact. There were certain businesses he had on hand that evening. He had practically made an appointment with a man at Bonneville; then, too, he was thinking of going up to San Francisco to-morrow and needed his sleep; would go to bed early; and besides all that, he was a very sick man; his stomach was out of whack; if he moved about it brought the gripes back. No, they must get along without him.

Magnus, knowing with whom he had to deal, did not urge the point, being convinced that Annixter would argue over the affair the rest of the morning. He re-settled himself in the buggy and Harran gathered up the reins.

"Well," he observed, "you know your business best. Come if you can. We dine at seven."

"I hear you are going to farm the whole of Los Muertos this season," remarked Annixter, with a certain note of challenge in his voice.

"We are thinking of it," replied Magnus.

Annixter grunted scornfully.

"Did you get the message I sent you by Presley?" he began.

Tactless, blunt, and direct, Annixter was quite capable of calling even Magnus a fool to his face. But before he could proceed, S. Behrman in his single buggy turned into the gate, and driving leisurely up to the porch halted on the other side of Magnus's team.

"Good-morning, gentlemen," he remarked, nodding to the two Derricks as though he had not seen them earlier in the day. "Mr. Annixter, how do you do?"

"What in hell do YOU want?" demanded Annixter with a stare.

S. Behrman hiccoughed slightly and passed a fat hand over his waistcoat.

"Why, not very much, Mr. Annixter," he replied, ignoring the belligerency in the young ranchman's voice, "but I will have to lodge a protest against you, Mr. Annixter, in the matter of keeping your line fence in repair. The sheep were all over the track last night, this side the Long Trestle, and I am afraid they have seriously disturbed our ballast along there. We—the railroad—can't fence along our right of way. The farmers have the prescriptive right of that, so we have to look to you to keep your fence in repair. I am sorry, but I shall have to protest— —" Annixter returned to the hammock and stretched himself out in it to his full length, remarking tranquilly:

"Go to the devil!"

"It is as much to your interest as to ours that the safety of the public— —"

"You heard what I said. Go to the devil!"

"That all may show obstinacy, Mr. Annixter, but— —"

Suddenly Annixter jumped up again and came to the edge of the porch; his face flamed scarlet to the roots of his stiff yellow hair. He thrust out his jaw aggressively, clenching his teeth.

"You," he vociferated, "I'll tell you what you are. You're a—a—a PIP!"

To his mind it was the last insult, the most outrageous calumny. He had no worse epithet at his command.

"— —may show obstinacy," pursued S. Behrman, bent upon finishing the phrase, "but it don't show common sense."

"I'll mend my fence, and then, again, maybe I won't mend my fence," shouted Annixter. "I know what you mean—that wild engine last night. Well, you've no right to run at that speed in the town limits."

"How the town limits? The sheep were this side the Long Trestle."

"Well, that's in the town limits of Guadalajara." "Why, Mr. Annixter, the Long Trestle is a good two miles out of Guadalajara."

Annixter squared himself, leaping to the chance of an argument.

"Two miles! It's not a mile and a quarter. No, it's not a mile. I'll leave it to Magnus here."

"Oh, I know nothing about it," declared Magnus, refusing to be involved.

"Yes, you do. Yes, you do, too. Any fool knows how far it is from Guadalajara to the Long Trestle. It's about five-eighths of a mile."

"From the depot of the town," remarked S. Behrman placidly, "to the head of the Long Trestle is about two miles."

"That's a lie and you know it's a lie," shouted the other, furious at S. Behrman's calmness, "and I can prove it's a lie. I've walked that distance on the Upper Road, and I know just how fast I walk, and if I can walk four miles in one hour."

Magnus and Harran drove on, leaving Annixter trying to draw S. Behrman into a wrangle.

When at length S. Behrman as well took himself away, Annixter returned to his hammock, finished the rest of his prunes and read another chapter of "Copperfield." Then he put the book, open, over his face and went to sleep.

An hour later, toward noon, his own terrific snoring woke him up suddenly, and he sat up, rubbing his face and blinking at the sunlight. There was a bad taste in his mouth from sleeping with it wide open, and going into the dining-room of the house, he mixed himself a drink of whiskey and soda and swallowed it in three great gulps. He told himself that he felt not only better but hungry, and pressed an electric button in the wall near the sideboard three times to let the kitchen—situated in a separate building near the ranch house—know that he was ready for his dinner. As he did so, an idea occurred to him. He wondered if Hilma Tree would bring up his dinner and wait on the table while he ate it.

In connection with his ranch, Annixter ran a dairy farm on a very small scale, making just enough butter and cheese for the consumption of the ranch's PERSONNEL. Old man Tree, his wife, and his daughter Hilma looked after the dairy. But there was not always work enough to keep the three of them occupied and Hilma at times made herself useful in other ways. As often as not she lent a hand in the kitchen, and two or three times a week she took her mother's place in looking after Annixter's house, making the beds, putting his room to rights, bringing his meals up from the kitchen. For the last summer she had been away visiting with relatives in one of the towns on the coast. But the week previous to this she had returned and Annixter had come upon her suddenly one day in the dairy, making cheese, the sleeves of her crisp blue shirt waist rolled back to her very shoulders. Annixter had carried away with him a clear-cut recollection of these smooth white arms of hers, bare to the shoulder, very round and cool and fresh. He would not have believed that a girl so young should have had arms so big and perfect. To his surprise he found himself thinking of her after he had gone to bed that night, and in the morning when he woke he was bothered to know whether he had dreamed about Hilma's fine white arms over night. Then abruptly he had lost patience with himself for being so occupied with the subject, raging and furious with all the breed of feemales—a fine way for a man to waste his time. He had had his experience with the timid little creature in the glove-cleaning establishment in Sacramento. That was enough. Feemales! Rot! None of them in HIS, thank you. HE had seen Hilma Tree give him a look in the dairy. Aha, he saw through her! She was trying to get a hold on him, was she? He would show her. Wait till he saw her again. He would send her about her business in a hurry. He resolved upon a terrible demeanour in the presence of the dairy girl—a great show of indifference, a fierce masculine nonchalance; and when, the next morning, she brought him his breakfast, he had been smitten dumb as soon as she entered the room, glueing his eyes upon his plate, his elbows close to his side, awkward, clumsy, overwhelmed with constraint.

While true to his convictions as a woman-hater and genuinely despising Hilma both as a girl and as an inferior, the idea of her worried him. Most of all, he was angry with himself because of his inane sheepishness when she was about. He at first had told himself that he was a fool not to be able to ignore her existence as hitherto, and then that he was a greater fool not to take advantage of his position. Certainly he had not the remotest idea of any affection, but Hilma was a fine looking girl. He imagined an affair with her.

As he reflected upon the matter now, scowling abstractedly at the button of the electric bell, turning the whole business over in his mind, he remembered that to-day was butter-making day and that Mrs. Tree would be occupied in the dairy. That meant that Hilma would take her place. He turned to the mirror of the sideboard, scrutinising his reflection with grim disfavour. After a moment, rubbing the roughened surface of his chin the wrong way, he muttered to his image in the glass:

"That a mug! Good Lord! what a looking mug!" Then, after a moment's silence, "Wonder if that fool feemale will be up here to-day."

He crossed over into his bedroom and peeped around the edge of the lowered curtain. The window looked out upon the skeleton-like tower of the artesian well and the cook-house and dairy-house close beside it. As he watched, he saw Hilma come out from the cook-house and hurry across toward the kitchen. Evidently, she was going to see about his dinner. But as she passed by the artesian well, she met young Delaney, one of Annixter's hands, coming up the trail by the irrigating ditch, leading his horse toward the stables, a great coil of barbed wire in his gloved hands and a pair of nippers thrust into his belt. No doubt, he had been mending the break in the line fence by the Long Trestle. Annixter saw him take off his wide-brimmed hat as he met Hilma, and the two stood there for some moments talking together. Annixter even heard Hilma laughing very gayly at something Delaney was saying. She patted his horse's neck affectionately, and Delaney, drawing the nippers from his belt, made as if to pinch her arm with them. She caught at his wrist and pushed him away, laughing again. To Annixter's mind the pair seemed astonishingly intimate. Brusquely his anger flamed up.

Ah, that was it, was it? Delaney and Hilma had an understanding between themselves. They carried on their affair right out there in the open, under his very eyes. It was absolutely disgusting. Had they no sense of decency, those two? Well, this ended it. He would stop that sort of thing short off; none of that on HIS ranch if he knew it. No, sir. He would pack that girl off before he was a day older. He wouldn't have that kind about the place. Not much! She'd have to get out. He would talk to old man Tree about it this afternoon. Whatever happened, HE insisted upon morality.

"And my dinner!" he suddenly exclaimed. "I've got to wait and go hungry—and maybe get sick again—while they carry on their disgusting love-making."

He turned about on the instant, and striding over to the electric bell, rang it again with all his might.

"When that feemale gets up here," he declared, "I'll just find out why I've got to wait like this. I'll take her down, to the Queen's taste. I'm lenient enough, Lord knows, but I don't propose to be imposed upon ALL the time."

A few moments later, while Annixter was pretending to read the county newspaper by the window in the dining-room, Hilma came in to set the table. At the time Annixter had his feet cocked on the window ledge and was smoking a cigar, but as soon as she entered the room he—without premeditation—brought his feet down to the floor and crushed out the lighted tip of his cigar under the window ledge. Over the top of the paper he glanced at her covertly from time to time.

Though Hilma was only nineteen years old, she was a large girl with all the development of a much older woman. There was a certain generous amplitude to the full, round curves of her hips and shoulders that suggested the precocious maturity of a healthy, vigorous animal life passed under the hot southern sun of a half-tropical country. She was, one knew at a glance, warm-blooded, full-blooded, with an even, comfortable balance of temperament. Her neck was thick, and sloped to her shoulders, with full, beautiful curves, and under her chin and under her ears the flesh was as white and smooth as floss satin, shading exquisitely to a faint delicate brown on her nape at the roots of her hair. Her throat rounded to meet her chin and cheek, with a soft swell of the skin, tinted pale amber in the shadows, but blending by barely perceptible gradations to the sweet, warm flush of her cheek. This colour on her temples was just touched with a certain blueness where the flesh was thin over the fine veining underneath. Her eyes were light brown, and so wide open that on the slightest provocation the full disc of the pupil was disclosed; the lids—just a fraction of a shade darker than the hue of her face—were edged with lashes that were almost black. While these lashes were not long, they were thick and rimmed her eyes with a fine, thin line. Her mouth was rather large, the lips shut tight, and nothing could have been more graceful, more charming than the outline of these full lips of hers, and her round white chin, modulating downward with a certain delicious roundness to her neck, her throat and the sweet feminine amplitude of her breast. The slightest movement of her head and shoulders sent a gentle undulation through all this beauty of soft outlines and smooth surfaces, the delicate amber shadows deepening or fading or losing themselves imperceptibly in the pretty rose-colour of her cheeks, or the dark, warm-tinted shadow of her thick brown hair.

Her hair seemed almost to have a life of its own, almost Medusa-like, thick, glossy and moist, lying in heavy, sweet-smelling masses over her forehead, over her small ears with their pink lobes, and far down upon her nape. Deep in between the coils and braids it was of a bitumen brownness, but in the sunlight it vibrated with a sheen like tarnished gold.

Like most large girls, her movements were not hurried, and this indefinite deliberateness of gesture, this slow grace, this certain ease of attitude, was a charm that was all her own.

But Hilma's greatest charm of all was her simplicity—a simplicity that was not only in the calm regularity of her face, with its statuesque evenness of contour, its broad surface of cheek and forehead and the masses of her straight smooth hair, but was apparent as well in the long line of her carriage, from her foot to her waist and the single deep swell from her waist to her shoulder. Almost unconsciously she dressed in harmony with this note of simplicity, and on this occasion wore a skirt of plain dark blue calico and a white shirt waist crisp from the laundry.

And yet, for all the dignity of this rigourous simplicity, there were about Hilma small contradictory suggestions of feminine daintiness, charming beyond words. Even Annixter could not help noticing that her feet were narrow and slender, and that the little steel buckles of her low shoes were polished bright, and that her fingertips and nails were of a fine rosy pink.

He found himself wondering how it was that a girl in Hilma's position should be able to keep herself so pretty, so trim, so clean and feminine, but he reflected that her work was chiefly in the dairy, and even there of the lightest order. She was on the ranch more for the sake of being with her parents than from any necessity of employment. Vaguely he seemed to understand that, in that great new land of the West, in the open-air, healthy life of the ranches, where the conditions of earning a livelihood were of the easiest, refinement among the younger women was easily to be found—not the refinement of education, nor culture, but the natural, intuitive refinement of the woman, not as yet defiled and crushed out by the sordid, strenuous life-struggle of over-populated districts. It was the original, intended and natural delicacy of an elemental existence, close to nature, close to life, close to the great, kindly earth.

As Hilma laid the table-spread, her arms opened to their widest reach, the white cloth setting a little glisten of reflected light underneath the chin, Annixter stirred in his place uneasily.

"Oh, it's you, is it, Miss Hilma?" he remarked, for the sake of saying something. "Good-morning. How do you do?"

"Good-morning, sir," she answered, looking up, resting for a moment on her outspread palms. "I hope you are better."

Her voice was low in pitch and of a velvety huskiness, seeming to come more from her chest than from her throat.

"Well, I'm some better," growled Annixter. Then suddenly he demanded, "Where's that dog?"

A decrepit Irish setter sometimes made his appearance in and about the ranch house, sleeping under the bed and eating when anyone about the place thought to give him a plate of bread.

Annixter had no particular interest in the dog. For weeks at a time he ignored its existence. It was not his dog. But to-day it seemed as if he could not let the subject rest. For no reason that he could explain even to himself, he recurred to it continually. He questioned Hilma minutely all about the dog. Who owned him? How old did she think he was? Did she imagine the dog was sick? Where had he got to? Maybe he had crawled off to die somewhere. He recurred to the subject all through the meal; apparently, he could talk of nothing else, and as she finally went away after clearing off the table, he went onto the porch and called after her:

"Say, Miss Hilma."

"Yes, sir."

"If that dog turns up again you let me know."

"Very well, sir."

Annixter returned to the dining-room and sat down in the chair he had just vacated. "To hell with the dog!" he muttered, enraged, he could not tell why.

When at length he allowed his attention to wander from Hilma Tree, he found that he had been staring fixedly at a thermometer upon the wall opposite, and this made him think that it had long been his intention to buy a fine barometer, an instrument that could be accurately depended on. But the barometer suggested the present condition of the weather and the likelihood of rain. In such case, much was to be done in the way of getting the seed ready and overhauling his ploughs and drills. He had not been away from the house in two days. It was time to be up and doing. He determined to put in the afternoon "taking a look around," and have a late supper. He would not go to Los Muertos; he would ignore Magnus Derrick's invitation. Possibly, though, it might be well to run over and see what was up.

"If I do," he said to himself, "I'll ride the buckskin." The buckskin was a half-broken broncho that fought like a fiend under the saddle until the quirt and spur brought her to her senses. But Annixter remembered that the Trees' cottage, next the dairy-house, looked out upon the stables, and perhaps Hilma would see him while he was mounting the horse and be impressed with his courage.

"Huh!" grunted Annixter under his breath, "I should like to see that fool Delaney try to bust that bronch. That's what I'D like to see."

However, as Annixter stepped from the porch of the ranch house, he was surprised to notice a grey haze over all the sky; the sunlight was gone; there was a sense of coolness in the air; the weather-vane on the barn—a fine golden trotting horse with flamboyant mane and tail—was veering in a southwest wind. Evidently the expected rain was close at hand.

Annixter crossed over to the stables reflecting that he could ride the buckskin to the Trees' cottage and tell Hilma that he would not be home to supper. The conference at Los Muertos would be an admirable excuse for this, and upon the spot he resolved to go over to the Derrick ranch house, after all.

As he passed the Trees' cottage, he observed with satisfaction that Hilma was going to and fro in the front room. If he busted the buckskin in the yard before the stable she could not help but see. Annixter found the stableman in the back of the barn greasing the axles of the buggy, and ordered him to put the saddle on the buckskin.

"Why, I don't think she's here, sir," answered the stableman, glancing into the stalls. "No, I remember now. Delaney took her out just after dinner. His other horse went lame and he wanted to go down by the Long Trestle to mend the fence. He started out, but had to come back."

"Oh, Delaney got her, did he?"

"Yes, sir. He had a circus with her, but he busted her right enough. When it comes to horse, Delaney can wipe the eye of any cow-puncher in the county, I guess."

"He can, can he?" observed Annixter. Then after a silence, "Well, all right, Billy; put my saddle on whatever you've got here. I'm going over to Los Muertos this afternoon."

"Want to look out for the rain, Mr. Annixter," remarked Billy. "Guess we'll have rain before night."

"I'll take a rubber coat," answered Annixter. "Bring the horse up to the ranch house when you're ready."

Annixter returned to the house to look for his rubber coat in deep disgust, not permitting himself to glance toward the dairy-house and the Trees' cottage. But as he reached the porch he heard the telephone ringing his call. It was Presley, who rang up from Los Muertos. He had heard from Harran that Annixter was, perhaps, coming over that evening. If he came, would he mind bringing over his—Presley's—bicycle. He had left it at the Quien Sabe ranch the day before and had forgotten to come back that way for it.

"Well," objected Annixter, a surly note in his voice, "I WAS going to RIDE over." "Oh, never mind, then," returned Presley easily. "I was to blame for forgetting it. Don't bother about it. I'll come over some of these days and get it myself."

Annixter hung up the transmitter with a vehement wrench and stamped out of the room, banging the door. He found his rubber coat hanging in the hallway and swung into it with a fierce movement of the shoulders that all but started the seams. Everything seemed to conspire to thwart him. It was just like that absent-minded, crazy poet, Presley, to forget his wheel. Well, he could come after it himself. He, Annixter, would ride SOME horse, anyhow. When he came out upon the porch he saw the wheel leaning against the fence where Presley had left it. If it stayed there much longer the rain would catch it. Annixter ripped out an oath. At every moment his ill-humour was increasing. Yet, for all that, he went back to the stable, pushing the bicycle before him, and countermanded his order, directing the stableman to get the buggy ready. He himself carefully stowed Presley's bicycle under the seat, covering it with a couple of empty sacks and a tarpaulin carriage cover.

While he was doing this, the stableman uttered an exclamation and paused in the act of backing the horse into the shafts, holding up a hand, listening.

From the hollow roof of the barn and from the thick velvet-like padding of dust over the ground outside, and from among the leaves of the few nearby trees and plants there came a vast, monotonous murmur that seemed to issue from all quarters of the horizon at once, a prolonged and subdued rustling sound, steady, even, persistent.

"There's your rain," announced the stableman. "The first of the season."

"And I got to be out in it," fumed Annixter, "and I suppose those swine will quit work on the big barn now."

When the buggy was finally ready, he put on his rubber coat, climbed in, and without waiting for the stableman to raise the top, drove out into the rain, a new-lit cigar in his teeth. As he passed the dairy-house, he saw Hilma standing in the doorway, holding out her hand to the rain, her face turned upward toward the grey sky, amused and interested at this first shower of the wet season. She was so absorbed that she did not see Annixter, and his clumsy nod in her direction passed unnoticed.

"She did it on purpose," Annixter told himself, chewing fiercely on his cigar. "Cuts me now, hey? Well, this DOES settle it. She leaves this ranch before I'm a day older."

He decided that he would put off his tour of inspection till the next day. Travelling in the buggy as he did, he must keep to the road which led to Derrick's, in very roundabout fashion, by way of Guadalajara. This rain would reduce the thick dust of the road to two feet of viscid mud. It would take him quite three hours to reach the ranch house on Los Muertos. He thought of Delaney and the buckskin and ground his teeth. And all this trouble, if you please, because of a fool feemale girl. A fine way for him to waste his time. Well, now he was done with it. His decision was taken now. She should pack.

Steadily the rain increased. There was no wind. The thick veil of wet descended straight from sky to earth, blurring distant outlines, spreading a vast sheen of grey over all the landscape. Its volume became greater, the prolonged murmuring note took on a deeper tone. At the gate to the road which led across Dyke's hop-fields toward Guadalajara, Annixter was obliged to descend and raise the top of the buggy. In doing so he caught the flesh of his hand in the joint of the iron elbow that supported the top and pinched it cruelly. It was the last misery, the culmination of a long train of wretchedness. On the instant he hated Hilma Tree so fiercely that his sharply set teeth all but bit his cigar in two.

While he was grabbing and wrenching at the buggy-top, the water from his hat brim dripping down upon his nose, the horse, restive under the drench of the rain, moved uneasily.

"Yah-h-h you!" he shouted, inarticulate with exasperation. "You—you—Gor-r-r, wait till I get hold of you. WHOA, you!"

But there was an interruption. Delaney, riding the buckskin, came around a bend in the road at a slow trot and Annixter, getting into the buggy again, found himself face to face with him.

"Why, hello, Mr. Annixter," said he, pulling up. "Kind of sort of wet, isn't it?"

Annixter, his face suddenly scarlet, sat back in his place abruptly, exclaiming:

"Oh—oh, there you are, are you?"

"I've been down there," explained Delaney, with a motion of his head toward the railroad, "to mend that break in the fence by the Long Trestle and I thought while I was about it I'd follow down along the fence toward Guadalajara to see if there were any more breaks. But I guess it's all right."

"Oh, you guess it's all right, do you?" observed Annixter through his teeth.

"Why—why—yes," returned the other, bewildered at the truculent ring in Annixter's voice. "I mended that break by the Long Trestle just now and— —

"Well, why didn't you mend it a week ago?" shouted Annixter wrathfully. "I've been looking for you all the morning, I have, and who told you you could take that buckskin? And the sheep were all over the right of way last night because of that break, and here that filthy pip, S. Behrman, comes down here this morning and wants to make trouble for me." Suddenly he cried out, "What do I FEED you for? What do I keep you around here for? Think it's just to fatten up your carcass, hey?"

"Why, Mr. Annixter— —" began Delaney.

"And don't TALK to me," vociferated the other, exciting himself with his own noise. "Don't you say a word to me even to apologise. If I've spoken to you once about that break, I've spoken fifty times."

"Why, sir," declared Delaney, beginning to get indignant, "the sheep did it themselves last night."

"I told you not to TALK to me," clamoured Annixter.

"But, say, look here— —"

"Get off the ranch. You get off the ranch. And taking that buckskin against my express orders. I won't have your kind about the place, not much. I'm easy-going enough, Lord knows, but I don't propose to be imposed on ALL the time. Pack off, you understand and do it lively. Go to the foreman and tell him I told him to pay you off and then clear out. And, you hear me," he concluded, with a menacing outthrust of his lower jaw, "you hear me, if

I catch you hanging around the ranch house after this, or if I so much as see you on Quien Sabe, I'll show you the way off of it, my friend, at the toe of my boot. Now, then, get out of the way and let me pass."

Angry beyond the power of retort, Delaney drove the spurs into the buckskin and passed the buggy in a single bound. Annixter gathered up the reins and drove on muttering to himself, and occasionally looking back to observe the buckskin flying toward the ranch house in a spattering shower of mud, Delaney urging her on, his head bent down against the falling rain.

"Huh," grunted Annixter with grim satisfaction, a certain sense of good humour at length returning to him, "that just about takes the saleratus out of YOUR dough, my friend."

A little farther on, Annixter got out of the buggy a second time to open another gate that let him out upon the Upper Road, not far distant from Guadalajara. It was the road that connected that town with Bonneville and that ran parallel with the railroad tracks. On the other side of the track he could see the infinite extension of the brown, bare land of Los Muertos, turning now to a soft, moist welter of fertility under the insistent caressing of the rain. The hard, sun-baked clods were decomposing, the crevices between drinking the wet with an eager, sucking noise. But the prospect was dreary; the distant horizons were blotted under drifting mists of rain; the eternal monotony of the earth lay open to the sombre low sky without a single adornment, without a single variation from its melancholy flatness. Near at hand the wires between the telegraph poles vibrated with a faint humming under the multitudinous fingering of the myriad of falling drops, striking among them and dripping off steadily from one to another. The poles themselves were dark and swollen and glistening with wet, while the little cones of glass on the transverse bars reflected the dull grey light of the end of the afternoon.

As Annixter was about to drive on, a freight train passed, coming from Guadalajara, going northward toward Bonneville, Fresno and San Francisco. It was a long train, moving slowly, methodically, with a measured coughing of its locomotive and a rhythmic cadence of its trucks over the interstices of the rails. On two or three of the flat cars near its end, Annixter plainly saw Magnus Derrick's ploughs, their bright coating of red and green paint setting a single brilliant note in all this array of grey and brown.

Annixter halted, watching the train file past, carrying Derrick's ploughs away from his ranch, at this very time of the first rain, when they would be most needed. He watched it, silent, thoughtful, and without articulate comment. Even after it passed he sat in his place a long time, watching it lose itself slowly in the distance, its prolonged rumble diminishing to a faint murmur. Soon he heard the engine sounding its whistle for the Long Trestle.

But the moving train no longer carried with it that impression of terror and destruction that had so thrilled Presley's imagination the night before. It passed slowly on its way with a mournful roll of wheels, like the passing of a cortege, like a file of artillery-caissons charioting dead bodies; the engine's smoke enveloping it in a mournful veil, leaving a sense of melancholy in its wake, moving past there, lugubrious, lamentable, infinitely sad under the grey sky and under the grey mist of rain which continued to fall with a subdued, rustling sound, steady, persistent, a vast monotonous murmur that seemed to come from all quarters of the horizon at once.

CHAPTER III

When Annixter arrived at the Los Muertos ranch house that same evening, he found a little group already assembled in the dining-room. Magnus Derrick, wearing the frock coat of broadcloth that he had put on for the occasion, stood with his back to the fireplace. Harran sat close at hand, one leg thrown over the arm of his chair. Presley lounged on the sofa, in corduroys and high laced boots, smoking cigarettes. Broderson leaned on his folded arms at one corner of the dining table, and Genslinger, editor and proprietor of the principal newspaper of the county, the "Bonneville Mercury," stood with his hat and driving gloves under his arm, opposite Derrick, a half-emptied glass of whiskey and water in his hand.

As Annixter entered he heard Genslinger observe: "I'll have a leader in the 'Mercury' to-morrow that will interest you people. There's some talk of your ranch lands being graded in value this winter. I suppose you will all buy?"

In an instant the editor's words had riveted upon him the attention of every man in the room. Annixter broke the moment's silence that followed with the remark:

"Well, it's about time they graded these lands of theirs."

The question in issue in Genslinger's remark was of the most vital interest to the ranchers around Bonneville and Guadalajara. Neither Magnus Derrick, Broderson, Annixter, nor Osterman actually owned all the ranches which they worked. As yet, the vast majority of these wheat lands were the property of the P. and S. W. The explanation of this condition of affairs went back to the early history of the Pacific and Southwestern, when, as a bonus for the construction of the road, the national government had granted to the company the odd numbered sections of land on either side of the proposed line of route for a distance of twenty miles. Indisputably, these sections belonged to the P. and S. W. The even-numbered sections being government property could be and had been taken up by the ranchers, but the railroad sections, or, as they were called, the "alternate sections," would have to be purchased direct from the railroad itself.

But this had not prevented the farmers from "coming in" upon that part of the San Joaquin. Long before this the railroad had thrown open these lands, and, by means of circulars, distributed broadcast throughout the State, had expressly invited settlement thereon. At that time patents had not been issued to the railroad for their odd-numbered sections, but as soon as the land was patented the railroad would grade it in value and offer it for sale, the first occupants having the first chance of purchase. The price of these lands was to be fixed by the price the government put upon its own adjoining lands—about two dollars and a half per acre.

With cultivation and improvement the ranches must inevitably appreciate in value. There was every chance to make fortunes. When the railroad lands about Bonneville had been thrown open, there had been almost a rush in the matter of settlement, and Broderson, Annixter, Derrick, and Osterman, being foremost with their claims, had secured the pick of the country. But the land once settled upon, the P. and S. W. seemed to be in no hurry as to fixing exactly the value of its sections included in the various ranches and offering them for sale. The matter dragged along from year to year, was forgotten for months together, being only brought to mind on such occasions as this, when the rumour spread that the General Office was about to take definite action in the affair.

"As soon as the railroad wants to talk business with me," observed Annixter, "about selling me their interest in Quien Sabe, I'm ready. The land has more than quadrupled in value. I'll bet I could sell it to-morrow for fifteen dollars an acre, and if I buy of the railroad for two and a half an acre, there's boodle in the game."

"For two and a half!" exclaimed Genslinger. "You don't suppose the railroad will let their land go for any such figure as that, do you? Wherever did you get that idea?"

"From the circulars and pamphlets," answered Harran, "that the railroad issued to us when they opened these lands. They are pledged to that. Even the P. and S. W. couldn't break such a pledge as that. You are new in the country, Mr. Genslinger. You don't remember the conditions upon which we took up this land."

"And our improvements," exclaimed Annixter. "Why, Magnus and I have put about five thousand dollars between us into that irrigating ditch already. I guess we are not improving the land just to make it valuable for the railroad people. No matter how much we improve the land, or how much it increases in value, they have got to stick by their agreement on the basis of two-fifty per acre. Here's one case where the P. and S. W. DON'T get everything in sight."

Genslinger frowned, perplexed.

"I AM new in the country, as Harran says," he answered, "but it seems to me that there's no fairness in that proposition. The presence of the railroad has helped increase the value of your ranches quite as much as your improvements. Why should you get all the benefit of the rise in value and the railroad nothing? The fair way would be to share it between you."

"I don't care anything about that," declared Annixter. "They agreed to charge but two-fifty, and they've got to stick to it."

"Well," murmured Genslinger, "from what I know of the affair, I don't believe the P. and S. W. intends to sell for two-fifty an acre, at all. The managers of the road want the best price they can get for everything in these hard times."

"Times aren't ever very hard for the railroad," hazards old Broderson.

Broderson was the oldest man in the room. He was about sixty-five years of age, venerable, with a white beard, his figure bent earthwards with hard work.

He was a narrow-minded man, painfully conscientious in his statements lest he should be unjust to somebody; a slow thinker, unable to let a subject drop when once he had started upon it. He had no sooner uttered his remark about hard times than he was moved to qualify it.

"Hard times," he repeated, a troubled, perplexed note in his voice; "well, yes—yes. I suppose the road DOES have hard times, maybe. Everybody does—of course. I didn't mean that exactly. I believe in being just and fair to everybody. I mean that we've got to use their lines and pay their charges good years AND bad years, the P. and S. W. being the only road in the State. That is—well, when I say the only road—no, I won't say the ONLY road. Of course there are other roads. There's the D. P. and M. and the San Francisco and North Pacific, that runs up to Ukiah. I got a brother-in-law in Ukiah. That's not much of a wheat country round Ukiah though they DO grow SOME wheat there, come to think. But I guess it's too far north. Well, of course there isn't MUCH. Perhaps sixty thousand acres in the whole county—if you include barley and oats. I don't know; maybe it's nearer forty thousand. I don't remember very well. That's a good many years ago. I——"

But Annixter, at the end of all patience, turned to Genslinger, cutting short the old man:

"Oh, rot! Of course the railroad will sell at two-fifty," he cried. "We've got the contracts."

"Look to them, then, Mr. Annixter," retorted Genslinger significantly, "look to them. Be sure that you are protected."

Soon after this Genslinger took himself away, and Derrick's Chinaman came in to set the table.

"What do you suppose he meant?" asked Broderson, when Genslinger was gone.

"About this land business?" said Annixter. "Oh, I don't know. Some tom fool idea. Haven't we got their terms printed in black and white in their circulars? There's their pledge."

"Oh, as to pledges," murmured Broderson, "the railroad is not always TOO much hindered by those."

"Where's Osterman?" demanded Annixter, abruptly changing the subject as if it were not worth discussion. "Isn't that goat Osterman coming down here to-night?"

"You telephoned him, didn't you, Presley?" inquired Magnus.

Presley had taken Princess Nathalie upon his knee stroking her long, sleek hair, and the cat, stupefied with beatitude, had closed her eyes to two fine lines, clawing softly at the corduroy of Presley's trousers with alternate paws.

"Yes, sir," returned Presley. "He said he would be here."

And as he spoke, young Osterman arrived.

He was a young fellow, but singularly inclined to baldness. His ears, very red and large, stuck out at right angles from either side of his head, and his mouth, too, was large—a great horizontal slit beneath his nose. His cheeks were of a brownish red, the cheek bones a little salient. His face was that of a comic actor, a singer of songs, a man never at a loss for an answer, continually striving to make a laugh. But he took no great interest in ranching and left the management of his land to his superintendents and foremen, he, himself, living in Bonneville. He was a poser, a wearer of clothes, forever acting a part, striving to create an impression, to draw attention to himself. He was not without a certain energy, but he devoted it to small ends, to perfecting himself in little accomplishments, continually running after some new thing, incapable of persisting long in any one course. At one moment his mania would be fencing; the next, sleight-of-hand tricks; the next, archery. For upwards of one month he had devoted himself to learning how to play two banjos simultaneously, then abandoning this had developed a sudden passion for stamped leather work and had made a quantity of purses, tennis belts, and hat bands, which he presented to young ladies of his acquaintance. It was his policy never to make an enemy. He was liked far better than he was respected. People spoke of him as "that goat Osterman," or "that fool Osterman kid," and invited him to dinner. He was of the sort who somehow cannot be ignored. If only because of his clamour he made himself important. If he had one abiding trait, it was his desire of astonishing people, and in some way, best known to himself, managed to cause the circulation of the most extraordinary stories wherein he, himself, was the chief actor. He was glib, voluble, dexterous, ubiquitous, a teller of funny stories, a cracker of jokes.

Naturally enough, he was heavily in debt, but carried the burden of it with perfect nonchalance. The year before S. Behrman had held mortgages for fully a third of his crop and had squeezed him viciously for interest. But for all that, Osterman and S. Behrman were continually seen arm-in-arm on the main street of Bonneville. Osterman was accustomed to slap S. Behrman on his fat back, declaring:

"You're a good fellow, old jelly-belly, after all, hey?"

As Osterman entered from the porch, after hanging his cavalry poncho and dripping hat on the rack outside, Mrs. Derrick appeared in the door that opened from the dining-room into the glass-roofed hallway just beyond. Osterman saluted her with effusive cordiality and with ingratiating blandness.

"I am not going to stay," she explained, smiling pleasantly at the group of men, her pretty, wide-open brown eyes, with their look of inquiry and innocence, glancing from face to face, "I only came to see if you wanted anything and to say how do you do."

She began talking to old Broderson, making inquiries as to his wife, who had been sick the last week, and Osterman turned to the company, shaking hands all around, keeping up an incessant stream of conversation.

"Hello, boys and girls. Hello, Governor. Sort of a gathering of the clans to-night. Well, if here isn't that man Annixter. Hello, Buck. What do you know? Kind of dusty out to-night."

At once Annixter began to get red in the face, retiring towards a corner of the room, standing in an awkward position by the case of stuffed birds, shambling and confused, while Mrs. Derrick was present, standing rigidly on both feet, his elbows close to his sides. But he was angry with Osterman, muttering imprecations to himself, horribly vexed that the young fellow should call him "Buck" before Magnus's wife. This goat Osterman! Hadn't he any sense, that fool? Couldn't he ever learn how to behave before a feemale? Calling him "Buck" like that while Mrs. Derrick was there. Why a stable-boy would know better; a hired man would have better manners. All through the dinner that followed Annixter was out of sorts, sulking in his place, refusing to eat by way of vindicating his self-respect, resolving to bring Osterman up with a sharp turn if he called him "Buck" again.

The Chinaman had made a certain kind of plum pudding for dessert, and Annixter, who remembered other dinners at the Derrick's, had been saving himself for this, and had meditated upon it all through the meal. No doubt, it would restore all his good humour, and he believed his stomach was so far recovered as to be able to stand it.

But, unfortunately, the pudding was served with a sauce that he abhorred—a thick, gruel-like, colourless mixture, made from plain water and sugar. Before he could interfere, the Chinaman had poured a quantity of it upon his plate.

"Faugh!" exclaimed Annixter. "It makes me sick. Such—such SLOOP. Take it away. I'll have mine straight, if you don't mind."

"That's good for your stomach, Buck," observed young Osterman; "makes it go down kind of sort of slick; don't you see? Sloop, hey? That's a good name."

"Look here, don't you call me Buck. You don't seem to have any sense, and, besides, it ISN'T good for my stomach. I know better. What do YOU know about my stomach, anyhow? Just looking at sloop like that makes me sick."

A little while after this the Chinaman cleared away the dessert and brought in coffee and cigars. The whiskey bottle and the syphon of soda-water reappeared. The men eased themselves in their places, pushing back from the table, lighting their cigars, talking of the beginning of the rains and the prospects of a rise in wheat. Broderson began an elaborate mental calculation, trying to settle in his mind the exact date of his visit to Ukiah, and Osterman did sleight-of-hand tricks with bread pills. But Princess Nathalie, the cat, was uneasy. Annixter was occupying her own particular chair in which she slept every night. She could not go to sleep, but spied upon him continually, watching his every movement with her lambent, yellow eyes, clear as amber.

Then, at length, Magnus, who was at the head of the table, moved in his place, assuming a certain magisterial attitude. "Well, gentlemen," he observed, "I have lost my case against the railroad, the grain-rate case. Ulsteen decided against me, and now I hear rumours to the effect that rates for the hauling of grain are to be advanced."

When Magnus had finished, there was a moment's silence, each member of the group maintaining his attitude of attention and interest. It was Harran who first spoke.

"S. Behrman manipulated the whole affair. There's a big deal of some kind in the air, and if there is, we all know who is back of it; S. Behrman, of course, but who's back of him? It's Shelgrim."

Shelgrim! The name fell squarely in the midst of the conversation, abrupt, grave, sombre, big with suggestion, pregnant with huge associations. No one in the group who was not familiar with it; no one, for that matter, in the county, the State, the whole reach of the West, the entire Union, that did not entertain convictions as to the man who carried it; a giant figure in the end-of-the-century finance, a product of circumstance, an inevitable result of conditions, characteristic, typical, symbolic of ungovernable forces. In the New Movement, the New Finance, the reorganisation of capital, the amalgamation of powers, the consolidation of enormous enterprises—no one individual was more constantly in the eye of the world; no one was more hated, more dreaded, no one more compelling of unwilling tribute to his commanding genius, to the colossal intellect operating the width of an entire continent than the president and owner of the Pacific and Southwestern.

"I don't think, however, he has moved yet," said Magnus.

"The thing for us, then," exclaimed Osterman, "is to stand from under before he does."

"Moved yet!" snorted Annixter. "He's probably moved so long ago that we've never noticed it."

"In any case," hazarded Magnus, "it is scarcely probable that the deal—whatever it is to be—has been consummated. If we act quickly, there may be a chance."

"Act quickly! How?" demanded Annixter. "Good Lord! what can you do? We're cinched already. It all amounts to just this: YOU CAN'T BUCK AGAINST THE RAILROAD. We've tried it and tried it, and we are stuck every time. You, yourself, Derrick, have just lost your grain-rate case. S. Behrman did you up. Shelgrim owns the courts. He's got men like Ulsteen in his pocket. He's got the Railroad Commission in his pocket. He's got the Governor of the State in his pocket. He keeps a million-dollar lobby at Sacramento every minute of the time the legislature is in session; he's got his own men on the floor of the United States Senate. He has the whole thing organised like an army corps. What ARE you going to do? He sits in his office in San Francisco and pulls the strings and we've got to dance."

"But—well—but," hazarded Broderson, "but there's the Interstate Commerce Commission. At least on long-haul rates they——"

"Hoh, yes, the Interstate Commerce Commission," shouted Annixter, scornfully, "that's great, ain't it? The greatest Punch and Judy; show on earth. It's almost as good as the Railroad Commission. There never was and there never will be a California Railroad Commission not in the pay of the P. and S. W."

"It is to the Railroad Commission, nevertheless," remarked Magnus, "that the people of the State must look for relief. That is our only hope. Once elect Commissioners who would be loyal to the people, and the whole system of excessive rates falls to the ground."

"Well, why not HAVE a Railroad Commission of our own, then?" suddenly declared young Osterman.

"Because it can't be done," retorted Annixter. "YOU CAN'T BUCK AGAINST THE RAILROAD and if you could you can't organise the farmers in the San Joaquin. We tried it once, and it was enough to turn your stomach. The railroad quietly bought delegates through S. Behrman and did us up."

"Well, that's the game to play," said Osterman decisively, "buy delegates."

"It's the only game that seems to win," admitted Harran gloomily. "Or ever will win," exclaimed Osterman, a sudden excitement seeming to take possession of him. His face—the face of a comic actor, with its great slit of mouth and stiff, red ears—went abruptly pink.

"Look here," he cried, "this thing is getting desperate. We've fought and fought in the courts and out and we've tried agitation and—and all the rest of it and S. Behrman sacks us every time. Now comes the time when there's a prospect of a big crop; we've had no rain for two years and the land has had a long rest. If there is any rain at all this winter, we'll have a bonanza year, and just at this very moment when we've got our chance—a chance to pay off our mortgages and get clear of debt and make a strike— here is Shelgrim making a deal to cinch us and put up rates. And now here's the primaries coming off and a new Railroad Commission going in. That's why Shelgrim chose this time to make his deal. If we wait till Shelgrim pulls it off, we're done for, that's flat. I tell you we're in a fix if we don't keep an eye open. Things are getting desperate. Magnus has just said that the key to the whole thing is the Railroad Commission. Well, why not have a Commission of our own? Never mind how we get it, let's get it. If it's got to be bought, let's buy it and put our own men on it and dictate what the rates will be. Suppose it costs a hundred thousand dollars. Well, we'll get back more than that in cheap rates."

"Mr. Osterman," said Magnus, fixing the young man with a swift glance, "Mr. Osterman, you are proposing a scheme of bribery, sir."

"I am proposing," repeated Osterman, "a scheme of bribery. Exactly so."

"And a crazy, wild-eyed scheme at that," said Annixter gruffly. "Even supposing you bought a Railroad Commission and got your schedule of low rates, what happens? The P. and S. W. crowd get out an injunction and tie you up."

"They would tie themselves up, too. Hauling at low rates is better than no hauling at all. The wheat has got to be moved." "Oh, rot!" cried Annixter. "Aren't you ever going to learn any sense? Don't you know that cheap transportation would benefit the Liverpool buyers and not us? Can't it be FED into you that you can't buck against the railroad? When you try to buy a Board of Commissioners don't you see that you'll have to bid against the railroad, bid against a corporation that can chuck out millions to our thousands? Do you think you can bid against the P. and S. W.?"

"The railroad don't need to know we are in the game against them till we've got our men seated."

"And when you've got them seated, what's to prevent the corporation buying them right over your head?"

"If we've got the right kind of men in they could not be bought that way," interposed Harran. "I don't know but what there's something in what Osterman says. We'd have the naming of the Commission and we'd name honest men."

Annixter struck the table with his fist in exasperation.

"Honest men!" he shouted; "the kind of men you could get to go into such a scheme would have to be DIS-honest to begin with."

Broderson, shifting uneasily in his place, fingering his beard with a vague, uncertain gesture, spoke again:

"It would be the CHANCE of them—our Commissioners—selling out against the certainty of Shelgrim doing us up. That is," he hastened to add, "ALMOST a certainty; pretty near a certainty."

"Of course, it would be a chance," exclaimed Osterman. "But it's come to the point where we've got to take chances, risk a big stake to make a big strike, and risk is better than sure failure."

"I can be no party to a scheme of avowed bribery and corruption, Mr. Osterman," declared Magnus, a ring of severity in his voice. "I am surprised, sir, that you should even broach the subject in my hearing."

"And," cried Annixter, "it can't be done."

"I don't know," muttered Harran, "maybe it just wants a little spark like this to fire the whole train."

Magnus glanced at his son in considerable surprise. He had not expected this of Harran. But so great was his affection for his son, so accustomed had he become to listening to his advice, to respecting his opinions, that, for the moment, after the first shock of surprise and disappointment, he was influenced to give a certain degree of attention to this new proposition. He in no way countenanced it. At any moment he was prepared to rise in his place and denounce it and Osterman both. It was trickery of the most contemptible order, a thing he believed to be unknown to the old school of politics and statesmanship to which he was proud to belong; but since Harran, even for one moment, considered it, he, Magnus, who trusted Harran implicitly, would do likewise—if it was only to oppose and defeat it in its very beginnings.

And abruptly the discussion began. Gradually Osterman, by dint of his clamour, his strident reiteration, the plausibility of his glib, ready assertions, the ease with which he extricated himself when apparently driven to a corner, completely won over old Broderson to his way of thinking. Osterman bewildered him with his volubility, the lightning rapidity with which he leaped from one subject to another, garrulous, witty, flamboyant, terrifying the old man with pictures of the swift approach of ruin, the imminence of danger.

Annixter, who led the argument against him—loving argument though he did—appeared to poor advantage, unable to present his side effectively. He called Osterman a fool, a goat, a senseless, crazy-headed jackass, but was unable to refute his assertions. His debate was the clumsy heaving of brickbats, brutal, direct. He contradicted everything Osterman said as a matter of principle, made conflicting assertions, declarations that were absolutely inconsistent, and when Osterman or Harran used these against him, could only exclaim:

"Well, in a way it's so, and then again in a way it isn't."

But suddenly Osterman discovered a new argument. "If we swing this deal," he cried, "we've got old jelly-belly Behrman right where we want him."

"He's the man that does us every time," cried Harran. "If there is dirty work to be done in which the railroad doesn't wish to appear, it is S. Behrman who does it. If the freight rates are to be 'adjusted' to squeeze us a little harder, it is S. Behrman who regulates what we can stand. If there's a judge to be bought, it is S. Behrman who does the bargaining. If there is a jury to be bribed, it is S. Behrman who handles the money. If there is an election to be jobbed, it is S. Behrman who manipulates it. It's Behrman here and Behrman there. It is Behrman we come against every time we make a move. It is Behrman who has the grip of us and will never let go till he has squeezed us bone dry. Why, when I think of it all sometimes I wonder I keep my hands off the man."

Osterman got on his feet; leaning across the table, gesturing wildly with his right hand, his serio-comic face, with its bald forehead and stiff, red ears, was inflamed with excitement. He took the floor, creating an impression, attracting all attention to himself, playing to the gallery, gesticulating, clamourous, full of noise.

"Well, now is your chance to get even," he vociferated. "It is now or never. You can take it and save the situation for yourselves and all California or you can leave it and rot on your own ranches. Buck, I know you. I know you're not afraid of anything that wears skin. I know you've got sand all through you, and I know if I showed you how we could put our deal through and seat a Commission of our own, you wouldn't hang back. Governor, you're a brave man. You know the advantage of prompt and fearless action. You are not the sort to shrink from taking chances. To play for big stakes is just your game—to stake a fortune on the turn of a card. You didn't get the reputation of being the strongest poker player in El

Dorado County for nothing. Now, here's the biggest gamble that ever came your way. If we stand up to it like men with guts in us, we'll win out. If we hesitate, we're lost."

"I don't suppose you can help playing the goat, Osterman," remarked Annixter, "but what's your idea? What do you think we can do? I'm not saying," he hastened to interpose, "that you've anyways convinced me by all this cackling. I know as well as you that we are in a hole. But I knew that before I came here to-night. YOU'VE not done anything to make me change my mind. But just what do you propose? Let's hear it."

"Well, I say the first thing to do is to see Disbrow. He's the political boss of the Denver, Pueblo, and Mojave road. We will have to get in with the machine some way and that's particularly why I want Magnus with us. He knows politics better than any of us and if we don't want to get sold again we will have to have some one that's in the know to steer us."

"The only politics I understand, Mr. Osterman," answered Magnus sternly, "are honest politics. You must look elsewhere for your political manager. I refuse to have any part in this matter. If the Railroad Commission can be nominated legitimately, if your arrangements can be made without bribery, I am with you to the last iota of my ability."

"Well, you can't get what you want without paying for it," contradicted Annixter.

Broderson was about to speak when Osterman kicked his foot under the table. He, himself, held his peace. He was quick to see that if he could involve Magnus and Annixter in an argument, Annixter, for the mere love of contention, would oppose the Governor and, without knowing it, would commit himself to his—Osterman's—scheme.

This was precisely what happened. In a few moments Annixter was declaring at top voice his readiness to mortgage the crop of Quien Sabe, if necessary, for the sake of "busting S. Behrman." He could see no great obstacle in the way of controlling the nominating convention so far as securing the naming of two Railroad Commissioners was concerned. Two was all they needed. Probably it WOULD cost money. You didn't get something for nothing. It would cost them all a good deal more if they sat like lumps on a log and played tiddledy-winks while Shelgrim sold out from under them. Then there was this, too: the P. and S. W. were hard up just then. The shortage on the State's wheat crop for the last two years had affected them, too. They were retrenching in expenditures all along the line. Hadn't they just cut wages in all departments? There was this affair of

Dyke's to prove it. The railroad didn't always act as a unit, either. There was always a party in it that opposed spending too much money. He would bet that party was strong just now. He was kind of sick himself of being kicked by S. Behrman. Hadn't that pip turned up on his ranch that very day to bully him about his own line fence? Next he would be telling him what kind of clothes he ought to wear. Harran had the right idea. Somebody had got to be busted mighty soon now and he didn't propose that it should be he.

"Now you are talking something like sense," observed Osterman. "I thought you would see it like that when you got my idea."

"Your idea, YOUR idea!" cried Annixter. "Why, I've had this idea myself for over three years."

"What about Disbrow?" asked Harran, hastening to interrupt. "Why do we want to see Disbrow?"

"Disbrow is the political man for the Denver, Pueblo, and Mojave," answered Osterman, "and you see it's like this: the Mojave road don't run up into the valley at all. Their terminus is way to the south of us, and they don't care anything about grain rates through the San Joaquin. They don't care how anti-railroad the Commission is, because the Commission's rulings can't affect them. But they divide traffic with the P. and S. W. in the southern part of the State and they have a good deal of influence with that road. I want to get the Mojave road, through Disbrow, to recommend a Commissioner of our choosing to the P. and S. W. and have the P. and S. W. adopt him as their own."

"Who, for instance?"

"Darrell, that Los Angeles man—remember?"

"Well, Darrell is no particular friend of Disbrow," said Annixter. "Why should Disbrow take him up?"

"PREE-cisely," cried Osterman. "We make it worth Disbrow's while to do it. We go to him and say, 'Mr. Disbrow, you manage the politics for the Mojave railroad, and what you say goes with your Board of Directors. We want you to adopt our candidate for Railroad Commissioner for the third district. How much do you want for doing it?' I KNOW we can buy Disbrow. That gives us one Commissioner. We need not bother about that any more. In the first district we don't make any move at all. We let the political managers of the P. and S. W. nominate whoever they like. Then we concentrate all our efforts to putting in our man in the second district. There is where the big fight will come."

"I see perfectly well what you mean, Mr. Osterman," observed Magnus, "but make no mistake, sir, as to my attitude in this business. You may count me as out of it entirely."

"Well, suppose we win," put in Annixter truculently, already acknowledging himself as involved in the proposed undertaking; "suppose we win and get low rates for hauling grain. How about you, then? You count yourself IN then, don't you? You get all the benefit of lower rates without sharing any of the risks we take to secure them. No, nor any of the expense, either. No, you won't dirty your fingers with helping us put this deal through, but you won't be so cursed particular when it comes to sharing the profits, will you?"

Magnus rose abruptly to his full height, the nostrils of his thin, hawk-like nose vibrating, his smooth-shaven face paler than ever.

"Stop right where you are, sir," he exclaimed. "You forget yourself, Mr. Annixter. Please understand that I tolerate such words as you have permitted yourself to make use of from no man, not even from my guest. I shall ask you to apologise."

In an instant he dominated the entire group, imposing a respect that was as much fear as admiration. No one made response. For the moment he was the Master again, the Leader. Like so many delinquent school-boys, the others cowered before him, ashamed, put to confusion, unable to find their tongues. In that brief instant of silence following upon Magnus's outburst, and while he held them subdued and over-mastered, the fabric of their scheme of corruption and dishonesty trembled to its base. It was the last protest of the Old School, rising up there in denunciation of the new order of things, the statesman opposed to the politician; honesty, rectitude, uncompromising integrity, prevailing for the last time against the devious manoeuvring, the evil communications, the rotten expediency of a corrupted institution.

For a few seconds no one answered. Then, Annixter, moving abruptly and uneasily in his place, muttered:

"I spoke upon provocation. If you like, we'll consider it unsaid. I don't know what's going to become of us—go out of business, I presume."

"I understand Magnus all right," put in Osterman. "He don't have to go into this thing, if it's against his conscience. That's all right. Magnus can stay out if he wants to, but that won't prevent us going ahead and seeing what we can do. Only there's this about it." He turned again to Magnus, speaking with every degree of earnestness, every appearance of conviction. "I did not deny, Governor, from the very start that this would mean bribery. But you don't suppose that I like the idea either. If there was one legitimate hope that was yet left untried, no matter how forlorn it was, I would try it. But there's not. It is literally and soberly true that every means of help—every honest means—has been attempted. Shelgrim is going to cinch us. Grain rates are increasing, while, on the other hand, the price of wheat is sagging lower and lower all the time. If we don't do something we are ruined."

Osterman paused for a moment, allowing precisely the right number of seconds to elapse, then altering and lowering his voice, added:

"I respect the Governor's principles. I admire them. They do him every degree of credit." Then, turning directly to Magnus, he concluded with, "But I only want you to ask yourself, sir, if, at such a crisis, one ought to think of oneself, to consider purely personal motives in such a desperate situation as this? Now, we want you with us, Governor; perhaps not openly, if you don't wish it, but tacitly, at least. I won't ask you for an answer to-night, but what I do ask of you is to consider this matter seriously and think over the whole business. Will you do it?"

Osterman ceased definitely to speak, leaning forward across the table, his eyes fixed on Magnus's face. There was a silence. Outside, the rain fell continually with an even, monotonous murmur. In the group of men around the table no one stirred nor spoke. They looked steadily at Magnus, who, for the moment, kept his glance fixed thoughtfully upon the table before him. In another moment he raised his head and looked from face to face around the group. After all, these were his neighbours, his friends, men with whom he had been upon the closest terms of association. In a way they represented what now had come to be his world. His single swift glance took in the men, one after another. Annixter, rugged, crude, sitting awkwardly and uncomfortably in his chair, his unhandsome face, with its outthrust lower lip and deeply cleft masculine chin, flushed and eager, his yellow hair disordered, the one tuft on the crown standing stiffly forth like the feather in an Indian's scalp lock; Broderson, vaguely combing at his long beard with a persistent maniacal gesture, distressed, troubled and uneasy; Osterman, with his comedy face, the face of a music-hall singer, his head bald and set off by his great red ears, leaning back in his place, softly cracking the knuckle of a forefinger, and, last of all and close to his elbow, his son, his support, his confidant and companion, Harran, so like himself, with his own erect, fine carriage, his thin, beak-like nose and his blond hair, with its tendency to curl in a forward direction in front of the ears, young, strong, courageous, full of the promise of the future years. His blue eyes looked straight into his father's with what Magnus could fancy a glance of appeal. Magnus could see that expression in the faces of the others very plainly. They looked to him as their natural leader, their chief who was to bring them out from this abominable trouble which was closing in upon them, and in them all he saw many types. They—these men around his table on that night of the first rain of a coming season—seemed to stand in his imagination for many others—all the farmers, ranchers, and wheat growers of the great San Joaquin. Their words were the words of a whole community; their distress, the distress of an entire State, harried beyond the bounds of endurance, driven to the wall, coerced, exploited, harassed to the limits of exasperation. "I will think of it," he said, then hastened to add, "but I can tell you beforehand that you may expect only a refusal."

After Magnus had spoken, there was a prolonged silence. The conference seemed of itself to have come to an end for that evening. Presley lighted another cigarette from the butt of the one he had been smoking, and the cat, Princess Nathalie, disturbed by his movement and by a whiff of drifting smoke, jumped from his knee to the floor and picking her way across the room to Annixter, rubbed gently against his legs, her tail in the air, her back delicately arched. No doubt she thought it time to settle herself for the night, and as Annixter gave no indication of vacating his chair, she chose this way of cajoling him into ceding his place to her. But Annixter was irritated at the Princess's attentions, misunderstanding their motive.

"Get out!" he exclaimed, lifting his feet to the rung of the chair. "Lord love me, but I sure do hate a cat."

"By the way," observed Osterman, "I passed Genslinger by the gate as I came in to-night. Had he been here?"

"Yes, he was here," said Harran, "and—" but Annixter took the words out of his mouth.

"He says there's some talk of the railroad selling us their sections this winter."

"Oh, he did, did he?" exclaimed Osterman, interested at once. "Where did he hear that?"

"Where does a railroad paper get its news? From the General Office, I suppose."

"I hope he didn't get it straight from headquarters that the land was to be graded at twenty dollars an acre," murmured Broderson.

"What's that?" demanded Osterman. "Twenty dollars! Here, put me on, somebody. What's all up? What did Genslinger say?"

"Oh, you needn't get scared," said Annixter. "Genslinger don't know, that's all. He thinks there was no understanding that the price of the land should not be advanced when the P. and S. W. came to sell to us."

"Oh," muttered Osterman relieved. Magnus, who had gone out into the office on the other side of the glass-roofed hallway, returned with a long, yellow envelope in his hand, stuffed with newspaper clippings and thin, closely printed pamphlets.

"Here is the circular," he remarked, drawing out one of the pamphlets. "The conditions of settlement to which the railroad obligated itself are very explicit."

He ran over the pages of the circular, then read aloud:

"'The Company invites settlers to go upon its lands before patents are issued or the road is completed, and intends in such cases to sell to them in preference to any other applicants and at a price based upon the value of the land without improvements,' and on the other page here," he remarked, "they refer to this again. 'In ascertaining the value of the lands, any improvements that a settler or any other person may have on the lands will not be taken into consideration, neither will the price be increased in consequence thereof.... Settlers are thus insured that in addition to being accorded the first privilege of purchase, at the graded price, they will also be protected in their improvements.' And here," he commented, "in Section IX. it reads, 'The lands are not uniform in price, but are offered at various figures from $2.50 upward per acre. Usually land covered with tall timber is held at $5.00 per acre, and that with pine at $10.00. Most is for sale at $2.50 and $5.00.'"

"When you come to read that carefully," hazarded old Broderson, "it—it's not so VERY REASSURING. 'MOST is for sale at two-fifty an acre,' it says. That don't mean 'ALL,' that only means SOME. I wish now that I had secured a more iron-clad agreement from the P. and S. W. when I took up its sections on my ranch, and—and Genslinger is in a position to know the intentions of the railroad. At least, he—he—he is in TOUCH with them. All newspaper men are. Those, I mean, who are subsidised by the General Office. But, perhaps, Genslinger isn't subsidised, I don't know. I—I am not sure. Maybe—perhaps"

"Oh, you don't know and you do know, and maybe and perhaps, and you're not so sure," vociferated Annixter. "How about ignoring the value of our improvements? Nothing hazy about THAT statement, I guess. It says in so many words that any improvements we make will not be considered when the land is appraised and that's the same thing, isn't it? The unimproved land is worth two-fifty an acre; only timber land is worth more and there's none too much timber about here."

"Well, one thing at a time," said Harran. "The thing for us now is to get into this primary election and the convention and see if we can push our men for Railroad Commissioners."

"Right," declared Annixter. He rose, stretching his arms above his head. "I've about talked all the wind out of me," he said. "Think I'll be moving along. It's pretty near midnight."

But when Magnus's guests turned their attention to the matter of returning to their different ranches, they abruptly realised that the downpour had doubled and trebled in its volume since earlier in the evening. The fields and roads were veritable seas of viscid mud, the night absolutely black-dark; assuredly not a night in which to venture out. Magnus insisted that the three ranchers should put up at Los Muertos. Osterman accepted at once, Annixter, after an interminable discussion, allowed himself to be persuaded, in the end accepting as though granting a favour. Broderson protested that his wife, who was not well, would expect him to return that night and would, no doubt, fret if he did not appear. Furthermore, he lived close by, at the junction of the County and Lower Road. He put a sack over his head and shoulders, persistently declining Magnus's offered umbrella and rubber coat, and hurried away, remarking that he had no foreman on his ranch and had to be up and about at five the next morning to put his men to work.

"Fool!" muttered Annixter when the old man had gone. "Imagine farming a ranch the size of his without a foreman."

Harran showed Osterman and Annixter where they were to sleep, in adjoining rooms. Magnus soon afterward retired.

Osterman found an excuse for going to bed, but Annixter and Harran remained in the latter's room, in a haze of blue tobacco smoke, talking, talking. But at length, at the end of all argument, Annixter got up, remarking:

"Well, I'm going to turn in. It's nearly two o'clock."

He went to his room, closing the door, and Harran, opening his window to clear out the tobacco smoke, looked out for a moment across the country toward the south.

The darkness was profound, impenetrable; the rain fell with an uninterrupted roar. Near at hand one could hear the sound of dripping eaves and foliage and the eager, sucking sound of the drinking earth, and abruptly while Harran stood looking out, one hand upon the upraised sash, a great puff of the outside air invaded the room, odourous with the reek of the soaking earth, redolent with fertility, pungent, heavy, tepid. He closed the window again and sat for a few moments on the edge of the bed, one shoe in his hand, thoughtful and absorbed, wondering if his father would involve himself in this new scheme, wondering if, after all, he wanted him to.

But suddenly he was aware of a commotion, issuing from the direction of Annixter's room, and the voice of Annixter himself upraised in expostulation and exasperation. The door of the room to which Annixter had been assigned opened with a violent wrench and an angry voice exclaimed to anybody who would listen:

"Oh, yes, funny, isn't it? In a way, it's funny, and then, again, in a way it isn't."

The door banged to so that all the windows of the house rattled in their frames.

Harran hurried out into the dining-room and there met Presley and his father, who had been aroused as well by Annixter's clamour. Osterman was there, too, his bald head gleaming like a bulb of ivory in the light of the lamp that Magnus carried.

"What's all up?" demanded Osterman. "Whatever in the world is the matter with Buck?"

Confused and terrible sounds came from behind the door of Annixter's room. A prolonged monologue of grievance, broken by explosions of wrath and the vague noise of some one in a furious hurry. All at once and before Harran had a chance to knock on the door, Annixter flung it open. His face was blazing with anger, his outthrust lip more prominent than ever, his wiry, yellow hair in disarray, the tuft on the crown sticking straight into the air like the upraised hackles of an angry hound. Evidently he had been dressing himself with the most headlong rapidity; he had not yet put on his coat and vest, but carried them over his arm, while with his disengaged hand he kept hitching his suspenders over his shoulders with a persistent and hypnotic gesture. Without a moment's pause he gave vent to his indignation in a torrent of words.

"Ah, yes, in my bed, sloop, aha! I know the man who put it there," he went on, glaring at Osterman, "and that man is a PIP. Sloop! Slimy, disgusting stuff; you heard me say I didn't like it when the Chink passed it to me at dinner—and just for that reason you put it in my bed, and I stick my feet into it when I turn in. Funny, isn't it? Oh, yes, too funny for any use. I'd laugh a little louder if I was you."

"Well, Buck," protested Harran, as he noticed the hat in Annixter's hand, "you're not going home just for— —"

Annixter turned on him with a shout.

"I'll get plumb out of here," he trumpeted. "I won't stay here another minute."

He swung into his waistcoat and coat, scrabbling at the buttons in the violence of his emotions. "And I don't know but what it will make me sick again to go out in a night like this. NO, I won't stay. Some things are funny, and then, again, there are some things that are not. Ah, yes, sloop! Well, that's all right. I can be funny, too, when you come to that. You don't get a cent of money out of me. You can do your dirty bribery in your own dirty way. I won't come into this scheme at all. I wash my hands of the whole business. It's rotten and it's wild-eyed; it's dirt from start to finish; and you'll all land in State's prison. You can count me out."

"But, Buck, look here, you crazy fool," cried Harran, "I don't know who put that stuff in your bed, but I'm not going; to let you go back to Quien Sabe in a rain like this."

"I know who put it in," clamoured the other, shaking his fists, "and don't call me Buck and I'll do as I please. I WILL go back home. I'll get plumb out of here. Sorry I came. Sorry I ever lent myself to such a disgusting, dishonest, dirty bribery game as this all to-night. I won't put a dime into it, no, not a penny."

He stormed to the door leading out upon the porch, deaf to all reason. Harran and Presley followed him, trying to dissuade him from going home at that time of night and in such a storm, but Annixter was not to be placated. He stamped across to the barn where his horse and buggy had been stabled, splashing through the puddles under foot, going out of his way to drench himself, refusing even to allow Presley and Harran to help him harness the horse.

"What's the use of making a fool of yourself, Annixter?" remonstrated Presley, as Annixter backed the horse from the stall. "You act just like a ten-year-old boy. If Osterman wants to play the goat, why should you help him out?"

"He's a PIP," vociferated Annixter. "You don't understand, Presley. It runs in my family to hate anything sticky. It's—it's—it's heredity. How would you like to get into bed at two in the morning and jam your feet down into a slimy mess like that? Oh, no. It's not so funny then. And you mark my words, Mr. Harran Derrick," he continued, as he climbed into the buggy, shaking the whip toward Harran, "this business we talked over to-night—I'm OUT of it. It's yellow. It's too CURSED dishonest."

He cut the horse across the back with the whip and drove out into the pelting rain. In a few seconds the sound of his buggy wheels was lost in the muffled roar of the downpour.

Harran and Presley closed the barn and returned to the house, sheltering themselves under a tarpaulin carriage cover. Once inside, Harran went to remonstrate with Osterman, who was still up. Magnus had again retired. The house had fallen quiet again.

As Presley crossed the dining-room on the way to his own apartment in the second story of the house, he paused for a moment, looking about him. In the dull light of the lowered lamps, the redwood panelling of the room showed a dark crimson as though stained with blood. On the massive slab of the dining table the half-emptied glasses and bottles stood about in the confusion in which they had been left, reflecting themselves deep into the polished wood; the glass doors of the case of stuffed birds was a subdued shimmer; the many-coloured Navajo blanket over the couch seemed a mere patch of brown.

Around the table the chairs in which the men had sat throughout the evening still ranged themselves in a semi-circle, vaguely suggestive of the conference of the past few hours, with all its possibilities of good and evil, its significance of a future big with portent. The room was still. Only on the cushions of the chair that Annixter had occupied, the cat, Princess Nathalie, at last comfortably settled in her accustomed place, dozed complacently, her paws tucked under her breast, filling the deserted room with the subdued murmur of her contented purr.

CHAPTER IV

On the Quien Sabe ranch, in one of its western divisions, near the line fence that divided it from the Osterman holding, Vanamee was harnessing the horses to the plough to which he had been assigned two days before, a stable-boy from the division barn helping him.

Promptly discharged from the employ of the sheep-raisers after the lamentable accident near the Long Trestle, Vanamee had presented himself to Harran, asking for employment. The season was beginning; on all the ranches work was being resumed. The rain had put the ground into admirable condition for ploughing, and Annixter, Broderson, and Osterman all had their gangs at work. Thus, Vanamee was vastly surprised to find Los Muertos idle, the horses still in the barns, the men gathering in the shade of the bunk-house and eating-house, smoking, dozing, or going aimlessly about, their arms dangling. The ploughs for which Magnus and Harran were waiting in a fury of impatience had not yet arrived, and since the management of Los Muertos had counted upon having these in hand long before this time, no provision had been made for keeping the old stock in repair; many of these old ploughs were useless, broken, and out of order; some had been sold. It could not be said definitely when the new ploughs would arrive. Harran had decided to wait one week longer, and then, in case of their non-appearance, to buy a consignment of the old style of plough from the dealers in Bonneville. He could afford to lose the money better than he could afford to lose the season.

Failing of work on Los Muertos, Vanamee had gone to Quien Sabe. Annixter, whom he had spoken to first, had sent him across the ranch to one of his division superintendents, and this latter, after assuring himself of Vanamee's familiarity with horses and his previous experience—even though somewhat remote—on Los Muertos, had taken him on as a driver of one of the gang ploughs, then at work on his division.

The evening before, when the foreman had blown his whistle at six o'clock, the long line of ploughs had halted upon the instant, and the drivers, unharnessing their teams, had taken them back to the division barns—leaving the ploughs as they were in the furrows. But an hour after daylight the next morning the work was resumed. After breakfast, Vanamee, riding one horse and leading the others, had returned to the line of ploughs together with the other drivers. Now he was busy harnessing the team. At the division blacksmith shop—temporarily put up—he had been obliged to wait while one of his lead horses was shod, and he had thus been delayed quite five minutes. Nearly all the other teams were harnessed, the drivers on their seats, waiting for the foreman's signal.

"All ready here?" inquired the foreman, driving up to Vanamee's team in his buggy.

"All ready, sir," answered Vanamee, buckling the last strap.

He climbed to his seat, shaking out the reins, and turning about, looked back along the line, then all around him at the landscape inundated with the brilliant glow of the early morning.

The day was fine. Since the first rain of the season, there had been no other. Now the sky was without a cloud, pale blue, delicate, luminous, scintillating with morning. The great brown earth turned a huge flank to it, exhaling the moisture of the early dew. The atmosphere, washed clean of dust and mist, was translucent as crystal. Far off to the east, the hills on the other side of Broderson Creek stood out against the pallid saffron of the horizon as flat and as sharply outlined as if pasted on the sky. The campanile of the ancient Mission of San Juan seemed as fine as frost work. All about between the horizons, the carpet of the land unrolled itself to infinity. But now it was no longer parched with heat, cracked and warped by a merciless sun, powdered with dust. The rain had done its work; not a clod that was not swollen with fertility, not a fissure that did not exhale the sense of fecundity. One could not take a dozen steps upon the ranches without the brusque sensation that underfoot the land was alive; roused at last from its sleep, palpitating with the desire of reproduction. Deep down there in the recesses of the soil, the great heart throbbed once more, thrilling with passion, vibrating with desire, offering itself to the caress of the plough, insistent, eager, imperious. Dimly one felt the deep-seated trouble of the earth, the uneasy agitation of its members, the hidden tumult of its womb, demanding to be made fruitful, to reproduce, to disengage the eternal renascent germ of Life that stirred and struggled in its loins.

The ploughs, thirty-five in number, each drawn by its team of ten, stretched in an interminable line, nearly a quarter of a mile in length, behind and ahead of Vanamee. They were arranged, as it were, en echelon, not in file—not one directly behind the other, but each succeeding plough its own width farther in the field than the one in front of it. Each of these ploughs held five shears, so that when the entire company was in motion, one hundred and seventy-five furrows were made at the same instant. At a distance, the ploughs resembled a great column of field artillery. Each driver was in his place, his glance alternating between his horses and the foreman nearest at hand. Other foremen, in their buggies or buckboards, were at intervals along the line, like battery lieutenants. Annixter himself, on horseback, in boots and campaign hat, a cigar in his teeth, overlooked the scene.

The division superintendent, on the opposite side of the line, galloped past to a position at the head. For a long moment there was a silence. A sense of preparedness ran from end to end of the column. All things were ready, each man in his place. The day's work was about to begin.

Suddenly, from a distance at the head of the line came the shrill trilling of a whistle. At once the foreman nearest Vanamee repeated it, at the same time turning down the line, and waving one arm. The signal was repeated, whistle answering whistle, till the sounds lost themselves in the distance. At once the line of ploughs lost its immobility, moving forward, getting slowly under way, the horses straining in the traces. A prolonged movement rippled from team to team, disengaging in its passage a multitude of sounds—-the click of buckles, the creak of straining leather, the subdued clash of machinery, the cracking of whips, the deep breathing of nearly four hundred horses, the abrupt commands and cries of the drivers, and, last of all, the prolonged, soothing murmur of the thick brown earth turning steadily from the multitude of advancing shears.

The ploughing thus commenced, continued. The sun rose higher. Steadily the hundred iron hands kneaded and furrowed and stroked the brown, humid earth, the hundred iron teeth bit deep into the Titan's flesh. Perched on his seat, the moist living reins slipping and tugging in his hands, Vanamee, in the midst of this steady confusion of constantly varying sensation, sight interrupted by sound, sound mingling with sight, on this swaying, vibrating seat, quivering with the prolonged thrill of the earth, lapsed to a sort of pleasing numbness, in a sense, hypnotised by the weaving maze of things in which he found himself involved. To keep his team at an even, regular gait, maintaining the precise interval, to run his furrows as closely as possible to those already made by the plough in front—this for the moment was the entire sum of his duties. But while one part of his brain, alert and watchful, took cognisance of these matters, all the greater part was lulled and stupefied with the long monotony of the affair.

The ploughing, now in full swing, enveloped him in a vague, slow-moving whirl of things. Underneath him was the jarring, jolting, trembling machine; not a clod was turned, not an obstacle encountered, that he did not receive the swift impression of it through all his body, the very friction of the damp soil, sliding incessantly from the shiny surface of the shears, seemed to reproduce itself in his finger-tips and along the back of his head. He heard the horse-hoofs by the myriads crushing down easily, deeply, into the loam, the prolonged clinking of trace-chains, the working of the smooth brown flanks in the harness, the clatter of wooden hames, the champing of bits, the click of iron shoes against pebbles, the brittle stubble of the surface ground crackling and snapping as the furrows turned, the sonorous, steady breaths wrenched from the deep, labouring chests, strap-bound, shining with sweat, and all along the line the voices of the men talking to the horses. Everywhere there were visions of glossy brown backs, straining, heaving, swollen with muscle; harness streaked with specks of froth, broad, cup-shaped hoofs, heavy with brown loam, men's faces red with tan, blue overalls spotted with axle-grease; muscled hands, the knuckles whitened in their grip on the reins, and through it all the ammoniacal smell of the horses, the bitter reek of perspiration of beasts and men, the aroma of warm leather, the scent of dead stubble—and stronger and more penetrating than everything else, the heavy, enervating odour of the upturned, living earth.

At intervals, from the tops of one of the rare, low swells of the land, Vanamee overlooked a wider horizon. On the other divisions of Quien Sabe the same work was in progress. Occasionally he could see another column of ploughs in the adjoining division—sometimes so close at hand that the subdued murmur of its movements reached his ear; sometimes so distant that it resolved itself into a long, brown streak upon the grey of the ground. Farther off to the west on the Osterman ranch other columns came and went, and, once, from the crest of the highest swell on his division, Vanamee caught a distant glimpse of the Broderson ranch. There, too, moving specks indicated that the ploughing was under way. And farther away still, far off there beyond the fine line of the horizons, over the curve of the globe, the shoulder of the earth, he knew were other ranches, and beyond these others, and beyond these still others, the immensities multiplying to infinity.

Everywhere throughout the great San Joaquin, unseen and unheard, a thousand ploughs up-stirred the land, tens of thousands of shears clutched deep into the warm, moist soil.

It was the long stroking caress, vigorous, male, powerful, for which the Earth seemed panting. The heroic embrace of a multitude of iron hands, gripping deep into the brown, warm flesh of the land that quivered responsive and passionate under this rude advance, so robust as to be almost an assault, so violent as to be veritably brutal. There, under the sun and under the speckless sheen of the sky, the wooing of the Titan began, the vast primal passion, the two world-forces, the elemental Male and Female, locked in a colossal embrace, at grapples in the throes of an infinite desire, at once terrible and divine, knowing no law, untamed, savage, natural, sublime.

From time to time the gang in which Vanamee worked halted on the signal from foreman or overseer. The horses came to a standstill, the vague clamour of the work lapsed away. Then the minutes passed. The whole work hung suspended. All up and down the line one demanded what had happened. The division superintendent galloped past, perplexed and anxious. For the moment, one of the ploughs was out of order, a bolt had slipped, a lever refused to work, or a machine had become immobilised in heavy ground, or a horse had lamed himself. Once, even, toward noon, an entire plough was taken out of the line, so out of gear that a messenger had to be sent to the division forge to summon the machinist.

Annixter had disappeared. He had ridden farther on to the other divisions of his ranch, to watch the work in progress there. At twelve o'clock, according to his orders, all the division superintendents put themselves in communication with him by means of the telephone wires that connected each of the division houses, reporting the condition of the work, the number of acres covered, the prospects of each plough traversing its daily average of twenty miles.

At half-past twelve, Vanamee and the rest of the drivers ate their lunch in the field, the tin buckets having been distributed to them that morning after breakfast. But in the evening, the routine of the previous day was repeated, and Vanamee, unharnessing his team, riding one horse and leading the others, returned to the division barns and bunk-house.

It was between six and seven o'clock. The half hundred men of the gang threw themselves upon the supper the Chinese cooks had set out in the shed of the eating-house, long as a bowling alley, unpainted, crude, the seats benches, the table covered with oil cloth. Overhead a half-dozen kerosene lamps flared and smoked.

The table was taken as if by assault; the clatter of iron knives upon the tin plates was as the reverberation of hail upon a metal roof. The ploughmen rinsed their throats with great draughts of wine, and, their elbows wide, their foreheads flushed, resumed the attack upon the beef and bread, eating as though they would never have enough. All up and down the long table, where the kerosene lamps reflected themselves deep in the oil-cloth cover, one heard the incessant sounds of mastication, and saw the uninterrupted movement of great jaws. At every moment one or another of the men demanded a fresh portion of beef, another pint of wine, another half-loaf of bread. For upwards of an hour the gang ate. It was no longer a supper. It was a veritable barbecue, a crude and primitive feasting, barbaric, homeric.

But in all this scene Vanamee saw nothing repulsive. Presley would have abhorred it—this feeding of the People, this gorging of the human animal, eager for its meat. Vanamee, simple, uncomplicated, living so close to nature and the rudimentary life, understood its significance. He knew very well that within a short half-hour after this meal the men would throw themselves down in their bunks to sleep without moving, inert and stupefied with fatigue, till the morning. Work, food, and sleep, all life reduced to its bare essentials, uncomplex, honest, healthy. They were strong, these men, with the strength of the soil they worked, in touch with the essential things, back again to the starting point of civilisation, coarse, vital, real, and sane.

For a brief moment immediately after the meal, pipes were lit, and the air grew thick with fragrant tobacco smoke. On a corner of the dining-room table, a game of poker was begun. One of the drivers, a Swede, produced an accordion; a group on the steps of the bunk-house listened, with alternate gravity and shouts of laughter, to the acknowledged story-teller of the gang. But soon the men began to turn in, stretching themselves at full length on the horse blankets in the racklike bunks. The sounds of heavy breathing increased steadily, lights were put out, and before the afterglow had faded from the sky, the gang was asleep.

Vanamee, however, remained awake. The night was fine, warm; the sky silver-grey with starlight. By and by there would be a moon. In the first watch after the twilight, a faint puff of breeze came up out of the south. From all around, the heavy penetrating smell of the new-turned earth exhaled steadily into the darkness. After a while, when the moon came up, he could see the vast brown breast of the earth turn toward it. Far off, distant objects came into view: The giant oak tree at Hooven's ranch house near the irrigating ditch on Los Muertos, the skeleton-like tower of the windmill on Annixter's Home ranch, the clump of willows along Broderson Creek close to the Long Trestle, and, last of all, the venerable tower of the Mission of San Juan on the high ground beyond the creek.

Thitherward, like homing pigeons, Vanamee's thoughts turned irresistibly. Near to that tower, just beyond, in the little hollow, hidden now from his sight, was the Seed ranch where Angele Varian had lived. Straining his eyes, peering across the intervening levels, Vanamee fancied he could almost see the line of venerable pear trees in whose shadow she had been accustomed to wait for him. On many such a night as this he had crossed the ranches to find her there. His mind went back to that wonderful time of his life sixteen years before this, when Angele was alive, when they two were involved in the sweet intricacies of a love so fine, so pure, so marvellous that it seemed to them a miracle, a manifestation, a thing veritably divine, put into the life of them and the hearts of them by God Himself. To that they had been born. For this love's sake they had come into the world, and the mingling of their lives was to be the Perfect Life, the intended, ordained union of the soul of man with the soul of woman, indissoluble, harmonious as music, beautiful beyond all thought, a foretaste of Heaven, a hostage of immortality.

No, he, Vanamee, could never, never forget, never was the edge of his grief to lose its sharpness, never would the lapse of time blunt the tooth of his pain. Once more, as he sat there, looking off across the ranches, his eyes fixed on the ancient campanile of the Mission church, the anguish that would not die leaped at his throat, tearing at his heart, shaking him and rending him with a violence as fierce and as profound as if it all had been but yesterday. The ache returned to his heart a physical keen pain; his hands gripped tight together, twisting, interlocked, his eyes filled with tears, his whole body shaken and riven from head to heel.

He had lost her. God had not meant it, after all. The whole matter had been a mistake. That vast, wonderful love that had come upon them had been only the flimsiest mockery. Abruptly Vanamee rose. He knew the night that was before him. At intervals throughout the course of his prolonged wanderings, in the desert, on the mesa, deep in the canon, lost and forgotten on the flanks of unnamed mountains, alone under the stars and under the moon's white eye, these hours came to him, his grief recoiling upon him like the recoil of a vast and terrible engine. Then he must fight out the night, wrestling with his sorrow, praying sometimes, incoherent, hardly conscious, asking "Why" of the night and of the stars.

Such another night had come to him now. Until dawn he knew he must struggle with his grief, torn with memories, his imagination assaulted with visions of a vanished happiness. If this paroxysm of sorrow was to assail him again that night, there was but one place for him to be. He would go to the Mission—he would see Father Sarria; he would pass the night in the deep shadow of the aged pear trees in the Mission garden.

He struck out across Quien Sabe, his face, the face of an ascetic, lean, brown, infinitely sad, set toward the Mission church. In about an hour he reached and crossed the road that led northward from Guadalajara toward the Seed ranch, and, a little farther on, forded Broderson Creek where it ran through one corner of the Mission land. He climbed the hill and halted, out of breath from his brisk wall, at the end of the colonnade of the Mission itself.

Until this moment Vanamee had not trusted himself to see the Mission at night. On the occasion of his first daytime visit with Presley, he had hurried away even before the twilight had set in, not daring for the moment to face the crowding phantoms that in his imagination filled the Mission garden after dark. In the daylight, the place had seemed strange to him. None of his associations with the old building and its surroundings were those of sunlight and brightness. Whenever, during his long sojourns in the wilderness of the Southwest, he had called up the picture in the eye of his mind, it had always appeared to him in the dim mystery of moonless nights, the venerable pear trees black with shadow, the fountain a thing to be heard rather than seen.

But as yet he had not entered the garden. That lay on the other side of the Mission. Vanamee passed down the colonnade, with its uneven pavement of worn red bricks, to the last door by the belfry tower, and rang the little bell by pulling the leather thong that hung from a hole in the door above the knob.

But the maid-servant, who, after a long interval opened the door, blinking and confused at being roused from her sleep, told Vanamee that Sarria was not in his room. Vanamee, however, was known to her as the priest's protege and great friend, and she allowed him to enter, telling him that, no doubt, he would find Sarria in the church itself. The servant led the way down the cool adobe passage to a larger room that occupied the entire width of the bottom of the belfry tower, and whence a flight of aged steps led upward into the dark. At the foot of the stairs was a door opening into the church. The servant admitted Vanamee, closing the door behind her.

The interior of the Mission, a great oblong of white-washed adobe with a flat ceiling, was lighted dimly by the sanctuary lamp that hung from three long chains just over the chancel rail at the far end of the church, and by two or three cheap kerosene lamps in brackets of imitation bronze. All around the walls was the inevitable series of pictures representing the Stations of the Cross. They were of a hideous crudity of design and composition, yet were wrought out with an innocent, unquestioning sincerity that was not without its charm. Each picture framed alike in gilt, bore its suitable inscription in staring black letters. "Simon, The Cyrenean, Helps Jesus to Carry His Cross." "Saint Veronica Wipes the Face of Jesus." "Jesus Falls for the Fourth Time," and so on. Half-way up the length of the church the pews began, coffin-like boxes of blackened oak, shining from years of friction, each with its door; while over them, and built out from the wall, was the pulpit, with its tarnished gilt sounding-board above it, like the raised cover of a great hat-box. Between the pews, in the aisle, the violent vermilion of a strip of ingrain carpet assaulted the eye. Farther on were the steps to the altar, the chancel rail of worm-riddled oak, the high altar, with its napery from the bargain counters of a San Francisco store, the massive silver candlesticks, each as much as one man could lift, the gift of a dead Spanish queen, and, last, the pictures of the chancel, the Virgin in a glory, a Christ in agony on the cross, and St. John the Baptist, the patron saint of the Mission, the San Juan Bautista, of the early days, a gaunt grey figure, in skins, two fingers upraised in the gesture of benediction.

The air of the place was cool and damp, and heavy with the flat, sweet scent of stale incense smoke. It was of a vault-like stillness, and the closing of the door behind Vanamee reechoed from corner to corner with a prolonged reverberation of thunder.

However, Father Sarria was not in the church. Vanamee took a couple of turns the length of the aisle, looking about into the chapels on either side of the chancel. But the building was deserted. The priest had been there recently, nevertheless, for the altar furniture was in disarray, as though he had been rearranging it but a moment before. On both sides of the church and half-way up their length, the walls were pierced by low archways, in which were massive wooden doors, clamped with iron bolts. One of these doors, on the pulpit side of the church, stood ajar, and stepping to it and pushing it wide open, Vanamee looked diagonally across a little patch of vegetables—beets, radishes, and lettuce—to the rear of the building that had once contained the cloisters, and through an open window saw Father Sarria diligently polishing the silver crucifix that usually stood on the high altar. Vanamee did not call to the priest. Putting a finger to either temple, he fixed his eyes steadily upon him for a moment as he moved about at his work. In a few seconds he closed his eyes, but only part way. The pupils contracted; his forehead lowered to an expression of poignant intensity. Soon afterward he saw the priest pause abruptly in the act of drawing the cover over the crucifix, looking about him from side to side. He turned again to his work, and again came to a stop, perplexed, curious. With uncertain steps, and evidently wondering why he did so, he came to the door of the room and opened it, looking out into the night. Vanamee, hidden in the deep shadow of the archway, did not move, but his eyes closed, and the intense expression deepened on his face. The priest hesitated, moved forward a step, turned back, paused again, then came straight across the garden patch, brusquely colliding with Vanamee, still motionless in the recess of the archway.

Sarria gave a great start, catching his breath.

"Oh—oh, it's you. Was it you I heard calling? No, I could not have heard—I remember now. What a strange power! I am not sure that it is right to do this thing, Vanamee. I—I HAD to come. I do not know why. It is a great force—a power—I don't like it. Vanamee, sometimes it frightens me."

Vanamee put his chin in the air.

"If I had wanted to, sir, I could have made you come to me from back there in the Quien Sabe ranch."

The priest shook his head.

"It troubles me," he said, "to think that my own will can count for so little. Just now I could not resist. If a deep river had been between us, I must have crossed it. Suppose I had been asleep now?" "It would have been all the easier," answered Vanamee. "I understand as little of these things as you. But I think if you had been asleep, your power of resistance would have been so much the more weakened."

"Perhaps I should not have waked. Perhaps I should have come to you in my sleep."

"Perhaps."

Sarria crossed himself. "It is occult," he hazarded. "No; I do not like it. Dear fellow," he put his hand on Vanamee's shoulder, "don't—call me that way again; promise. See," he held out his hand, "I am all of a tremble. There, we won't speak of it further. Wait for me a moment. I have only to put the cross in its place, and a fresh altar cloth, and then I am done. To-morrow is the feast of The Holy Cross, and I am preparing against it. The night is fine. We will smoke a cigar in the cloister garden."

A few moments later the two passed out of the door on the other side of the church, opposite the pulpit, Sarria adjusting a silk skull cap on his tonsured head. He wore his cassock now, and was far more the churchman in appearance than when Vanamee and Presley had seen him on a former occasion.

They were now in the cloister garden. The place was charming. Everywhere grew clumps of palms and magnolia trees. A grapevine, over a century old, occupied a trellis in one angle of the walls which surrounded the garden on two sides. Along the third side was the church itself, while the fourth was open, the wall having crumbled away, its site marked only by a line of eight great pear trees, older even than the grapevine, gnarled, twisted, bearing no fruit. Directly opposite the pear trees, in the south wall of the garden, was a round, arched portal, whose gate giving upon the esplanade in front of the Mission was always closed. Small gravelled walks, well kept, bordered with mignonette, twisted about among the flower beds, and underneath the magnolia trees. In the centre was a little fountain in a stone basin green with moss, while just beyond, between the fountain and the pear trees, stood what was left of a sun dial, the bronze gnomon, green with the beatings of the weather, the figures on the half-circle of the dial worn away, illegible.

But on the other side of the fountain, and directly opposite the door of the Mission, ranged against the wall, were nine graves—three with headstones, the rest with slabs. Two of Sarria's predecessors were buried here; three of the graves were those of Mission Indians. One was thought to contain a former alcalde of Guadalajara; two more held the bodies of De La Cuesta and his young wife (taking with her to the grave the illusion of her husband's love), and the last one, the ninth, at the end of the line, nearest the pear trees, was marked by a little headstone, the smallest of any, on which, together with the proper dates—only sixteen years apart—was cut the name "Angele Varian."

But the quiet, the repose, the isolation of the little cloister garden was infinitely delicious. It was a tiny corner of the great valley that stretched in all directions around it—shut off, discreet, romantic, a garden of dreams, of enchantments, of illusions. Outside there, far off, the great grim world went clashing through its grooves, but in here never an echo of the grinding of its wheels entered to jar upon the subdued modulation of the fountain's uninterrupted murmur.

Sarria and Vanamee found their way to a stone bench against the side wall of the Mission, near the door from which they had just issued, and sat down, Sarria lighting a cigar, Vanamee rolling and smoking cigarettes in Mexican fashion.

All about them widened the vast calm night. All the stars were out. The moon was coming up. There was no wind, no sound. The insistent flowing of the fountain seemed only as the symbol of the passing of time, a thing that was understood rather than heard, inevitable, prolonged. At long intervals, a faint breeze, hardly more than a breath, found its way into the garden over the enclosing walls, and passed overhead, spreading everywhere the delicious, mingled perfume of magnolia blossoms, of mignonette, of moss, of grass, and all the calm green life silently teeming within the enclosure of the walls.

From where he sat, Vanamee, turning his head, could look out underneath the pear trees to the north. Close at hand, a little valley lay between the high ground on which the Mission was built, and the line of low hills just beyond Broderson Creek on the Quien Sabe. In here was the Seed ranch, which Angele's people had cultivated, a unique and beautiful stretch of five hundred acres, planted thick with roses, violets, lilies, tulips, iris, carnations, tube-roses, poppies, heliotrope—all manner and description of flowers, five hundred acres of them, solid, thick, exuberant; blooming and fading, and leaving their seed or slips to be marketed broadcast all over the United States. This had been the vocation of Angele's parents—raising flowers for their seeds. All over the country the Seed ranch was known. Now it was arid, almost dry, but when in full flower, toward the middle of summer, the sight of these half-thousand acres royal with colour— vermilion, azure, flaming yellow—was a marvel. When an east wind blew, men on the streets of Bonneville, nearly twelve miles away, could catch the scent of this valley of flowers, this chaos of perfume.

And into this life of flowers, this world of colour, this atmosphere oppressive and clogged and cloyed and thickened with sweet odour, Angele had been born. There she had lived her sixteen years. There she had died. It was not surprising that Vanamee, with his intense, delicate sensitiveness to beauty, his almost abnormal capacity for great happiness, had been drawn to her, had loved her so deeply.

She came to him from out of the flowers, the smell of the roses in her hair of gold, that hung in two straight plaits on either side of her face; the reflection of the violets in the profound dark blue of her eyes, perplexing, heavy-lidded, almond-shaped, oriental; the aroma and the imperial red of the carnations in her lips, with their almost Egyptian fulness; the whiteness of the lilies, the perfume of the lilies, and the lilies' slender balancing grace in her neck. Her hands disengaged the odour of the heliotropes. The folds of her dress gave off the enervating scent of poppies. Her feet were redolent of hyacinths.

For a long time after sitting down upon the bench, neither the priest nor Vanamee spoke. But after a while Sarria took his cigar from his lips, saying:

"How still it is! This is a beautiful old garden, peaceful, very quiet. Some day I shall be buried here. I like to remember that; and you, too, Vanamee."

"Quien sabe?"

"Yes, you, too. Where else? No, it is better here, yonder, by the side of the little girl."

"I am not able to look forward yet, sir. The things that are to be are somehow nothing to me at all. For me they amount to nothing."

"They amount to everything, my boy."

"Yes, to one part of me, but not to the part of me that belonged to Angele—the best part. Oh, you don't know," he exclaimed with a sudden movement, "no one can understand. What is it to me when you tell me that sometime after I shall die too, somewhere, in a vague place you call Heaven, I shall see her again? Do you think that the idea of that ever made any one's sorrow easier to bear? Ever took the edge from any one's grief?"

"But you believe that——"

"Oh, believe, believe!" echoed the other. "What do I believe? I don't know. I believe, or I don't believe. I can remember what she WAS, but I cannot hope what she will be. Hope, after all, is only memory seen reversed. When I try to see her in another life—whatever you call it—in Heaven—beyond the grave—this vague place of yours; when I try to see her there, she comes to my imagination only as what she was, material, earthly, as I loved her. Imperfect, you say; but that is as I saw her, and as I saw her, I loved her; and as she WAS, material, earthly, imperfect, she loved me. It's that, that I want," he exclaimed. "I don't want her changed. I don't want her spiritualised, exalted, glorified, celestial. I want HER. I think it is only this feeling that has kept me from killing myself. I would rather be unhappy in the memory of what she actually was, than be happy in the realisation of her transformed, changed, made celestial. I am only human. Her soul! That was beautiful, no doubt. But, again, it was something very vague, intangible, hardly more than a phrase. But the touch of her hand was real, the sound of her voice was real, the clasp of her arms about my neck was real. Oh," he cried, shaken with a sudden wrench of passion, "give those back to me. Tell your God to give those back to me—the sound of her voice, the touch of her hand, the clasp of her dear arms, REAL, REAL, and then you may talk to me of Heaven."

Sarria shook his head. "But when you meet her again," he observed, "in Heaven, you, too, will be changed. You will see her spiritualised, with spiritual eyes. As she is now, she does not appeal to you. I understand that. It is because, as you say, you are only human, while she is divine. But when you come to be like her, as she is now, you will know her as she really is, not as she seemed to be, because her voice was sweet, because her hair was pretty, because her hand was warm in yours. Vanamee, your talk is that of a foolish child. You are like one of the Corinthians to whom Paul wrote. Do you remember? Listen now. I can recall the words, and such words, beautiful and terrible at the same time, such a majesty. They march like soldiers with trumpets. 'But some man will say'—as you have said just now—'How are the dead raised up? And with what body do they come? Thou fool! That which thou sowest is not quickened except it die, and that which thou sowest, thou sowest not that body that shall be, but bare grain. It may chance of wheat, or of some other grain. But God giveth it a body as it hath pleased him, and to every seed his own body.... It is sown a natural body; it is raised a spiritual body.' It is because you are a natural body that you cannot understand her, nor wish for her as a spiritual body, but when you are both spiritual, then you shall know each other as you are—know as you never knew before. Your grain of wheat is your symbol of immortality. You bury it in the earth. It dies, and rises again a thousand times more beautiful. Vanamee, your dear girl was only a grain of humanity that we have buried here, and the end is not yet. But all this is so old, so old. The world learned it a thousand years ago, and yet each man that has ever stood by the open grave of any one he loved must learn it all over again from the beginning."

Vanamee was silent for a moment, looking off with unseeing eyes between the trunks of the pear trees, over the little valley.

"That may all be as you say," he answered after a while. "I have not learned it yet, in any case. Now, I only know that I love her—oh, as if it all were yesterday—and that I am suffering, suffering, always."

He leaned forward, his head supported on his clenched fists, the infinite sadness of his face deepening like a shadow, the tears brimming in his deep-set eyes. A question that he must ask, which involved the thing that was scarcely to be thought of, occurred to him at this moment. After hesitating for a long moment, he said:

"I have been away a long time, and I have had no news of this place since I left. Is there anything to tell, Father? Has any discovery been made, any suspicion developed, as to—the Other?"

The priest shook his head.

"Not a word, not a whisper. It is a mystery. It always will be."

Vanamee clasped his head between his clenched fists, rocking himself to and fro.

"Oh, the terror of it," he murmured. "The horror of it. And she—think of it, Sarria, only sixteen, a little girl; so innocent, that she never knew what wrong meant, pure as a little child is pure, who believed that all things were good; mature only in her love. And to be struck down like that, while your God looked down from Heaven and would not take her part." All at once he seemed to lose control of himself. One of those furies of impotent grief and wrath that assailed him from time to time, blind, insensate, incoherent, suddenly took possession of him. A torrent of words issued from his lips, and he flung out an arm, the fist clenched, in a fierce, quick gesture, partly of despair, partly of defiance, partly of supplication. "No, your God would not take her part. Where was God's mercy in that? Where was Heaven's protection in that? Where was the loving kindness you preach about? Why did God give her life if it was to be stamped out? Why did God give her the power of love if it was to come to nothing? Sarria, listen to me. Why did God make her so divinely pure if He permitted that abomination? Ha!" he exclaimed bitterly, "your God! Why, an Apache buck would have been more merciful. Your God! There is no God. There is only the Devil. The Heaven you pray to is only a joke, a wretched trick, a delusion. It is only Hell that is real."

Sarria caught him by the arm.

"You are a fool and a child," he exclaimed, "and it is blasphemy that you are saying. I forbid it. You understand? I forbid it."

Vanamee turned on him with a sudden cry. "Then, tell your God to give her back to me!"

Sarria started away from him, his eyes widening in astonishment, surprised out of all composure by the other's outburst. Vanamee's swarthy face was pale, the sunken cheeks and deep-set eyes were marked with great black shadows. The priest no longer recognised him. The face, that face of the ascetic, lean, framed in its long black hair and pointed beard, was quivering with the excitement of hallucination. It was the face of the inspired shepherds of the Hebraic legends, living close to nature, the younger prophets of Israel, dwellers in the wilderness, solitary, imaginative, believing in the Vision, having strange delusions, gifted with strange powers. In a brief second of thought, Sarria understood. Out into the wilderness, the vast arid desert of the Southwest, Vanamee had carried his grief. For days, for weeks, months even, he had been alone, a solitary speck lost in the immensity of the horizons; continually he was brooding, haunted with his sorrow, thinking, thinking, often hard put to it for food. The body was ill-nourished, and the mind, concentrated forever upon one subject, had recoiled upon itself, had preyed upon the naturally nervous temperament, till the imagination had become exalted, morbidly active, diseased, beset with hallucinations, forever in search of the manifestation, of the miracle. It was small wonder that, bringing a fancy so distorted back to the scene of a vanished happiness, Vanamee should be racked with the most violent illusions, beset in the throes of a veritable hysteria.

"Tell your God to give her back to me," he repeated with fierce insistence.

It was the pitch of mysticism, the imagination harassed and goaded beyond the normal round, suddenly flipping from the circumference, spinning off at a tangent, out into the void, where all things seemed possible, hurtling through the dark there, groping for the supernatural, clamouring for the miracle. And it was also the human, natural protest against the inevitable, the irrevocable; the spasm of revolt under the sting of death, the rebellion of the soul at the victory of the grave.

"He can give her back to me if He only will," Vanamee cried. "Sarria, you must help me. I tell you—I warn you, sir, I can't last much longer under it. My head is all wrong with it—I've no more hold on my mind. Something must happen or I shall lose my senses. I am breaking down under it all, my body and my mind alike. Bring her to me; make God show her to me. If all tales are true, it would not be the first time. If I cannot have her, at least let me see her as she was, real, earthly, not her spirit, her ghost. I want her real self, undefiled again. If this is dementia, then let me be demented. But help me, you and your God; create the delusion, do the miracle."

"Stop!" cried the priest again, shaking him roughly by the shoulder. "Stop. Be yourself. This is dementia; but I shall NOT let you be demented. Think of what you are saying. Bring her back to you! Is that the way of God? I thought you were a man; this is the talk of a weak-minded girl."

Vanamee stirred abruptly in his place, drawing a long breath and looking about him vaguely, as if he came to himself.

"You are right," he muttered. "I hardly know what I am saying at times. But there are moments when my whole mind and soul seem to rise up in rebellion against what has happened; when it seems to me that I am stronger than death, and that if I only knew how to use the strength of my will, concentrate my power of thought—volition—that I could—I don't know—not call her back—but—something——"

"A diseased and distorted mind is capable of hallucinations, if that is what you mean," observed Sarria.

"Perhaps that is what I mean. Perhaps I want only the delusion, after all."

Sarria did not reply, and there was a long silence. In the damp south corners of the walls a frog began to croak at exact intervals. The little fountain rippled monotonously, and a magnolia flower dropped from one of the trees, falling straight as a plummet through the motionless air, and settling upon the gravelled walk with a faint rustling sound. Otherwise the stillness was profound.

A little later, the priest's cigar, long since out, slipped from his fingers to the ground. He began to nod gently. Vanamee touched his arm.

"Asleep, sir?"

The other started, rubbing his eyes.

"Upon my word, I believe I was."

"Better go to bed, sir. I am not tired. I think I shall sit out here a little longer."

"Well, perhaps I would be better off in bed. YOUR bed is always ready for you here whenever you want to use it."

"No—I shall go back to Quien Sabe—later. Good-night, sir."

"Good-night, my boy."

Vanamee was left alone. For a long time he sat motionless in his place, his elbows on his knees, his chin propped in his hands. The minutes passed—then the hours. The moon climbed steadily higher among the stars. Vanamee rolled and smoked cigarette after cigarette, the blue haze of smoke hanging motionless above his head, or drifting in slowly weaving filaments across the open spaces of the garden.

But the influence of the old enclosure, this corner of romance and mystery, this isolated garden of dreams, savouring of the past, with its legends, its graves, its crumbling sun dial, its fountain with its rime of moss, was not to be resisted. Now that the priest had left him, the same exaltation of spirit that had seized upon Vanamee earlier in the evening, by degrees grew big again in his mind and imagination. His sorrow assaulted him like the flagellations of a fine whiplash, and his love for Angele rose again in his heart, it seemed to him never so deep, so tender, so infinitely strong. No doubt, it was his familiarity with the Mission garden, his clear-cut remembrance of it, as it was in the days when he had met Angele there, tallying now so exactly with the reality there under his eyes, that brought her to his imagination so vividly. As yet he dared not trust himself near her grave, but, for the moment, he rose and, his hands clasped behind him, walked slowly from point to point amid the tiny gravelled walks, recalling the incidents of eighteen years ago. On the bench he had quitted he and Angele had often sat. Here by the crumbling sun dial, he recalled the night when he had kissed her for the first time. Here, again, by the rim of the fountain, with its fringe of green, she once had paused, and, baring her arm to the shoulder, had thrust it deep into the water, and then withdrawing it, had given it to him to kiss, all wet and cool; and here, at last, under the shadow of the pear trees they had sat, evening after evening, looking off over the little valley below them, watching the night build itself, dome-like, from horizon to zenith.

Brusquely Vanamee turned away from the prospect. The Seed ranch was dark at this time of the year, and flowerless. Far off toward its centre, he had caught a brief glimpse of the house where Angele had lived, and a faint light burning in its window. But he turned from it sharply. The deep-seated travail of his grief abruptly reached the paroxysm. With long strides he crossed the garden and reentered the Mission church itself, plunging into the coolness of its atmosphere as into a bath. What he searched for he did not know, or, rather, did not define. He knew only that he was suffering, that a longing for Angele, for some object around which his great love could enfold itself, was tearing at his heart with iron teeth. He was ready to be deluded; craved the hallucination; begged pitifully for the illusion; anything rather than the empty, tenantless night, the voiceless silence, the vast loneliness of the overspanning arc of the heavens.

Before the chancel rail of the altar, under the sanctuary lamp, Vanamee sank upon his knees, his arms folded upon the rail, his head bowed down upon them. He prayed, with what words he could not say for what he did not understand—for help, merely, for relief, for an Answer to his cry.

It was upon that, at length, that his disordered mind concentrated itself, an Answer—he demanded, he implored an Answer. Not a vague visitation of Grace, not a formless sense of Peace; but an Answer, something real, even if the reality were fancied, a voice out of the night, responding to his, a hand in the dark clasping his groping fingers, a breath, human, warm, fragrant, familiar, like a soft, sweet caress on his shrunken cheeks. Alone there in the dim half-light of the decaying Mission, with its crumbling plaster, its naive crudity of ornament and picture, he wrestled fiercely with his desires—words, fragments of sentences, inarticulate, incoherent, wrenched from his tight-shut teeth.

But the Answer was not in the church. Above him, over the high altar, the Virgin in a glory, with downcast eyes and folded hands, grew vague and indistinct in the shadow, the colours fading, tarnished by centuries of incense smoke. The Christ in agony on the Cross was but a lamentable vision of tormented anatomy, grey flesh, spotted with crimson. The St. John, the San Juan Bautista, patron saint of the Mission, the gaunt figure in skins, two fingers upraised in the gesture of benediction, gazed stolidly out into the half-gloom under the ceiling, ignoring the human distress that beat itself in vain against the altar rail below, and Angele remained as before—only a memory, far distant, intangible, lost.

Vanamee rose, turning his back upon the altar with a vague gesture of despair. He crossed the church, and issuing from the low-arched door opposite the pulpit, once more stepped out into the garden. Here, at least, was reality. The warm, still air descended upon him like a cloak, grateful, comforting, dispelling the chill that lurked in the damp mould of plaster and crumbling adobe.

But now he found his way across the garden on the other side of the fountain, where, ranged against the eastern wall, were nine graves. Here Angele was buried, in the smallest grave of them all, marked by the little headstone, with its two dates, only sixteen years apart. To this spot, at last, he had returned, after the years spent in the desert, the wilderness—after all the wanderings of the Long Trail. Here, if ever, he must have a sense of her nearness. Close at hand, a short four feet under that mound of grass, was the form he had so often held in the embrace of his arms; the face, the very face he had kissed, that face with the hair of gold making three-cornered the round white forehead, the violet-blue eyes, heavy-lidded, with their strange oriental slant upward toward the temples; the sweet full lips, almost Egyptian in their fulness—all that strange, perplexing, wonderful beauty, so troublous, so enchanting, so out of all accepted standards.

He bent down, dropping upon one knee, a hand upon the headstone, and read again the inscription. Then instinctively his hand left the stone and rested upon the low mound of turf, touching it with the softness of a caress; and then, before he was aware of it, he was stretched at full length upon the earth, beside the grave, his arms about the low mound, his lips pressed against the grass with which it was covered. The pent-up grief of nearly twenty years rose again within his heart, and overflowed, irresistible, violent, passionate. There was no one to see, no one to hear. Vanamee had no thought of restraint. He no longer wrestled with his pain—strove against it. There was even a sense of relief in permitting himself to be overcome. But the reaction from this outburst was equally violent. His revolt against the inevitable, his protest against the grave, shook him from head to foot, goaded him beyond all bounds of reason, hounded him on and into the domain of hysteria, dementia. Vanamee was no longer master of himself—no longer knew what he was doing.

At first, he had been content with merely a wild, unreasoned cry to Heaven that Angele should be restored to him, but the vast egotism that seems to run through all forms of disordered intelligence gave his fancy another turn. He forgot God. He no longer reckoned with Heaven. He arrogated their powers to himself—struggled to be, of his own unaided might, stronger than death, more powerful than the grave. He had demanded of Sarria that God should restore Angele to him, but now he appealed directly to Angele herself. As he lay there, his arms clasped about her grave, she seemed so near to him that he fancied she MUST hear. And suddenly, at this moment, his recollection of his strange compelling power—the same power by which he had called Presley to him half-way across the Quien Sabe ranch, the same power which had brought Sarria to his side that very evening—recurred to him. Concentrating his mind upon the one object with which it had so long been filled, Vanamee, his eyes closed, his face buried in his arms, exclaimed:

"Come to me—Angele—don't you hear? Come to me."

But the Answer was not in the Grave. Below him the voiceless Earth lay silent, moveless, withholding the secret, jealous of that which it held so close in its grip, refusing to give up that which had been confided to its keeping, untouched by the human anguish that above there, on its surface, clutched with despairing hands at a grave long made. The Earth that only that morning had been so eager, so responsive to the lightest summons, so vibrant with Life, now at night, holding death within its embrace, guarding inviolate the secret of the Grave, was deaf to all entreaty, refused the Answer, and Angele remained as before, only a memory, far distant, intangible, lost.

Vanamee lifted his head, looking about him with unseeing eyes, trembling with the exertion of his vain effort. But he could not as yet allow himself to despair. Never before had that curious power of attraction failed him. He felt himself to be so strong in this respect that he was persuaded if he exerted himself to the limit of his capacity, something—he could not say what—must come of it. If it was only a self-delusion, an hallucination, he told himself that he would be content.

Almost of its own accord, his distorted mind concentrated itself again, every thought, all the power of his will riveting themselves upon Angele. As if she were alive, he summoned her to him. His eyes, fixed upon the name cut into the headstone, contracted, the pupils growing small, his fists shut tight, his nerves braced rigid.

For a few seconds he stood thus, breathless, expectant, awaiting the manifestation, the Miracle. Then, without knowing why, hardly conscious of what was transpiring, he found that his glance was leaving the headstone, was turning from the grave. Not only this, but his whole body was following the direction of his eyes. Before he knew it, he was standing with his back to Angele's grave, was facing the north, facing the line of pear trees and the little valley where the Seed ranch lay. At first, he thought this was because he had allowed his will to weaken, the concentrated power of his mind to grow slack. And once more turning toward the grave, he banded all his thoughts together in a consummate effort, his teeth grinding together, his hands pressed to his forehead. He forced himself to the notion that Angele was alive, and to this creature of his imagination he addressed himself:

"Angele!" he cried in a low voice; "Angele, I am calling you—do you hear? Come to me—come to me now, now."

Instead of the Answer he demanded, that inexplicable counter-influence cut across the current of his thought. Strive as he would against it, he must veer to the north, toward the pear trees. Obeying it, he turned, and, still wondering, took a step in that direction, then another and another. The next moment he came abruptly to himself, in the black shadow of the pear trees themselves, and, opening his eyes, found himself looking off over the Seed ranch, toward the little house in the centre where Angele had once lived.

Perplexed, he returned to the grave, once more calling upon the resources of his will, and abruptly, so soon as these reached a certain point, the same cross-current set in. He could no longer keep his eyes upon the headstone, could no longer think of the grave and what it held. He must face the north; he must be drawn toward the pear trees, and there left standing in their shadow, looking out aimlessly over the Seed ranch, wondering, bewildered.

Farther than this the influence never drew him, but up to this point—the line of pear trees—it was not to be resisted.

For a time the peculiarity of the affair was of more interest to Vanamee than even his own distress of spirit, and once or twice he repeated the attempt, almost experimentally, and invariably with the same result: so soon as he seemed to hold Angele in the grip of his mind, he was moved to turn about toward the north, and hurry toward the pear trees on the crest of the hill that over-looked the little valley.

But Vanamee's unhappiness was too keen this night for him to dwell long upon the vagaries of his mind. Submitting at length, and abandoning the grave, he flung himself down in the black shade of the pear trees, his chin in his hands, and resigned himself finally and definitely to the inrush of recollection and the exquisite grief of an infinite regret.

To his fancy, she came to him again. He put himself back many years. He remembered the warm nights of July and August, profoundly still, the sky encrusted with stars, the little Mission garden exhaling the mingled perfumes that all through the scorching day had been distilled under the steady blaze of a summer's sun. He saw himself as another person, arriving at this, their rendezvous. All day long she had been in his mind. All day long he had looked forward to this quiet hour that belonged to her. It was dark. He could see nothing, but, by and by, he heard a step, a gentle rustle of the grass on the slope of the hill pressed under an advancing foot. Then he saw the faint gleam of pallid gold of her hair, a barely visible glow in the starlight, and heard the murmur of her breath in the lapse of the over-passing breeze. And then, in the midst of the gentle perfumes of the garden, the perfumes of the magnolia flowers, of the mignonette borders, of the crumbling walls, there expanded a new odour, or the faint mingling of many odours, the smell of the roses that lingered in her hair, of the lilies that exhaled from her neck, of the heliotrope that disengaged itself from her hands and arms, and of the hyacinths with which her little feet were redolent, And then, suddenly, it was herself—her eyes, heavy-lidded, violet blue, full of the love of him; her sweet full lips speaking his name; her hands clasping his hands, his shoulders, his neck—her whole dear body giving itself into his embrace; her lips against his; her hands holding his head, drawing his face down to hers.

Vanamee, as he remembered all this, flung out an arm with a cry of pain, his eyes searching the gloom, all his mind in strenuous mutiny against the triumph of Death. His glance shot swiftly out across the night, unconsciously following the direction from which Angele used to come to him.

"Come to me now," he exclaimed under his breath, tense and rigid with the vast futile effort of his will. "Come to me now, now. Don't you hear me, Angele? You must, you must come."

Suddenly Vanamee returned to himself with the abruptness of a blow. His eyes opened. He half raised himself from the ground. Swiftly his scattered wits readjusted themselves. Never more sane, never more himself, he rose to his feet and stood looking off into the night across the Seed ranch.

"What was it?" he murmured, bewildered.

He looked around him from side to side, as if to get in touch with reality once more. He looked at his hands, at the rough bark of the pear tree next which he stood, at the streaked and rain-eroded walls of the Mission and garden. The exaltation of his mind calmed itself; the unnatural strain under which he laboured slackened. He became thoroughly master of himself again, matter-of-fact, practical, keen.

But just so sure as his hands were his own, just so sure as the bark of the pear tree was rough, the mouldering adobe of the Mission walls damp—just so sure had Something occurred. It was vague, intangible, appealing only to some strange, nameless sixth sense, but none the less perceptible. His mind, his imagination, sent out from him across the night, across the little valley below him, speeding hither and thither through the dark, lost, confused, had suddenly paused, hovering, had found Something. It had not returned to him empty-handed. It had come back, but now there was a change— mysterious, illusive. There were no words for this that had transpired. But for the moment, one thing only was certain. The night was no longer voiceless, the dark was no longer empty. Far off there, beyond the reach of vision, unlocalised, strange, a ripple had formed on the still black pool of the night, had formed, flashed one instant to the stars, then swiftly faded again. The night shut down once more. There was no sound—nothing stirred.

For the moment, Vanamee stood transfixed, struck rigid in his place, stupefied, his eyes staring, breathless with utter amazement. Then, step by step, he shrank back into the deeper shadow, treading with the infinite precaution of a prowling leopard. A qualm of something very much like fear seized upon him. But immediately on the heels of this first impression came the doubt of his own senses. Whatever had happened had been so ephemeral, so faint, so intangible, that now he wondered if he had not deceived himself, after all. But the reaction followed. Surely, there had been Something. And from that moment began for him the most poignant uncertainty of mind. Gradually he drew back into the garden, holding his breath, listening to every faintest sound, walking upon tiptoe. He reached the fountain, and wetting his hands, passed them across his forehead and eyes. Once more he stood listening. The silence was profound.

Troubled, disturbed, Vanamee went away, passing out of the garden, descending the hill. He forded Broderson Creek where it intersected the road to Guadalajara, and went on across Quien Sabe, walking slowly, his head bent down, his hands clasped behind his back, thoughtful, perplexed.

CHAPTER V

At seven o'clock, in the bedroom of his ranch house, in the white-painted iron bedstead with its blue-grey army blankets and red counterpane, Annixter was still asleep, his face red, his mouth open, his stiff yellow hair in wild disorder. On the wooden chair at the bed-head, stood the kerosene lamp, by the light of which he had been reading the previous evening. Beside it was a paper bag of dried prunes, and the limp volume of "Copperfield," the place marked by a slip of paper torn from the edge of the bag.

Annixter slept soundly, making great work of the business, unable to take even his rest gracefully. His eyes were shut so tight that the skin at their angles was drawn into puckers. Under his pillow, his two hands were doubled up into fists. At intervals, he gritted his teeth ferociously, while, from time to time, the abrupt sound of his snoring dominated the brisk ticking of the alarm clock that hung from the brass knob of the bed-post, within six inches of his ear.

But immediately after seven, this clock sprung its alarm with the abruptness of an explosion, and within the second, Annixter had hurled the bed-clothes from him and flung himself up to a sitting posture on the edge of the bed, panting and gasping, blinking at the light, rubbing his head, dazed and bewildered, stupefied at the hideous suddenness with which he had been wrenched from his sleep.

His first act was to take down the alarm clock and stifle its prolonged whirring under the pillows and blankets. But when this had been done, he continued to sit stupidly on the edge of the bed, curling his toes away from the cold of the floor; his half-shut eyes, heavy with sleep, fixed and vacant, closing and opening by turns. For upwards of three minutes he alternately dozed and woke, his head and the whole upper half of his body sagging abruptly sideways from moment to moment. But at length, coming more to himself, he straightened up, ran his fingers through his hair, and with a prodigious yawn, murmured vaguely:

"Oh, Lord! Oh-h, LORD!"

He stretched three or four times, twisting about in his place, curling and uncurling his toes, muttering from time to time between two yawns:

"Oh, Lord! Oh, Lord!"

He stared about the room, collecting his thoughts, readjusting himself for the day's work.

The room was barren, the walls of tongue-and-groove sheathing — alternate brown and yellow boards — like the walls of a stable, were adorned with two or three unframed lithographs, the Christmas "souvenirs" of weekly periodicals, fastened with great wire nails; a bunch of herbs or flowers, lamentably withered and grey with dust, was affixed to the mirror over the black walnut washstand by the window, and a yellowed photograph of Annixter's combined harvester — himself and his men in a group before it — hung close at hand. On the floor, at the bedside and before the bureau, were two oval rag-carpet rugs. In the corners of the room were muddy boots, a McClellan saddle, a surveyor's transit, an empty coal-hod and a box of iron bolts and nuts. On the wall over the bed, in a gilt frame, was Annixter's college diploma, while on the bureau, amid a litter of hair-brushes, dirty collars, driving gloves, cigars and the like, stood a broken machine for loading shells.

It was essentially a man's room, rugged, uncouth, virile, full of the odours of tobacco, of leather, of rusty iron; the bare floor hollowed by the grind of hob-nailed boots, the walls marred by the friction of heavy things of metal. Strangely enough, Annixter's clothes were disposed of on the single chair with the precision of an old maid. Thus he had placed them the night before; the boots set carefully side by side, the trousers, with the overalls still upon them, neatly folded upon the seat of the chair, the coat hanging from its back.

The Quien Sabe ranch house was a six-room affair, all on one floor. By no excess of charity could it have been called a home. Annixter was a wealthy man; he could have furnished his dwelling with quite as much elegance as that of Magnus Derrick. As it was, however, he considered his house merely as a place to eat, to sleep, to change his clothes in; as a shelter from the rain, an office where business was transacted — nothing more.

When he was sufficiently awake, Annixter thrust his feet into a pair of wicker slippers, and shuffled across the office adjoining his bedroom, to the bathroom just beyond, and stood under the icy shower a few minutes, his teeth chattering, fulminating oaths at the coldness of the water. Still shivering, he hurried into his clothes, and, having pushed the button of the electric bell to announce that he was ready for breakfast, immediately plunged into the business of the day. While he was thus occupied, the butcher's cart from Bonneville drove into the yard with the day's supply of meat. This cart also brought the Bonneville paper and the mail of the previous night. In the bundle of correspondence that the butcher handed to Annixter that morning, was a telegram from Osterman, at that time on his second trip to Los Angeles. It read:

"Flotation of company in this district assured. Have secured services of desirable party. Am now in position to sell you your share stock, as per original plan."

Annixter grunted as he tore the despatch into strips. "Well," he muttered, "that part is settled, then."

He made a little pile of the torn strips on the top of the unlighted stove, and burned them carefully, scowling down into the flicker of fire, thoughtful and preoccupied.

He knew very well what Osterman referred to by "Flotation of company," and also who was the "desirable party" he spoke of.

Under protest, as he was particular to declare, and after interminable argument, Annixter had allowed himself to be reconciled with Osterman, and to be persuaded to reenter the proposed political "deal." A committee had been formed to finance the affair—Osterman, old Broderson, Annixter himself, and, with reservations, hardly more than a looker-on, Harran Derrick. Of this committee, Osterman was considered chairman. Magnus Derrick had formally and definitely refused his adherence to the scheme. He was trying to steer a middle course. His position was difficult, anomalous. If freight rates were cut through the efforts of the members of the committee, he could not very well avoid taking advantage of the new schedule. He would be the gainer, though sharing neither the risk nor the expense. But, meanwhile, the days were passing; the primary elections were drawing nearer. The committee could not afford to wait, and by way of a beginning, Osterman had gone to Los Angeles, fortified by a large sum of money—a purse to which Annixter, Broderson and himself had contributed. He had put himself in touch with Disbrow, the political man of the Denver, Pueblo and Mojave road, and had had two interviews with him. The telegram that Annixter received that morning was to say that Disbrow had been bought over, and would adopt Parrell as the D., P. and M. candidate for Railroad Commissioner from the third district.

One of the cooks brought up Annixter's breakfast that morning, and he went through it hastily, reading his mail at the same time and glancing over the pages of the "Mercury," Genslinger's paper. The "Mercury," Annixter was persuaded, received a subsidy from the Pacific and Southwestern Railroad, and was hardly better than the mouthpiece by which Shelgrim and the General Office spoke to ranchers about Bonneville.

An editorial in that morning's issue said:

"It would not be surprising to the well-informed, if the long-deferred re-grade of the value of the railroad sections included in the Los Muertos, Quien Sabe, Osterman and Broderson properties was made before the first of the year. Naturally, the tenants of these lands feel an interest in the price which the railroad will put upon its holdings, and it is rumoured they expect the land will be offered to them for two dollars and fifty cents per acre. It needs no seventh daughter of a seventh daughter to foresee that these gentlemen will be disappointed."

"Rot!" vociferated Annixter to himself as he finished. He rolled the paper into a wad and hurled it from him.

"Rot! rot! What does Genslinger know about it? I stand on my agreement with the P. and S. W.—from two fifty to five dollars an acre—there it is in black and white. The road IS obligated. And my improvements! I made the land valuable by improving it, irrigating it, draining it, and cultivating it. Talk to ME. I know better."

The most abiding impression that Genslinger's editorial made upon him was, that possibly the "Mercury" was not subsidised by the corporation after all. If it was; Genslinger would not have been led into making his mistake as to the value of the land. He would have known that the railroad was under contract to sell at two dollars and a half an acre, and not only this, but that when the land was put upon the market, it was to be offered to the present holders first of all. Annixter called to mind the explicit terms of the agreement between himself and the railroad, and dismissed the matter from his mind. He lit a cigar, put on his hat and went out.

The morning was fine, the air nimble, brisk. On the summit of the skeleton-like tower of the artesian well, the windmill was turning steadily in a breeze from the southwest. The water in the irrigating ditch was well up. There was no cloud in the sky. Far off to the east and west, the bulwarks of the valley, the Coast Range and the foothills of the Sierras stood out, pale amethyst against the delicate pink and white sheen of the horizon. The sunlight was a veritable flood, crystal, limpid, sparkling, setting a feeling of gayety in the air, stirring up an effervescence in the blood, a tumult of exuberance in the veins.

But on his way to the barns, Annixter was obliged to pass by the open door of the dairy-house. Hilma Tree was inside, singing at her work; her voice of a velvety huskiness, more of the chest than of the throat, mingling with the liquid dashing of the milk in the vats and churns, and the clear, sonorous clinking of the cans and pans. Annixter turned into the dairy-house, pausing on the threshold, looking about him. Hilma stood bathed from head to foot in the torrent of sunlight that poured in upon her from the three wide-open windows. She was charming, delicious, radiant of youth, of health, of well-being. Into her eyes, wide open, brown, rimmed with their fine, thin line of intense black lashes, the sun set a diamond flash; the same golden light glowed all around her thick, moist hair, lambent, beautiful, a sheen of almost metallic lustre, and reflected itself upon her wet lips, moving with the words of her singing. The whiteness of her skin under the caress of this hale, vigorous morning light was dazzling, pure, of a fineness beyond words. Beneath the sweet modulation of her chin, the reflected light from the burnished copper vessel she was carrying set a vibration of pale gold. Overlaying the flush of rose in her cheeks, seen only when she stood against the sunlight, was a faint sheen of down, a lustrous floss, delicate as the pollen of a flower, or the impalpable powder of a moth's wing. She was moving to and fro about her work, alert, joyous, robust; and from all the fine, full amplitude of her figure, from her thick white neck, sloping downward to her shoulders, from the deep, feminine swell of her breast, the vigorous maturity of her hips, there was disengaged a vibrant note of gayety, of exuberant animal life, sane, honest, strong. She wore a skirt of plain blue calico and a shirtwaist of pink linen, clean, trim; while her sleeves turned back to her shoulders, showed her large, white arms, wet with milk, redolent and fragrant with milk, glowing and resplendent in the early morning light.

On the threshold, Annixter took off his hat.

"Good morning, Miss Hilma."

Hilma, who had set down the copper can on top of the vat, turned about quickly.

"Oh, GOOD morning, sir;" and, unconsciously, she made a little gesture of salutation with her hand, raising it part way toward her head, as a man would have done.

"Well," began Annixter vaguely, "how are you getting along down here?"

"Oh, very fine. To-day, there is not so much to do. We drew the whey hours ago, and now we are just done putting the curd to press. I have been cleaning. See my pans. Wouldn't they do for mirrors, sir? And the copper things. I have scrubbed and scrubbed. Oh, you can look into the tiniest corners, everywhere, you won't find so much as the littlest speck of dirt or grease. I love CLEAN things, and this room is my own particular place. Here I can do just as I please, and that is, to keep the cement floor, and the vats, and the churns and the separators, and especially the cans and coppers, clean; clean, and to see that the milk is pure, oh, so that a little baby could drink it; and to have the air always sweet, and the sun—oh, lots and lots of sun, morning, noon and afternoon, so that everything shines. You know, I never see the sun set that it don't make me a little sad; yes, always, just a little. Isn't it funny? I should want it to be day all the time. And when the day is gloomy and dark, I am just as sad as if a very good friend of mine had left me. Would you believe it? Just until within a few years, when I was a big girl, sixteen and over, mamma had to sit by my bed every night before I could go to sleep. I was afraid in the dark. Sometimes I am now. Just imagine, and now I am nineteen—a young lady."

"You were, hey?" observed Annixter, for the sake of saying something. "Afraid in the dark? What of—ghosts?"

"N-no; I don't know what. I wanted the light, I wanted——" She drew a deep breath, turning towards the window and spreading her pink finger-tips to the light. "Oh, the SUN. I love the sun. See, put your hand there—here on the top of the vat—like that. Isn't it warm? Isn't it fine? And don't you love to see it coming in like that through the windows, floods of it; and all the little dust in it shining? Where there is lots of sunlight, I think the people must be very good. It's only wicked people that love the dark. And the wicked things are always done and planned in the dark, I think. Perhaps, too, that's why I hate things that are mysterious—things that I can't see, that happen in the dark." She wrinkled her nose with a little expression of aversion. "I hate a mystery. Maybe that's why I am afraid in the dark—or was. I shouldn't like to think that anything could happen around me that I couldn't see or understand or explain."

She ran on from subject to subject, positively garrulous, talking in her low-pitched voice of velvety huskiness for the mere enjoyment of putting her ideas into speech, innocently assuming that they were quite as interesting to others as to herself. She was yet a great child, ignoring the fact that she had ever grown up, taking a child's interest in her immediate surroundings, direct, straightforward, plain. While speaking, she continued about her work, rinsing out the cans with a mixture of hot water and soda, scouring them bright, and piling them in the sunlight on top of the vat.

Obliquely, and from between his narrowed lids, Annixter scrutinised her from time to time, more and more won over by her adorable freshness, her clean, fine youth. The clumsiness that he usually experienced in the presence of women was wearing off. Hilma Tree's direct simplicity put him at his ease. He began to wonder if he dared to kiss Hilma, and if he did dare, how she would take it. A spark of suspicion flickered up in his mind. Did not her manner imply, vaguely, an invitation? One never could tell with feemales. That was why she was talking so much, no doubt, holding him there, affording the opportunity. Aha! She had best look out, or he would take her at her word.

"Oh, I had forgotten," suddenly exclaimed Hilma, "the very thing I wanted to show you—the new press. You remember I asked for one last month? This is it. See, this is how it works. Here is where the curds go; look. And this cover is screwed down like this, and then you work the lever this way." She grasped the lever in both hands, throwing her weight upon it, her smooth, bare arm swelling round and firm with the effort, one slim foot, in its low shoe set off with the bright, steel buckle, braced against the wall.

"My, but that takes strength," she panted, looking up at him and smiling. "But isn't it a fine press? Just what we needed."

"And," Annixter cleared his throat, "and where do you keep the cheeses and the butter?" He thought it very likely that these were in the cellar of the dairy.

"In the cellar," answered Hilma. "Down here, see?" She raised the flap of the cellar door at the end of the room. "Would you like to see? Come down; I'll show you."

She went before him down into the cool obscurity underneath, redolent of new cheese and fresh butter. Annixter followed, a certain excitement beginning to gain upon him. He was almost sure now that Hilma wanted him to kiss her. At all events, one could but try. But, as yet, he was not absolutely sure. Suppose he had been mistaken in her; suppose she should consider herself insulted and freeze him with an icy stare. Annixter winced at the very thought of it. Better let the whole business go, and get to work.

He was wasting half the morning. Yet, if she DID want to give him the opportunity of kissing her, and he failed to take advantage of it, what a ninny she would think him; she would despise him for being afraid. He afraid! He, Annixter, afraid of a fool, feemale girl. Why, he owed it to himself as a man to go as far as he could. He told himself that that goat Osterman would have kissed Hilma Tree weeks ago. To test his state of mind, he imagined himself as having decided to kiss her, after all, and at once was surprised to experience a poignant qualm of excitement, his heart beating heavily, his breath coming short. At the same time, his courage remained with him. He was not afraid to try. He felt a greater respect for himself because of this. His self-assurance hardened within him, and as Hilma turned to him, asking him to taste a cut from one of the ripe cheeses, he suddenly stepped close to her, throwing an arm about her shoulders, advancing his head.

But at the last second, he bungled, hesitated; Hilma shrank from him, supple as a young reed; Annixter clutched harshly at her arm, and trod his full weight upon one of her slender feet, his cheek and chin barely touching the delicate pink lobe of one of her ears, his lips brushing merely a fold of her shirt waist between neck and shoulder. The thing was a failure, and at once he realised that nothing had been further from Hilma's mind than the idea of his kissing her.

She started back from him abruptly, her hands nervously clasped against her breast, drawing in her breath sharply and holding it with a little, tremulous catch of the throat that sent a quivering vibration the length of her smooth, white neck. Her eyes opened wide with a childlike look, more of astonishment than anger. She was surprised, out of all measure, discountenanced, taken all aback, and when she found her breath, gave voice to a great "Oh" of dismay and distress.

For an instant, Annixter stood awkwardly in his place, ridiculous, clumsy, murmuring over and over again:

"Well—well—that's all right—who's going to hurt you? You needn't be afraid—who's going to hurt you—that's all right."

Then, suddenly, with a quick, indefinite gesture of one arm, he exclaimed:

"Good-bye, I—I'm sorry."

He turned away, striding up the stairs, crossing the dairy-room, and regained the open air, raging and furious. He turned toward the barns, clapping his hat upon his head, muttering the while under his breath:

"Oh, you goat! You beastly fool PIP. Good LORD, what an ass you've made of yourself now!"

Suddenly he resolved to put Hilma Tree out of his thoughts. The matter was interfering with his work. This kind of thing was sure not earning any money. He shook himself as though freeing his shoulders of an irksome burden, and turned his entire attention to the work nearest at hand.

The prolonged rattle of the shinglers' hammers upon the roof of the big barn attracted him, and, crossing over between the ranch house and the artesian well, he stood for some time absorbed in the contemplation of the vast building, amused and interested with the confusion of sounds—the clatter of hammers, the cadenced scrape of saws, and the rhythmic shuffle of planes—that issued from the gang of carpenters who were at that moment putting the finishing touches upon the roof and rows of stalls. A boy and two men were busy hanging the great sliding door at the south end, while the painters—come down from Bonneville early that morning—were engaged in adjusting the spray and force engine, by means of which Annixter had insisted upon painting the vast surfaces of the barn, condemning the use of brushes and pots for such work as old-fashioned and out-of-date.

He called to one of the foremen, to ask when the barn would be entirely finished, and was told that at the end of the week the hay and stock could be installed.

"And a precious long time you've been at it, too," Annixter declared.

"Well, you know the rain——"

"Oh, rot the rain! I work in the rain. You and your unions make me sick."

"But, Mr. Annixter, we couldn't have begun painting in the rain. The job would have been spoiled."

"Hoh, yes, spoiled. That's all very well. Maybe it would, and then, again, maybe it wouldn't."

But when the foreman had left him, Annixter could not forbear a growl of satisfaction. It could not be denied that the barn was superb, monumental even. Almost any one of the other barns in the county could be swung, bird-cage fashion, inside of it, with room to spare. In every sense, the barn was precisely what Annixter had hoped of it. In his pleasure over the success of his idea, even Hilma for the moment was forgotten.

"And, now," murmured Annixter, "I'll give that dance in it. I'll make 'em sit up."

It occurred to him that he had better set about sending out the invitations for the affair. He was puzzled to decide just how the thing should be managed, and resolved that it might be as well to consult Magnus and Mrs. Derrick.

"I want to talk of this telegram of the goat's with Magnus, anyhow," he said to himself reflectively, "and there's things I got to do in Bonneville before the first of the month."

He turned about on his heel with a last look at the barn, and set off toward the stable. He had decided to have his horse saddled and ride over to Bonneville by way of Los Muertos. He would make a day of it, would see Magnus, Harran, old Broderson and some of the business men of Bonneville.

A few moments later, he rode out of the barn and the stable-yard, a fresh cigar between his teeth, his hat slanted over his face against the rays of the sun, as yet low in the east. He crossed the irrigating ditch and gained the trail—the short cut over into Los Muertos, by way of Hooven's. It led south and west into the low ground overgrown by grey-green willows by Broderson Creek, at this time of the rainy season a stream of considerable volume, farther on dipping sharply to pass underneath the Long Trestle of the railroad. On the other side of the right of way, Annixter was obliged to open the gate in Derrick's line fence. He managed this without dismounting, swearing at the horse the while, and spurring him continually. But once inside the gate he cantered forward briskly.

This part of Los Muertos was Hooven's holding, some five hundred acres enclosed between the irrigating ditch and Broderson Creek, and half the way across, Annixter came up with Hooven himself, busily at work replacing a broken washer in his seeder. Upon one of the horses hitched to the machine, her hands gripped tightly upon the harness of the collar, Hilda, his little daughter, with her small, hob-nailed boots and boy's canvas overalls, sat, exalted and petrified with ecstasy and excitement, her eyes wide opened, her hair in a tangle.

"Hello, Bismarck," said Annixter, drawing up beside him. "What are YOU doing here? I thought the Governor was going to manage without his tenants this year."

"Ach, Meest'r Ennixter," cried the other, straightening up. "Ach, dat's you, eh? Ach, you bedt he doand menege mitout me. Me, I gotta stay. I talk der straighd talk mit der Governor. I fix 'em. Ach, you bedt. Sieben yahr I hef bei der rench ge-stopped; yais, sir. Efery oder sohn-of-a-guhn bei der plaice ged der sach bud me. Eh? Wat you tink von dose ting?"

"I think that's a crazy-looking monkey-wrench you've got there," observed Annixter, glancing at the instrument in Hooven's hand.

"Ach, dot wrainch," returned Hooven. "Soh! Wail, I tell you dose ting now whair I got 'em. Say, you see dot wrainch. Dat's not Emericen wrainch at alle. I got 'em at Gravelotte der day we licked der stuffun oudt der Frainch, ach, you bedt. Me, I pelong to der Wurtemberg redgimend, dot dey use to suppord der batterie von der Brince von Hohenlohe. Alle der day we lay down bei der stomach in der feildt behindt der batterie, und der schells von der Frainch cennon hef eggsblode—ach, donnerwetter!—I tink efery schell eggsblode bei der beckside my neck. Und dat go on der whole day, noddun else, noddun aber der Frainch schell, b-r-r, b-r-r b-r-r, b-r-AM, und der smoag, und unzer batterie, dat go off slow, steady, yoost like der glock, eins, zwei, boom! eins, zwei, boom! yoost like der glock, ofer und ofer again, alle der day. Den vhen der night come dey say we hev der great victorie made. I doand know. Vhat do I see von der bettle? Noddun. Den we gedt oop und maerch und maerch alle night, und in der morgen we hear dose cennon egain, hell oaf der way, far-off, I doand know vhair. Budt, nef'r mindt. Bretty qnick, ach, Gott—" his face flamed scarlet, "Ach, du lieber Gott! Bretty zoon, dere wass der Kaiser, glose bei, und Fritz, Unzer Fritz. Bei Gott, den I go grazy, und yell, ach, you bedt, der whole redgimend: 'Hoch der Kaiser! Hoch der Vaterland!' Und der dears come to der eyes, I doand know because vhy, und der mens gry und shaike der hend, und der whole redgimend maerch off like dat, fairy broudt, bei Gott, der head oop high, und sing 'Die Wacht am Rhein.' Dot wass Gravelotte."

"And the monkey-wrench?"

"Ach, I pick 'um oop vhen der batterie go. Der cennoniers hef forgedt und leaf 'um. I carry 'um in der sack. I tink I use 'um vhen I gedt home in der business. I was maker von vagons in Carlsruhe, und I nef'r gedt home again. Vhen der war hef godt over, I go beck to Ulm und gedt marriet, und den I gedt demn sick von der armie. Vhen I gedt der release, I clair oudt, you bedt. I come to Emerica. First, New Yor-ruk; den Milwaukee; den Sbringfieldt-Illinoy; den Galifornie, und heir I stay."

"And the Fatherland? Ever want to go back?"

"Wail, I tell you dose ting, Meest'r Ennixter. Alle-ways, I tink a lot oaf Shairmany, und der Kaiser, und nef'r I forgedt Gravelotte. Budt, say, I tell you dose ting. Vhair der wife is, und der kinder—der leedle girl Hilda— DERE IS DER VATERLAND. Eh? Emerica, dat's my gountry now, und dere," he pointed behind him to the house under the mammoth oak tree on the Lower Road, "dat's my home. Dat's goot enough Vaterland for me."

Annixter gathered up the reins, about to go on.

"So you like America, do you, Bismarck?" he said. "Who do you vote for?"

"Emerica? I doand know," returned the other, insistently. "Dat's my home yonder. Dat's my Vaterland. Alle von we Shairmens yoost like dot. Shairmany, dot's hell oaf some fine plaice, sure. Budt der Vaterland iss vhair der home und der wife und kinder iss. Eh? Yes? Voad? Ach, no. Me, I nef'r voad. I doand bodder der haid mit dose ting. I maig der wheat grow, und ged der braid fur der wife und Hilda, dot's all. Dot's me; dot's Bismarck."

"Good-bye," commented Annixter, moving off.

Hooven, the washer replaced, turned to his work again, starting up the horses. The seeder advanced, whirring.

"Ach, Hilda, leedle girl," he cried, "hold tight bei der shdrap on. Hey MULE! Hoop! Gedt oop, you."

Annixter cantered on. In a few moments, he had crossed Broderson Creek and had entered upon the Home ranch of Los Muertos. Ahead of him, but so far off that the greater portion of its bulk was below the horizon, he could see the Derricks' home, a roof or two between the dull green of cypress and eucalyptus. Nothing else was in sight. The brown earth, smooth, unbroken, was as a limitless, mud-coloured ocean. The silence was profound.

Then, at length, Annixter's searching eye made out a blur on the horizon to the northward; the blur concentrated itself to a speck; the speck grew by steady degrees to a spot, slowly moving, a note of dull colour, barely darker than the land, but an inky black silhouette as it topped a low rise of ground and stood for a moment outlined against the pale blue of the sky. Annixter turned his horse from the road and rode across the ranch land to meet this new object of interest. As the spot grew larger, it resolved itself into constituents, a collection of units; its shape grew irregular, fragmentary. A disintegrated, nebulous confusion advanced toward Annixter, preceded, as he discovered on nearer approach, by a medley of faint sounds. Now it was no longer a spot, but a column, a column that moved, accompanied by spots. As Annixter lessened the distance, these spots resolved themselves into buggies or men on horseback that kept pace with the advancing column. There were horses in the column itself. At first glance, it appeared as if there were nothing else, a riderless squadron tramping steadily over the upturned plough land of the ranch. But it drew nearer. The horses were in lines, six abreast, harnessed to machines. The noise increased, defined itself. There was a shout or two; occasionally a horse blew through his nostrils with a prolonged, vibrating snort. The click and clink of metal work was incessant, the machines throwing off a continual rattle of wheels and cogs and clashing springs. The column approached nearer; was close at hand. The noises mingled to a subdued uproar, a bewildering confusion; the impact of innumerable hoofs was a veritable rumble. Machine after machine appeared; and Annixter, drawing to one side, remained for nearly ten minutes watching and interested, while, like an array of chariots— clattering, jostling, creaking, clashing, an interminable procession, machine succeeding machine, six-horse team succeeding six-horse team—bustling, hurried—Magnus Derrick's thirty-three grain drills, each with its eight hoes, went clamouring past, like an advance of military, seeding the ten thousand acres of the great ranch; fecundating the living soil; implanting deep in the dark womb of the Earth the germ of life, the sustenance of a whole world, the food of an entire People.

When the drills had passed, Annixter turned and rode back to the Lower Road, over the land now thick with seed. He did not wonder that the seeding on Los Muertos seemed to be hastily conducted. Magnus and Harran Derrick had not yet been able to make up the time lost at the beginning of the season, when they had waited so long for the ploughs to arrive. They had been behindhand all the time. On Annixter's ranch, the land had not only been harrowed, as well as seeded, but in some cases, cross-harrowed as well. The labour of putting in the vast crop was over. Now there was nothing to do but wait, while the seed silently germinated; nothing to do but watch for the wheat to come up.

When Annixter reached the ranch house of Los Muertos, under the shade of the cypress and eucalyptus trees, he found Mrs. Derrick on the porch, seated in a long wicker chair. She had been washing her hair, and the light brown locks that yet retained so much of their brightness, were carefully spread in the sun over the back of her chair. Annixter could not but remark that, spite of her more than fifty years, Annie Derrick was yet rather pretty. Her eyes were still those of a young girl, just touched with an uncertain expression of innocence and inquiry, but as her glance fell upon him, he found that that expression changed to one of uneasiness, of distrust, almost of aversion.

The night before this, after Magnus and his wife had gone to bed, they had lain awake for hours, staring up into the dark, talking, talking. Magnus had not long been able to keep from his wife the news of the coalition that was forming against the railroad, nor the fact that this coalition was determined to gain its ends by any means at its command. He had told her of Osterman's scheme of a fraudulent election to seat a Board of Railroad Commissioners, who should be nominees of the farming interests. Magnus and his wife had talked this matter over and over again; and the same discussion, begun immediately after supper the evening before, had lasted till far into the night.

At once, Annie Derrick had been seized with a sudden terror lest Magnus, after all, should allow himself to be persuaded; should yield to the pressure that was every day growing stronger. None better than she knew the iron integrity of her husband's character. None better than she remembered how his dearest ambition, that of political preferment, had been thwarted by his refusal to truckle, to connive, to compromise with his ideas of right. Now, at last, there seemed to be a change. Long continued oppression, petty tyranny, injustice and extortion had driven him to exasperation. S. Behrman's insults still rankled. He seemed nearly ready to countenance Osterman's scheme. The very fact that he was willing to talk of it to her so often and at such great length, was proof positive that it occupied his mind. The pity of it, the tragedy of it! He, Magnus, the "Governor," who had been so staunch, so rigidly upright, so loyal to his convictions, so bitter in his denunciation of the New Politics, so scathing in his attacks on bribery and corruption in high places; was it possible that now, at last, he could be brought to withhold his condemnation of the devious intrigues of the unscrupulous, going on there under his very eyes? That Magnus should not command Harran to refrain from all intercourse with the conspirators, had been a matter of vast surprise to Mrs. Derrick. Time was when Magnus would have forbidden his son to so much as recognise a dishonourable man.

But besides all this, Derrick's wife trembled at the thought of her husband and son engaging in so desperate a grapple with the railroad—that great monster, iron-hearted, relentless, infinitely powerful. Always it had issued triumphant from the fight; always S. Behrman, the Corporation's champion, remained upon the field as victor, placid, unperturbed, unassailable. But now a more terrible struggle than any hitherto loomed menacing over the rim of the future; money was to be spent like water; personal reputations were to be hazarded in the issue; failure meant ruin in all directions, financial ruin, moral ruin, ruin of prestige, ruin of character. Success, to her mind, was almost impossible. Annie Derrick feared the railroad. At night, when everything else was still, the distant roar of passing trains echoed across Los Muertos, from Guadalajara, from Bonneville, or from the Long Trestle, straight into her heart. At such moments she saw very plainly the galloping terror of steam and steel, with its single eye, cyclopean, red, shooting from horizon to horizon, symbol of a vast power, huge and terrible; the leviathan with tentacles of steel, to oppose which meant to be ground to instant destruction beneath the clashing wheels. No, it was better to submit, to resign oneself to the inevitable. She obliterated herself, shrinking from the harshness of the world, striving, with vain hands, to draw her husband back with her.

Just before Annixter's arrival, she had been sitting, thoughtful, in her long chair, an open volume of poems turned down upon her lap, her glance losing itself in the immensity of Los Muertos that, from the edge of the lawn close by, unrolled itself, gigantic, toward the far, southern horizon, wrinkled and serrated after the season's ploughing. The earth, hitherto grey with dust, was now upturned and brown. As far as the eye could reach, it was empty of all life, bare, mournful, absolutely still; and, as she looked, there seemed to her morbid imagination—diseased and disturbed with long brooding, sick with the monotony of repeated sensation—to be disengaged from all this immensity, a sense of a vast oppression, formless, disquieting. The terror of sheer bigness grew slowly in her mind; loneliness beyond words gradually enveloped her. She was lost in all these limitless reaches of space. Had she been abandoned in mid-ocean, in an open boat, her terror could hardly have been greater. She felt vividly that certain uncongeniality which, when all is said, forever remains between humanity and the earth which supports it. She recognised the colossal indifference of nature, not hostile, even kindly and friendly, so long as the human ant-swarm was submissive, working with it, hurrying along at its side in the mysterious march of the centuries. Let, however, the insect rebel, strive to make head against the power of this nature, and at once it became relentless, a gigantic engine, a vast power, huge, terrible; a leviathan with a heart of steel, knowing no compunction, no forgiveness, no tolerance; crushing out the human atom with sound less calm, the agony of destruction sending never a jar, never the faintest tremour through all that prodigious mechanism of wheels and cogs.

Such thoughts as these did not take shape distinctly in her mind. She could not have told herself exactly what it was that disquieted her. She only received the vague sensation of these things, as it were a breath of wind upon her face, confused, troublous, an indefinite sense of hostility in the air.

The sound of hoofs grinding upon the gravel of the driveway brought her to herself again, and, withdrawing her gaze from the empty plain of Los Muertos, she saw young Annixter stopping his horse by the carriage steps. But the sight of him only diverted her mind to the other trouble. She could not but regard him with aversion. He was one of the conspirators, was one of the leaders in the battle that impended; no doubt, he had come to make a fresh attempt to win over Magnus to the unholy alliance.

However, there was little trace of enmity in her greeting. Her hair was still spread, like a broad patch of back, and she made that her excuse for not getting up. In answer to Annixter's embarrassed inquiry after Magnus, she sent the Chinese cook to call him from the office; and Annixter, after tying his horse to the ring driven into the trunk of one of the eucalyptus trees, came up to the porch, and, taking off his hat, sat down upon the steps.

"Is Harran anywhere about?" he asked. "I'd like to see Harran, too."

"No," said Mrs. Derrick, "Harran went to Bonneville early this morning."

She glanced toward Annixter nervously, without turning her head, lest she should disturb her outspread hair.

"What is it you want to see Mr. Derrick about?" she inquired hastily. "Is it about this plan to elect a Railroad Commission? Magnus does not approve of it," she declared with energy. "He told me so last night."

Annixter moved about awkwardly where he sat, smoothing down with his hand the one stiff lock of yellow hair that persistently stood up from his crown like an Indian's scalp-lock. At once his suspicions were all aroused. Ah! this feemale woman was trying to get a hold on him, trying to involve him in a petticoat mess, trying to cajole him. Upon the instant, he became very crafty; an excess of prudence promptly congealed his natural impulses. In an actual spasm of caution, he scarcely trusted himself to speak, terrified lest he should commit himself to something. He glanced about apprehensively, praying that Magnus might join them speedily, relieving the tension.

"I came to see about giving a dance in my new barn," he answered, scowling into the depths of his hat, as though reading from notes he had concealed there. "I wanted to ask how I should send out the invites. I thought of just putting an ad. in the 'Mercury.'"

But as he spoke, Presley had come up behind Annixter in time to get the drift of the conversation, and now observed:

"That's nonsense, Buck. You're not giving a public ball. You MUST send out invitations."

"Hello, Presley, you there?" exclaimed Annixter, turning round. The two shook hands.

"Send out invitations?" repeated Annixter uneasily. "Why must I?"

"Because that's the only way to do."

"It is, is it?" answered Annixter, perplexed and troubled. No other man of his acquaintance could have so contradicted Annixter without provoking a quarrel upon the instant. Why the young rancher, irascible, obstinate, belligerent, should invariably defer to the poet, was an inconsistency never to be explained. It was with great surprise that Mrs. Derrick heard him continue:

"Well, I suppose you know what you're talking about, Pres. Must have written invites, hey?"

"Of course."

"Typewritten?"

"Why, what an ass you are, Buck," observed Presley calmly. "Before you get through with it, you will probably insult three-fourths of the people you intend to invite, and have about a hundred quarrels on your hands, and a lawsuit or two."

However, before Annixter could reply, Magnus came out on the porch, erect, grave, freshly shaven. Without realising what he was doing, Annixter instinctively rose to his feet. It was as though Magnus was a commander-in-chief of an unseen army, and he a subaltern. There was some little conversation as to the proposed dance, and then Annixter found an excuse for drawing the Governor aside. Mrs. Derrick watched the two with eyes full of poignant anxiety, as they slowly paced the length of the gravel driveway to the road gate, and stood there, leaning upon it, talking earnestly; Magnus tall, thin-lipped, impassive, one hand in the breast of his frock coat, his head bare, his keen, blue eyes fixed upon Annixter's face. Annixter came at once to the main point.

"I got a wire from Osterman this morning, Governor, and, well—we've got Disbrow. That means that the Denver, Pueblo and Mojave is back of us. There's half the fight won, first off."

"Osterman bribed him, I suppose," observed Magnus.

Annixter raised a shoulder vexatiously.

"You've got to pay for what you get," he returned. "You don't get something for nothing, I guess. Governor," he went on, "I don't see how you can stay out of this business much longer. You see how it will be. We're going to win, and I don't see how you can feel that it's right of you to let us do all the work and stand all the expense. There's never been a movement of any importance that went on around you that you weren't the leader in it. All Tulare County, all the San Joaquin, for that matter, knows you. They want a leader, and they are looking to you. I know how you feel about politics nowadays. But, Governor, standards have changed since your time; everybody plays the game now as we are playing it—the most honourable men. You can't play it any other way, and, pshaw! if the right wins out in the end, that's the main thing. We want you in this thing, and we want you bad. You've been chewing on this affair now a long time. Have you made up your mind? Do you come in? I tell you what, you've got to look at these things in a large way. You've got to judge by results. Well, now, what do you think? Do you come in?"

Magnus's glance left Annixter's face, and for an instant sought the ground. His frown lowered, but now it was in perplexity, rather than in anger. His mind was troubled, harassed with a thousand dissensions.

But one of Magnus's strongest instincts, one of his keenest desires, was to be, if only for a short time, the master. To control men had ever been his ambition; submission of any kind, his greatest horror. His energy stirred within him, goaded by the lash of his anger, his sense of indignity, of insult. Oh for one moment to be able to strike back, to crush his enemy, to defeat the railroad, hold the Corporation in the grip of his fist, put down S. Behrman, rehabilitate himself, regain his self-respect. To be once more powerful, to command, to dominate. His thin lips pressed themselves together; the nostrils of his prominent hawk-like nose dilated, his erect, commanding figure stiffened unconsciously. For a moment, he saw himself controlling the situation, the foremost figure in his State, feared, respected, thousands of men beneath him, his ambition at length gratified; his career, once apparently brought to naught, completed; success a palpable achievement. What if this were his chance, after all, come at last after all these years. His chance! The instincts of the old-time gambler, the most redoubtable poker player of El Dorado County, stirred at the word. Chance! To know it when it came, to recognise it as it passed fleet as a wind-flurry, grip at it, catch at it, blind, reckless, staking all upon the hazard of the issue, that was genius. Was this his Chance? All of a sudden, it seemed to him that it was. But his honour! His cherished, lifelong integrity, the unstained purity of his principles? At this late date, were they to be sacrificed? Could he now go counter to all the firm built fabric of his character? How, afterward, could he bear to look Harran and Lyman in the face? And, yet—and, yet—back swung the pendulum—to neglect his Chance meant failure; a life begun in promise, and ended in obscurity, perhaps in financial ruin, poverty even. To seize it meant achievement, fame, influence, prestige, possibly great wealth.

"I am so sorry to interrupt," said Mrs. Derrick, as she came up. "I hope Mr. Annixter will excuse me, but I want Magnus to open the safe for me. I have lost the combination, and I must have some money. Phelps is going into town, and I want him to pay some bills for me. Can't you come right away, Magnus? Phelps is ready and waiting."

Annixter struck his heel into the ground with a suppressed oath. Always these fool feemale women came between him and his plans, mixing themselves up in his affairs. Magnus had been on the very point of saying something, perhaps committing himself to some course of action, and, at precisely the wrong moment, his wife had cut in. The opportunity was lost. The three returned toward the ranch house; but before saying good-bye, Annixter had secured from Magnus a promise to the effect that, before coming to a definite decision in the matter under discussion, he would talk further with him.

Presley met him at the porch. He was going into town with Phelps, and proposed to Annixter that he should accompany them.

"I want to go over and see old Broderson," Annixter objected.

But Presley informed him that Broderson had gone to Bonneville earlier in the morning. He had seen him go past in his buckboard. The three men set off, Phelps and Annixter on horseback, Presley on his bicycle.

When they had gone, Mrs. Derrick sought out her husband in the office of the ranch house. She was at her prettiest that morning, her cheeks flushed with excitement, her innocent, wide-open eyes almost girlish. She had fastened her hair, still moist, with a black ribbon tied at the back of her head, and the soft mass of light brown reached to below her waist, making her look very young.

"What was it he was saying to you just now," she exclaimed, as she came through the gate in the green-painted wire railing of the office. "What was Mr. Annixter saying? I know. He was trying to get you to join him, trying to persuade you to be dishonest, wasn't that it? Tell me, Magnus, wasn't that it?"

Magnus nodded.

His wife drew close to him, putting a hand on his shoulder.

"But you won't, will you? You won't listen to him again; you won't so much as allow him—anybody—to even suppose you would lend yourself to bribery? Oh, Magnus, I don't know what has come over you these last few weeks. Why, before this, you would have been insulted if any one thought you would even consider anything like dishonesty. Magnus, it would break my heart if you joined Mr. Annixter and Mr. Osterman. Why, you couldn't be the same man to me afterward; you, who have kept yourself so clean till now. And the boys; what would Lyman say, and Harran, and every one who knows you and respects you, if you lowered yourself to be just a political adventurer!"

For a moment, Derrick leaned his head upon his hand, avoiding her gaze. At length, he said, drawing a deep breath: "I am troubled, Annie. These are the evil days. I have much upon my mind."

"Evil days or not," she insisted, "promise me this one thing, that you will not join Mr. Annixter's scheme." She had taken his hand in both of hers and was looking into his face, her pretty eyes full of pleading.

"Promise me," she repeated; "give me your word. Whatever happens, let me always be able to be proud of you, as I always have been. Give me your word. I know you never seriously thought of joining Mr. Annixter, but I am so nervous and frightened sometimes. Just to relieve my mind, Magnus, give me your word."

"Why—you are right," he answered. "No, I never thought seriously of it. Only for a moment, I was ambitious to be—I don't know what—what I had hoped to be once—well, that is over now. Annie, your husband is a disappointed man."

"Give me your word," she insisted. "We can talk about other things afterward."

Again Magnus wavered, about to yield to his better instincts and to the entreaties of his wife. He began to see how perilously far he had gone in this business. He was drifting closer to it every hour. Already he was entangled, already his foot was caught in the mesh that was being spun. Sharply he recoiled. Again all his instincts of honesty revolted. No, whatever happened, he would preserve his integrity. His wife was right. Always she had influenced his better side. At that moment, Magnus's repugnance of the proposed political campaign was at its pitch of intensity. He wondered how he had ever allowed himself to so much as entertain the idea of joining with the others. Now, he would wrench free, would, in a single instant of power, clear himself of all compromising relations. He turned to his wife. Upon his lips trembled the promise she implored. But suddenly there came to his mind the recollection of his new-made pledge to Annixter. He had given his word that before arriving at a decision he would have a last interview with him. To Magnus, his given word was sacred. Though now he wanted to, he could not as yet draw back, could not promise his wife that he would decide to do right. The matter must be delayed a few days longer.

Lamely, he explained this to her. Annie Derrick made but little response when he had done. She kissed his forehead and went out of the room, uneasy, depressed, her mind thronging with vague fears, leaving Magnus before his office desk, his head in his hands, thoughtful, gloomy, assaulted by forebodings.

Meanwhile, Annixter, Phelps, and Presley continued on their way toward Bonneville. In a short time they had turned into the County Road by the great watering-tank, and proceeded onward in the shade of the interminable line of poplar trees, the wind-break that stretched along the roadside bordering the Broderson ranch. But as they drew near to Caraher's saloon and grocery, about half a mile outside of Bonneville, they recognised Harran's horse tied to the railing in front of it. Annixter left the others and went in to see Harran.

"Harran," he said, when the two had sat down on either side of one of the small tables, "you've got to make up your mind one way or another pretty soon. What are you going to do? Are you going to stand by and see the rest of the Committee spending money by the bucketful in this thing and keep your hands in your pockets? If we win, you'll benefit just as much as the rest of us. I suppose you've got some money of your own—you have, haven't you? You are your father's manager, aren't you?"

Disconcerted at Annixter's directness, Harran stammered an affirmative, adding:

"It's hard to know just what to do. It's a mean position for me, Buck. I want to help you others, but I do want to play fair. I don't know how to play any other way. I should like to have a line from the Governor as to how to act, but there's no getting a word out of him these days. He seems to want to let me decide for myself."

"Well, look here," put in Annixter. "Suppose you keep out of the thing till it's all over, and then share and share alike with the Committee on campaign expenses."

Harran fell thoughtful, his hands in his pockets, frowning moodily at the toe of his boot. There was a silence. Then:

"I don't like to go it blind," he hazarded. "I'm sort of sharing the responsibility of what you do, then. I'm a silent partner. And, then—I don't want to have any difficulties with the Governor. We've always got along well together. He wouldn't like it, you know, if I did anything like that." "Say," exclaimed Annixter abruptly, "if the Governor says he will keep his hands off, and that you can do as you please, will you come in? For God's sake, let us ranchers act together for once. Let's stand in with each other in ONE fight."

Without knowing it, Annixter had touched the right spring.

"I don't know but what you're right," Harran murmured vaguely. His sense of discouragement, that feeling of what's-the-use, was never more oppressive. All fair means had been tried. The wheat grower was at last with his back to the wall. If he chose his own means of fighting, the responsibility must rest upon his enemies, not on himself.

"It's the only way to accomplish anything," he continued, "standing in with each other... well,... go ahead and see what you can do. If the Governor is willing, I'll come in for my share of the campaign fund."

"That's some sense," exclaimed Annixter, shaking him by the hand. "Half the fight is over already. We've got Disbrow you know; and the next thing is to get hold of some of those rotten San Francisco bosses. Osterman will——" But Harran interrupted him, making a quick gesture with his hand.

"Don't tell me about it," he said. "I don't want to know what you and Osterman are going to do. If I did, I shouldn't come in."

Yet, for all this, before they said good-bye Annixter had obtained Harran's promise that he would attend the next meeting of the Committee, when Osterman should return from Los Angeles and make his report. Harran went on toward Los Muertos. Annixter mounted and rode into Bonneville.

Bonneville was very lively at all times. It was a little city of some twenty or thirty thousand inhabitants, where, as yet, the city hall, the high school building, and the opera house were objects of civic pride. It was well governed, beautifully clean, full of the energy and strenuous young life of a new city. An air of the briskest activity pervaded its streets and sidewalks. The business portion of the town, centring about Main Street, was always crowded. Annixter, arriving at the Post Office, found himself involved in a scene of swiftly shifting sights and sounds. Saddle horses, farm wagons—the inevitable Studebakers—buggies grey with the dust of country roads, buckboards with squashes and grocery packages stowed under the seat, two-wheeled sulkies and training carts, were hitched to the gnawed railings and zinc-sheathed telegraph poles along the curb. Here and there, on the edge of the sidewalk, were bicycles, wedged into bicycle racks painted with cigar advertisements. Upon the asphalt sidewalk itself, soft and sticky with the morning's heat, was a continuous movement. Men with large stomachs, wearing linen coats but no vests, laboured ponderously up and down. Girls in lawn skirts, shirt waists, and garden hats, went to and fro, invariably in couples, coming in and out of the drug store, the grocery store, and haberdasher's, or lingering in front of the Post Office, which was on a corner under the I.O.O.F. hall. Young men, in shirt sleeves, with brown, wicker cuff-protectors over their forearms, and pencils behind their ears, bustled in front of the grocery store, anxious and preoccupied. A very old man, a Mexican, in ragged white trousers and bare feet, sat on a horse-block in front of the barber shop, holding a horse by a rope around its neck. A Chinaman went by, teetering under the weight of his market baskets slung on a pole across his shoulders. In the neighbourhood of the hotel, the Yosemite House, travelling salesmen, drummers for jewelry firms of San Francisco, commercial agents, insurance men, well-dressed, metropolitan, debonair, stood about cracking jokes, or hurried in and out of the flapping white doors of the Yosemite barroom. The Yosemite 'bus and City 'bus passed up the street, on the way from the morning train, each with its two or three passengers. A very narrow wagon, belonging to the Cole & Colemore Harvester Works, went by, loaded with long strips of iron that made a horrible din as they jarred over the unevenness of the pavement.

The electric car line, the city's boast, did a brisk business, its cars whirring from end to end of the street, with a jangling of bells and a moaning plaint of gearing. On the stone bulkheads of the grass plat around the new City Hall, the usual loafers sat, chewing tobacco, swapping stories. In the park were the inevitable array of nursemaids, skylarking couples, and ragged little boys. A single policeman, in grey coat and helmet, friend and acquaintance of every man and woman in the town, stood by the park entrance, leaning an elbow on the fence post, twirling his club.

But in the centre of the best business block of the street was a three-story building of rough brown stone, set off with plate glass windows and gold-lettered signs. One of these latter read, "Pacific and Southwestern Railroad, Freight and Passenger Office," while another much smaller, beneath the windows of the second story bore the inscription, "P. and S. W. Land Office."

Annixter hitched his horse to the iron post in front of this building, and tramped up to the second floor, letting himself into an office where a couple of clerks and bookkeepers sat at work behind a high wire screen. One of these latter recognised him and came forward.

"Hello," said Annixter abruptly, scowling the while. "Is your boss in? Is Ruggles in?"

The bookkeeper led Annixter to the private office in an adjoining room, ushering him through a door, on the frosted glass of which was painted the name, "Cyrus Blakelee Ruggles." Inside, a man in a frock coat, shoestring necktie, and Stetson hat, sat writing at a roller-top desk. Over this desk was a vast map of the railroad holdings in the country about Bonneville and Guadalajara, the alternate sections belonging to the Corporation accurately plotted. Ruggles was cordial in his welcome of Annixter. He had a way of fiddling with his pencil continually while he talked, scribbling vague lines and fragments of words and names on stray bits of paper, and no sooner had Annixter sat down than he had begun to write, in full-bellied script, ANN ANN all over his blotting pad.

"I want to see about those lands of mine—I mean of yours—of the railroad's," Annixter commenced at once. "I want to know when I can buy. I'm sick of fooling along like this."

"Well, Mr. Annixter," observed Ruggles, writing a great L before the ANN, and finishing it off with a flourishing D. "The lands"—he crossed out one of the N's and noted the effect with a hasty glance—"the lands are practically yours. You have an option on them indefinitely, and, as it is, you don't have to pay the taxes."

"Rot your option! I want to own them," Annixter declared. "What have you people got to gain by putting off selling them to us. Here this thing has dragged along for over eight years. When I came in on Quien Sabe, the understanding was that the lands—your alternate sections—were to be conveyed to me within a few months."

"The land had not been patented to us then," answered Ruggles.

"Well, it has been now, I guess," retorted Annixter.

"I'm sure I couldn't tell you, Mr. Annixter."

Annixter crossed his legs wearily.

"Oh, what's the good of lying, Ruggles? You know better than to talk that way to me."

Ruggles's face flushed on the instant, but he checked his answer and laughed instead.

"Oh, if you know so much about it—" he observed.

"Well, when are you going to sell to me?"

"I'm only acting for the General Office, Mr. Annixter," returned Ruggles. "Whenever the Directors are ready to take that matter up, I'll be only too glad to put it through for you."

"As if you didn't know. Look here, you're not talking to old Broderson. Wake up, Ruggles. What's all this talk in Genslinger's rag about the grading of the value of our lands this winter and an advance in the price?"

Ruggles spread out his hands with a deprecatory gesture.

"I don't own the 'Mercury,'" he said.

"Well, your company does."

"If it does, I don't know anything about it."

"Oh, rot! As if you and Genslinger and S. Behrman didn't run the whole show down here. Come on, let's have it, Ruggles. What does S. Behrman pay Genslinger for inserting that three-inch ad. of the P. and S. W. in his paper? Ten thousand a year, hey?"

"Oh, why not a hundred thousand and be done with it?" returned the other, willing to take it as a joke.

Instead of replying, Annixter drew his check-book from his inside pocket.

"Let me take that fountain pen of yours," he said. Holding the book on his knee he wrote out a check, tore it carefully from the stub, and laid it on the desk in front of Ruggles.

"What's this?" asked Ruggles.

"Three-fourths payment for the sections of railroad land included in my ranch, based on a valuation of two dollars and a half per acre. You can have the balance in sixty-day notes."

Ruggles shook his head, drawing hastily back from the check as though it carried contamination.

"I can't touch it," he declared. "I've no authority to sell to you yet."

"I don't understand you people," exclaimed Annixter. "I offered to buy of you the same way four years ago and you sang the same song. Why, it isn't business. You lose the interest on your money. Seven per cent. of that capital for four years—you can figure it out. It's big money."

"Well, then, I don't see why you're so keen on parting with it. You can get seven per cent. the same as us."

"I want to own my own land," returned Annixter. "I want to feel that every lump of dirt inside my fence is my personal property. Why, the very house I live in now—the ranch house—stands on railroad ground."

"But, you've an option"

"I tell you I don't want your cursed option. I want ownership; and it's the same with Magnus Derrick and old Broderson and Osterman and all the ranchers of the county. We want to own our land, want to feel we can do as we blame please with it. Suppose I should want to sell Quien Sabe. I can't sell it as a whole till I've bought of you. I can't give anybody a clear title. The land has doubled in value ten times over again since I came in on it and improved it. It's worth easily twenty an acre now. But I can't take advantage of that rise in value so long as you won't sell, so long as I don't own it. You're blocking me."

"But, according to you, the railroad can't take advantage of the rise in any case. According to you, you can sell for twenty dollars, but we can only get two and a half."

"Who made it worth twenty?" cried Annixter. "I've improved it up to that figure. Genslinger seems to have that idea in his nut, too. Do you people think you can hold that land, untaxed, for speculative purposes until it goes up to thirty dollars and then sell out to some one else—sell it over our heads? You and Genslinger weren't in office when those contracts were drawn. You ask your boss, you ask S. Behrman, he knows. The General Office is pledged to sell to us in preference to any one else, for two and a half."

"Well," observed Ruggles decidedly, tapping the end of his pencil on his desk and leaning forward to emphasise his words, "we're not selling NOW. That's said and signed, Mr. Annixter."

"Why not? Come, spit it out. What's the bunco game this time?"

"Because we're not ready. Here's your check."

"You won't take it?"

"No."

"I'll make it a cash payment, money down—the whole of it—payable to Cyrus Blakelee Ruggles, for the P. and S. W."

"No."

"Third and last time."

"No."

"Oh, go to the devil!"

"I don't like your tone, Mr. Annixter," returned Ruggles, flushing angrily. "I don't give a curse whether you like it or not," retorted Annixter, rising and thrusting the check into his pocket, "but never you mind, Mr. Ruggles, you and S. Behrman and Genslinger and Shelgrim and the whole gang of thieves of you—you'll wake this State of California up some of these days by going just one little bit too far, and there'll be an election of Railroad Commissioners of, by, and for the people, that'll get a twist of you, my bunco-steering friend—you and your backers and cappers and swindlers and thimble-riggers, and smash you, lock, stock, and barrel. That's my tip to you and be damned to you, Mr. Cyrus Blackleg Ruggles."

Annixter stormed out of the room, slamming the door behind him, and Ruggles, trembling with anger, turned to his desk and to the blotting pad written all over with the words LANDS, TWENTY DOLLARS, TWO AND

A HALF, OPTION, and, over and over again, with great swelling curves and flourishes, RAILROAD, RAILROAD, RAILROAD.

But as Annixter passed into the outside office, on the other side of the wire partition he noted the figure of a man at the counter in conversation with one of the clerks. There was something familiar to Annixter's eye about the man's heavy built frame, his great shoulders and massive back, and as he spoke to the clerk in a tremendous, rumbling voice, Annixter promptly recognised Dyke.

There was a meeting. Annixter liked Dyke, as did every one else in and about Bonneville. He paused now to shake hands with the discharged engineer and to ask about his little daughter, Sidney, to whom he knew Dyke was devotedly attached.

"Smartest little tad in Tulare County," asserted Dyke. "She's getting prettier every day, Mr. Annixter. THERE'S a little tad that was just born to be a lady. Can recite the whole of 'Snow Bound' without ever stopping. You don't believe that, maybe, hey? Well, it's true. She'll be just old enough to enter the Seminary up at Marysville next winter, and if my hop business pays two per cent. on the investment, there's where she's going to go."

"How's it coming on?" inquired Annixter.

"The hop ranch? Prime. I've about got the land in shape, and I've engaged a foreman who knows all about hops. I've been in luck. Everybody will go into the business next year when they see hops go to a dollar, and they'll overstock the market and bust the price. But I'm going to get the cream of it now. I say two per cent. Why, Lord love you, it will pay a good deal more than that. It's got to. It's cost more than I figured to start the thing, so, perhaps, I may have to borrow somewheres; but then on such a sure game as this—and I do want to make something out of that little tad of mine."

"Through here?" inquired Annixter, making ready to move off.

"In just a minute," answered Dyke. "Wait for me and I'll walk down the street with you."

Annixter grumbled that he was in a hurry, but waited, nevertheless, while Dyke again approached the clerk.

"I shall want some empty cars of you people this fall," he explained. "I'm a hop-raiser now, and I just want to make sure what your rates on hops are. I've been told, but I want to make sure. Savvy?" There was a long delay while the clerk consulted the tariff schedules, and Annixter fretted impatiently. Dyke, growing uneasy, leaned heavily on his elbows, watching the clerk anxiously. If the tariff was exorbitant, he saw his plans brought to naught, his money jeopardised, the little tad, Sidney, deprived of her education. He began to blame himself that he had not long before determined definitely what the railroad would charge for moving his hops. He told himself he was not much of a business man; that he managed carelessly.

"Two cents," suddenly announced the clerk with a certain surly indifference.

"Two cents a pound?"

"Yes, two cents a pound—that's in car-load lots, of course. I won't give you that rate on smaller consignments."

"Yes, car-load lots, of course... two cents. Well, all right."

He turned away with a great sigh of relief.

"He sure did have me scared for a minute," he said to Annixter, as the two went down to the street, "fiddling and fussing so long. Two cents is all right, though. Seems fair to me. That fiddling of his was all put on. I know 'em, these railroad heelers. He knew I was a discharged employee first off, and he played the game just to make me seem small because I had to ask favours of him. I don't suppose the General Office tips its slavees off to act like swine, but there's the feeling through the whole herd of them. 'Ye got to come to us. We let ye live only so long as we choose, and what are ye going to do about it? If ye don't like it, git out.'"

Annixter and the engineer descended to the street and had a drink at the Yosemite bar, and Annixter went into the General Store while Dyke bought a little pair of red slippers for Sidney. Before the salesman had wrapped them up, Dyke slipped a dime into the toe of each with a wink at Annixter.

"Let the little tad find 'em there," he said behind his hand in a hoarse whisper. "That'll be one on Sid."

"Where to now?" demanded Annixter as they regained the street. "I'm going down to the Post Office and then pull out for the ranch. Going my way?"

Dyke hesitated in some confusion, tugging at the ends of his fine blonde beard.

"No, no. I guess I'll leave you here. I've got—got other things to do up the street. So long."

The two separated, and Annixter hurried through the crowd to the Post Office, but the mail that had come in on that morning's train was unusually heavy. It was nearly half an hour before it was distributed. Naturally enough, Annixter placed all the blame of the delay upon the railroad, and delivered himself of some pointed remarks in the midst of the waiting crowd. He was irritated to the last degree when he finally emerged upon the sidewalk again, cramming his mail into his pockets. One cause of his bad temper was the fact that in the bundle of Quien Sabe letters was one to Hilma Tree in a man's handwriting.

"Huh!" Annixter had growled to himself, "that pip Delaney. Seems now that I'm to act as go-between for 'em. Well, maybe that feemale girl gets this letter, and then, again, maybe she don't."

But suddenly his attention was diverted. Directly opposite the Post Office, upon the corner of the street, stood quite the best business building of which Bonneville could boast. It was built of Colusa granite, very solid, ornate, imposing. Upon the heavy plate of the window of its main floor, in gold and red letters, one read the words: "Loan and Savings Bank of Tulare County." It was of this bank that S. Behrman was president. At the street entrance of the building was a curved sign of polished brass, fixed upon the angle of the masonry; this sign bore the name, "S. Behrman," and under it in smaller letters were the words, "Real Estate, Mortgages."

As Annixter's glance fell upon this building, he was surprised to see Dyke standing upon the curb in front of it, apparently reading from a newspaper that he held in his hand. But Annixter promptly discovered that he was not reading at all. From time to time the former engineer shot a swift glance out of the corner of his eye up and down the street. Annixter jumped at a conclusion. An idea suddenly occurred to him. Dyke was watching to see if he was observed—was waiting an opportunity when no one who knew him should be in sight. Annixter stepped back a little, getting a telegraph pole somewhat between him and the other. Very interested, he watched what was going on. Pretty soon Dyke thrust the paper into his pocket and sauntered slowly to the windows of a stationery store, next the street entrance of S. Behrman's offices. For a few seconds he stood there, his back turned, seemingly absorbed in the display, but eyeing the street narrowly nevertheless; then he turned around, gave a last look about and stepped swiftly into the doorway by the great brass sign. He disappeared. Annixter came from behind the telegraph pole with a flush of actual shame upon his face. There had been something so slinking, so mean, in the movements and manner of this great, burly honest fellow of an engineer, that he could not help but feel ashamed for him. Circumstances were such that a simple business transaction was to Dyke almost culpable, a degradation, a thing to be concealed.

"Borrowing money of S. Behrman," commented Annixter, "mortgaging your little homestead to the railroad, putting your neck in the halter. Poor fool! The pity of it. Good Lord, your hops must pay you big, now, old man."

Annixter lunched at the Yosemite Hotel, and then later on, toward the middle of the afternoon, rode out of the town at a canter by the way of the Upper Road that paralleled the railroad tracks and that ran diametrically straight between Bonneville and Guadalajara. About half-way between the two places he overtook Father Sarria trudging back to San Juan, his long cassock powdered with dust. He had a wicker crate in one hand, and in the other, in a small square valise, the materials for the Holy Sacrament. Since early morning the priest had covered nearly fifteen miles on foot, in order to administer Extreme Unction to a moribund good-for-nothing, a greaser, half Indian, half Portuguese, who lived in a remote corner of Osterman's stock range, at the head of a canon there. But he had returned by way of Bonneville to get a crate that had come for him from San Diego. He had been notified of its arrival the day before.

Annixter pulled up and passed the time of day with the priest.

"I don't often get up your way," he said, slowing down his horse to accommodate Sarria's deliberate plodding. Sarria wiped the perspiration from his smooth, shiny face.

"You? Well, with you it is different," he answered. "But there are a great many Catholics in the county—some on your ranch. And so few come to the Mission. At High Mass on Sundays, there are a few—Mexicans and Spaniards from Guadalajara mostly; but weekdays, for matins, vespers, and the like, I often say the offices to an empty church—'the voice of one crying in the wilderness.' You Americans are not good churchmen. Sundays you sleep—you read the newspapers."

"Well, there's Vanamee," observed Annixter. "I suppose he's there early and late."

Sarria made a sharp movement of interest.

"Ah, Vanamee—a strange lad; a wonderful character, for all that. If there were only more like him. I am troubled about him. You know I am a very owl at night. I come and go about the Mission at all hours. Within the week, three times I have seen Vanamee in the little garden by the Mission, and at the dead of night. He had come without asking for me. He did not see me. It was strange. Once, when I had got up at dawn to ring for early matins, I saw him stealing away out of the garden. He must have been there all the night. He is acting queerly. He is pale; his cheeks are more sunken than ever. There is something wrong with him. I can't make it out. It is a mystery. Suppose you ask him?"

"Not I. I've enough to bother myself about. Vanamee is crazy in the head. Some morning he will turn up missing again, and drop out of sight for another three years. Best let him alone, Sarria. He's a crank. How is that greaser of yours up on Osterman's stock range?"

"Ah, the poor fellow—the poor fellow," returned the other, the tears coming to his eyes. "He died this morning—as you might say, in my arms, painfully, but in the faith, in the faith. A good fellow."

"A lazy, cattle-stealing, knife-in-his-boot Dago."

"You misjudge him. A really good fellow on better acquaintance."

Annixter grunted scornfully. Sarria's kindness and good-will toward the most outrageous reprobates of the ranches was proverbial. He practically supported some half-dozen families that lived in forgotten cabins, lost and all but inaccessible, in the far corners of stock range and canyon. This particular greaser was the laziest, the dirtiest, the most worthless of the lot. But in Sarria's mind, the lout was an object of affection, sincere, unquestioning. Thrice a week the priest, with a basket of provisions—cold ham, a bottle of wine, olives, loaves of bread, even a chicken or two—toiled over the interminable stretch of country between the Mission and his cabin. Of late, during the rascal's sickness, these visits had been almost daily. Hardly once did the priest leave the bedside that he did not slip a half-dollar into the palm of his wife or oldest daughter. And this was but one case out of many.

His kindliness toward animals was the same. A horde of mange-corroded curs lived off his bounty, wolfish, ungrateful, often marking him with their teeth, yet never knowing the meaning of a harsh word. A burro, over-fed, lazy, incorrigible, browsed on the hill back of the Mission, obstinately refusing to be harnessed to Sarria's little cart, squealing and biting whenever the attempt was made; and the priest suffered him, submitting to his humour, inventing excuses for him, alleging that the burro was foundered, or was in need of shoes, or was feeble from extreme age. The two peacocks, magnificent, proud, cold-hearted, resenting all familiarity, he served with the timorous, apologetic affection of a queen's lady-in-waiting, resigned to their disdain, happy if only they condescended to enjoy the grain he spread for them.

At the Long Trestle, Annixter and the priest left the road and took the trail that crossed Broderson Creek by the clumps of grey-green willows and led across Quien Sabe to the ranch house, and to the Mission farther on. They were obliged to proceed in single file here, and Annixter, who had allowed the priest to go in front, promptly took notice of the wicker basket he carried. Upon his inquiry, Sarria became confused. "It was a basket that he had had sent down to him from the city."

"Well, I know—but what's in it?"

"Why—I'm sure—ah, poultry—a chicken or two."

"Fancy breed?"

"Yes, yes, that's it, a fancy breed." At the ranch house, where they arrived toward five o'clock, Annixter insisted that the priest should stop long enough for a glass of sherry. Sarria left the basket and his small black valise at the foot of the porch steps, and sat down in a rocker on the porch itself, fanning himself with his broad-brimmed hat, and shaking the dust from his cassock. Annixter brought out the decanter of sherry and glasses, and the two drank to each other's health.

But as the priest set down his glass, wiping his lips with a murmur of satisfaction, the decrepit Irish setter that had attached himself to Annixter's house came out from underneath the porch, and nosed vigorously about the wicker basket. He upset it. The little peg holding down the cover slipped, the basket fell sideways, opening as it fell, and a cock, his head enclosed in a little chamois bag such as are used for gold watches, struggled blindly out into the open air. A second, similarly hooded, followed. The pair, stupefied in their headgear, stood rigid and bewildered in their tracks, clucking uneasily. Their tails were closely sheared. Their legs, thickly muscled, and extraordinarily long, were furnished with enormous cruel-looking spurs. The breed was unmistakable. Annixter looked once at the pair, then shouted with laughter.

"'Poultry'—'a chicken or two'—'fancy breed'—ho! yes, I should think so. Game cocks! Fighting cocks! Oh, you old rat! You'll be a dry nurse to a burro, and keep a hospital for infirm puppies, but you will fight game cocks. Oh, Lord! Why, Sarria, this is as good a grind as I ever heard. There's the Spanish cropping out, after all."

Speechless with chagrin, the priest bundled the cocks into the basket and catching up the valise, took himself abruptly away, almost running till he had put himself out of hearing of Annixter's raillery. And even ten minutes later, when Annixter, still chuckling, stood upon the porch steps, he saw the priest, far in the distance, climbing the slope of the high ground, in the direction of the Mission, still hurrying on at a great pace, his cassock flapping behind him, his head bent; to Annixter's notion the very picture of discomfiture and confusion.

As Annixter turned about to reenter the house, he found himself almost face to face with Hilma Tree. She was just going in at the doorway, and a great flame of the sunset, shooting in under the eaves of the porch, enveloped her from her head, with its thick, moist hair that hung low over her neck, to her slim feet, setting a golden flash in the little steel buckles of her low shoes. She had come to set the table for Annixter's supper. Taken all aback by the suddenness of the encounter, Annixter ejaculated an abrupt and senseless, "Excuse me." But Hilma, without raising her eyes, passed on unmoved into the dining-room, leaving Annixter trying to find his breath, and fumbling with the brim of his hat, that he was surprised to find he had taken from his head. Resolutely, and taking a quick advantage of his opportunity, he followed her into the dining-room.

"I see that dog has turned up," he announced with brisk cheerfulness. "That Irish setter I was asking about."

Hilma, a swift, pink flush deepening the delicate rose of her cheeks, did not reply, except by nodding her head. She flung the table-cloth out from under her arms across the table, spreading it smooth, with quick little caresses of her hands. There was a moment's silence. Then Annixter said:

"Here's a letter for you." He laid it down on the table near her, and Hilma picked it up. "And see here, Miss Hilma," Annixter continued, "about that—this morning—I suppose you think I am a first-class mucker. If it will do any good to apologise, why, I will. I want to be friends with you. I made a bad mistake, and started in the wrong way. I don't know much about women people. I want you to forget about that—this morning, and not think I am a galoot and a mucker. Will you do it? Will you be friends with me?"

Hilma set the plate and coffee cup by Annixter's place before answering, and Annixter repeated his question. Then she drew a deep, quick breath, the flush in her cheeks returning.

"I think it was—it was so wrong of you," she murmured. "Oh! you don't know how it hurt me. I cried—oh, for an hour."

"Well, that's just it," returned Annixter vaguely, moving his head uneasily. "I didn't know what kind of a girl you were—I mean, I made a mistake. I thought it didn't make much difference. I thought all feemales were about alike."

"I hope you know now," murmured Hilma ruefully. "I've paid enough to have you find out. I cried—you don't know. Why, it hurt me worse than anything I can remember. I hope you know now." "Well, I do know now," he exclaimed.

"It wasn't so much that you tried to do—what you did," answered Hilma, the single deep swell from her waist to her throat rising and falling in her emotion. "It was that you thought that you could—that anybody could that wanted to—that I held myself so cheap. Oh!" she cried, with a sudden sobbing catch in her throat, "I never can forget it, and you don't know what it means to a girl."

"Well, that's just what I do want," he repeated. "I want you to forget it and have us be good friends."

In his embarrassment, Annixter could think of no other words. He kept reiterating again and again during the pauses of the conversation:

"I want you to forget it. Will you? Will you forget it—that—this morning, and have us be good friends?"

He could see that her trouble was keen. He was astonished that the matter should be so grave in her estimation. After all, what was it that a girl should be kissed? But he wanted to regain his lost ground.

"Will you forget it, Miss Hilma? I want you to like me."

She took a clean napkin from the sideboard drawer and laid it down by the plate.

"I—I do want you to like me," persisted Annixter. "I want you to forget all about this business and like me."

Hilma was silent. Annixter saw the tears in her eyes.

"How about that? Will you forget it? Will you—will—will you LIKE me?"

She shook her head.

"No," she said.

"No what? You won't like me? Is that it?"

Hilma, blinking at the napkin through her tears, nodded to say, Yes, that was it. Annixter hesitated a moment, frowning, harassed and perplexed.

"You don't like me at all, hey?"

At length Hilma found her speech. In her low voice, lower and more velvety than ever, she said:

"No—I don't like you at all."

Then, as the tears suddenly overpowered her, she dashed a hand across her eyes, and ran from the room and out of doors.

Annixter stood for a moment thoughtful, his protruding lower lip thrust out, his hands in his pocket.

"I suppose she'll quit now," he muttered. "Suppose she'll leave the ranch—if she hates me like that. Well, she can go—that's all—she can go. Fool feemale girl," he muttered between his teeth, "petticoat mess." He was about to sit down to his supper when his eye fell upon the Irish setter, on his haunches in the doorway. There was an expectant, ingratiating look on the dog's face. No doubt, he suspected it was time for eating.

"Get out—YOU!" roared Annixter in a tempest of wrath.

The dog slunk back, his tail shut down close, his ears drooping, but instead of running away, he lay down and rolled supinely upon his back, the very image of submission, tame, abject, disgusting. It was the one thing to drive Annixter to a fury. He kicked the dog off the porch in a rolling explosion of oaths, and flung himself down to his seat before the table, fuming and panting.

"Damn the dog and the girl and the whole rotten business—and now," he exclaimed, as a sudden fancied qualm arose in his stomach, "now, it's all made me sick. Might have known it. Oh, it only lacked that to wind up the whole day. Let her go, I don't care, and the sooner the better."

He countermanded the supper and went to bed before it was dark, lighting his lamp, on the chair near the head of the bed, and opening his "Copperfield" at the place marked by the strip of paper torn from the bag of prunes. For upward of an hour he read the novel, methodically swallowing one prune every time he reached the bottom of a page. About nine o'clock he blew out the lamp and, punching up his pillow, settled himself for the night.

Then, as his mind relaxed in that strange, hypnotic condition that comes just before sleep, a series of pictures of the day's doings passed before his imagination like the roll of a kinetoscope.

First, it was Hilma Tree, as he had seen her in the dairy-house—charming, delicious, radiant of youth, her thick, white neck with its pale amber shadows under the chin; her wide, open eyes rimmed with fine, black lashes; the deep swell of her breast and hips, the delicate, lustrous floss on her cheek, impalpable as the pollen of a flower. He saw her standing there in the scintillating light of the morning, her smooth arms wet with milk, redolent and fragrant of milk, her whole, desirable figure moving in the golden glory of the sun, steeped in a lambent flame, saturated with it, glowing with it, joyous as the dawn itself.

Then it was Los Muertos and Hooven, the sordid little Dutchman, grimed with the soil he worked in, yet vividly remembering a period of military glory, exciting himself with recollections of Gravelotte and the Kaiser, but contented now in the country of his adoption, defining the Fatherland as the place where wife and children lived. Then came the ranch house of Los Muertos, under the grove of cypress and eucalyptus, with its smooth, gravelled driveway and well-groomed lawns; Mrs. Derrick with her wide-opened eyes, that so easily took on a look of uneasiness, of innocence, of anxious inquiry, her face still pretty, her brown hair that still retained so much of its brightness spread over her chair back, drying in the sun; Magnus, erect as an officer of cavalry, smooth-shaven, grey, thin-lipped, imposing, with his hawk-like nose and forward-curling grey hair; Presley with his dark face, delicate mouth and sensitive, loose lips, in corduroys and laced boots, smoking cigarettes—an interesting figure, suggestive of a mixed origin, morbid, excitable, melancholy, brooding upon things that had no names. Then it was Bonneville, with the gayety and confusion of Main Street, the whirring electric cars, the zinc-sheathed telegraph poles, the buckboards with squashes stowed under the seats; Ruggles in frock coat, Stetson hat and shoe-string necktie, writing abstractedly upon his blotting pad; Dyke, the engineer, big-boned. Powerful, deep-voiced, good-natured, with his fine blonde beard and massive arms, rehearsing the praises of his little daughter Sidney, guided only by the one ambition that she should be educated at a seminary, slipping a dime into the toe of her diminutive slipper, then, later, overwhelmed with shame, slinking into S. Behrman's office to mortgage his homestead to the heeler of the corporation that had discharged him. By suggestion, Annixter saw S. Behrman, too, fat, with a vast stomach, the check and neck meeting to form a great, tremulous jowl, the roll of fat over his collar, sprinkled with sparse, stiff hairs; saw his brown, round-topped hat of varnished straw, the linen vest stamped with innumerable interlocked horseshoes, the heavy watch chain, clinking against the pearl vest buttons; invariably placid, unruffled, never losing his temper, serene, unassailable, enthroned.

Then, at the end of all, it was the ranch again, seen in a last brief glance before he had gone to bed; the fecundated earth, calm at last, nursing the emplanted germ of life, ruddy with the sunset, the horizons purple, the small clamour of the day lapsing into quiet, the great, still twilight, building itself, dome-like, toward the zenith. The barn fowls were roosting in the trees near the stable, the horses crunching their fodder in the stalls, the day's work ceasing by slow degrees; and the priest, the Spanish churchman, Father Sarria, relic of a departed regime, kindly, benign, believing in all goodness, a lover of his fellows and of dumb animals, yet, for all that, hurrying away in confusion and discomfiture, carrying in one hand the vessels of the Holy Communion and in the other a basket of game cocks.

CHAPTER VI

It was high noon, and the rays of the sun, that hung poised directly overhead in an intolerable white glory, fell straight as plummets upon the roofs and streets of Guadalajara. The adobe walls and sparse brick sidewalks of the drowsing town radiated the heat in an oily, quivering shimmer. The leaves of the eucalyptus trees around the Plaza drooped motionless, limp and relaxed under the scorching, searching blaze. The shadows of these trees had shrunk to their smallest circumference, contracting close about the trunks. The shade had dwindled to the breadth of a mere line. The sun was everywhere. The heat exhaling from brick and plaster and metal met the heat that steadily descended blanketwise and smothering, from the pale, scorched sky. Only the lizards—they lived in chinks of the crumbling adobe and in interstices of the sidewalk—remained without, motionless, as if stuffed, their eyes closed to mere slits, basking, stupefied with heat. At long intervals the prolonged drone of an insect developed out of the silence, vibrated a moment in a soothing, somnolent, long note, then trailed slowly into the quiet again. Somewhere in the interior of one of the 'dobe houses a guitar snored and hummed sleepily. On the roof of the hotel a group of pigeons cooed incessantly with subdued, liquid murmurs, very plaintive; a cat, perfectly white, with a pink nose and thin, pink lips, dozed complacently on a fence rail, full in the sun. In a corner of the Plaza three hens wallowed in the baking hot dust their wings fluttering, clucking comfortably.

And this was all. A Sunday repose prevailed the whole moribund town, peaceful, profound. A certain pleasing numbness, a sense of grateful enervation exhaled from the scorching plaster. There was no movement, no sound of human business. The faint hum of the insect, the intermittent murmur of the guitar, the mellow complainings of the pigeons, the prolonged purr of the white cat, the contented clucking of the hens—all these noises mingled together to form a faint, drowsy bourdon, prolonged, stupefying, suggestive of an infinite quiet, of a calm, complacent life, centuries old, lapsing gradually to its end under the gorgeous loneliness of a cloudless, pale blue sky and the steady fire of an interminable sun.

In Solotari's Spanish-Mexican restaurant, Vanamee and Presley sat opposite each other at one of the tables near the door, a bottle of white wine, tortillas, and an earthen pot of frijoles between them. They were the sole occupants of the place. It was the day that Annixter had chosen for his barn-dance and, in consequence, Quien Sabe was in fete and work suspended. Presley and Vanamee had arranged to spend the day in each other's company, lunching at Solotari's and taking a long tramp in the afternoon. For the moment they sat back in their chairs, their meal all but finished. Solotari brought black coffee and a small carafe of mescal, and retiring to a corner of the room, went to sleep.

All through the meal Presley had been wondering over a certain change he observed in his friend. He looked at him again.

Vanamee's lean, spare face was of an olive pallor. His long, black hair, such as one sees in the saints and evangelists of the pre-Raphaelite artists, hung over his ears. Presley again remarked his pointed beard, black and fine, growing from the hollow cheeks. He looked at his face, a face like that of a young seer, like a half-inspired shepherd of the Hebraic legends, a dweller in the wilderness, gifted with strange powers. He was dressed as when Presley had first met him, herding his sheep, in brown canvas overalls, thrust into top boots; grey flannel shirt, open at the throat, showing the breast ruddy with tan; the waist encircled with a cartridge belt, empty of cartridges.

But now, as Presley took more careful note of him, he was surprised to observe a certain new look in Vanamee's deep-set eyes. He remembered now that all through the morning Vanamee had been singularly reserved. He was continually drifting into reveries, abstracted, distrait. Indubitably, something of moment had happened.

At length Vanamee spoke. Leaning back in his chair, his thumbs in his belt, his bearded chin upon his breast, his voice was the even monotone of one speaking in his sleep.

He told Presley in a few words what had happened during the first night he had spent in the garden of the old Mission, of the Answer, half-fancied, half-real, that had come to him.

"To no other person but you would I speak of this," he said, "but you, I think, will understand—will be sympathetic, at least, and I feel the need of unburdening myself of it to some one. At first I would not trust my own senses. I was sure I had deceived myself, but on a second night it happened again. Then I was afraid—or no, not afraid, but disturbed—oh, shaken to my very heart's core. I resolved to go no further in the matter, never again to put it to test. For a long time I stayed away from the Mission, occupying myself with my work, keeping it out of my mind. But the temptation was too strong. One night I found myself there again, under the black shadow of the pear trees calling for Angele, summoning her from out the dark, from out the night. This time the Answer was prompt, unmistakable. I cannot explain to you what it was, nor how it came to me, for there was no sound. I saw absolutely nothing but the empty night. There was no moon. But somewhere off there over the little valley, far off, the darkness was troubled; that ME that went out upon my thought—out from the Mission garden, out over the valley, calling for her, searching for her, found, I don't know what, but found a resting place—a companion. Three times since then I have gone to the Mission garden at night. Last night was the third time."

He paused, his eyes shining with excitement. Presley leaned forward toward him, motionless with intense absorption.

"Well—and last night," he prompted.

Vanamee stirred in his seat, his glance fell, he drummed an instant upon the table.

"Last night," he answered, "there was—there was a change. The Answer was—" he drew a deep breath—"nearer."

"You are sure?"

The other smiled with absolute certainty.

"It was not that I found the Answer sooner, easier. I could not be mistaken. No, that which has troubled the darkness, that which has entered into the empty night—is coming nearer to me—physically nearer, actually nearer."

His voice sank again. His face like the face of younger prophets, the seers, took on a half-inspired expression. He looked vaguely before him with unseeing eyes.

"Suppose," he murmured, "suppose I stand there under the pear trees at night and call her again and again, and each time the Answer comes nearer and nearer and I wait until at last one night, the supreme night of all, she—she——"

Suddenly the tension broke. With a sharp cry and a violent uncertain gesture of the hand Vanamee came to himself.

"Oh," he exclaimed, "what is it? Do I dare? What does it mean? There are times when it appals me and there are times when it thrills me with a sweetness and a happiness that I have not known since she died. The vagueness of it! How can I explain it to you, this that happens when I call to her across the night—that faint, far-off, unseen tremble in the darkness, that intangible, scarcely perceptible stir. Something neither heard nor seen, appealing to a sixth sense only. Listen, it is something like this: On Quien Sabe, all last week, we have been seeding the earth. The grain is there now under the earth buried in the dark, in the black stillness, under the clods. Can you imagine the first—the very first little quiver of life that the grain of wheat must feel after it is sown, when it answers to the call of the sun, down there in the dark of the earth, blind, deaf; the very first stir from the inert, long, long before any physical change has occurred,—long before the microscope could discover the slightest change,—when the shell first tightens with the first faint premonition of life? Well, it is something as illusive as that." He paused again, dreaming, lost in a reverie, then, just above a whisper, murmured:

"'That which thou sowest is not quickened except it die,'... and she, Angele... died."

"You could not have been mistaken?" said Presley. "You were sure that there was something? Imagination can do so much and the influence of the surroundings was strong. How impossible it would be that anything SHOULD happen. And you say you heard nothing, saw nothing."

"I believe," answered Vanamee, "in a sixth sense, or, rather, a whole system of other unnamed senses beyond the reach of our understanding. People who live much alone and close to nature experience the sensation of it. Perhaps it is something fundamental that we share with plants and animals. The same thing that sends the birds south long before the first colds, the same thing that makes the grain of wheat struggle up to meet the sun. And this sense never deceives. You may see wrong, hear wrong, but once touch this sixth sense and it acts with absolute fidelity, you are certain. No, I hear nothing in the Mission garden. I see nothing, nothing touches me, but I am CERTAIN for all that."

Presley hesitated for a moment, then he asked:

"Shall you go back to the garden again? Make the test again?" "I don't know."

"Strange enough," commented Presley, wondering.

Vanamee sank back in his chair, his eyes growing vacant again:

"Strange enough," he murmured.

There was a long silence. Neither spoke nor moved. There, in that moribund, ancient town, wrapped in its siesta, flagellated with heat, deserted, ignored, baking in a noon-day silence, these two strange men, the one a poet by nature, the other by training, both out of tune with their world, dreamers, introspective, morbid, lost and unfamiliar at that end-of-the-century time, searching for a sign, groping and baffled amidst the perplexing obscurity of the Delusion, sat over empty wine glasses, silent with the pervading silence that surrounded them, hearing only the cooing of doves and the drone of bees, the quiet so profound, that at length they could plainly distinguish at intervals the puffing and coughing of a locomotive switching cars in the station yard of Bonneville.

It was, no doubt, this jarring sound that at length roused Presley from his lethargy. The two friends rose; Solotari very sleepily came forward; they paid for the luncheon, and stepping out into the heat and glare of the streets of the town, passed on through it and took the road that led northward across a corner of Dyke's hop fields. They were bound for the hills in the northeastern corner of Quien Sabe. It was the same walk which Presley had taken on the previous occasion when he had first met Vanamee herding the sheep. This encompassing detour around the whole country-side was a favorite pastime of his and he was anxious that Vanamee should share his pleasure in it.

But soon after leaving Guadalajara, they found themselves upon the land that Dyke had bought and upon which he was to raise his famous crop of hops. Dyke's house was close at hand, a very pleasant little cottage, painted white, with green blinds and deep porches, while near it and yet in process of construction, were two great storehouses and a drying and curing house, where the hops were to be stored and treated. All about were evidences that the former engineer had already been hard at work. The ground had been put in readiness to receive the crop and a bewildering, innumerable multitude of poles, connected with a maze of wire and twine, had been set out. Farther on at a turn of the road, they came upon Dyke himself, driving a farm wagon loaded with more poles. He was in his shirt sleeves, his massive, hairy arms bare to the elbow, glistening with sweat, red with heat. In his bell-like, rumbling voice, he was calling to his foreman and a boy at work in stringing the poles together. At sight of Presley and Vanamee he hailed them jovially, addressing them as "boys," and insisting that they should get into the wagon with him and drive to the house for a glass of beer. His mother had only the day before returned from Marysville, where she had been looking up a seminary for the little tad. She would be delighted to see the two boys; besides, Vanamee must see how the little tad had grown since he last set eyes on her; wouldn't know her for the same little girl; and the beer had been on ice since morning. Presley and Vanamee could not well refuse.

They climbed into the wagon and jolted over the uneven ground through the bare forest of hop-poles to the house. Inside they found Mrs. Dyke, an old lady with a very gentle face, who wore a cap and a very old-fashioned gown with hoop skirts, dusting the what-not in a corner of the parlor. The two men were presented and the beer was had from off the ice.

"Mother," said Dyke, as he wiped the froth from his great blond beard, "ain't Sid anywhere about? I want Mr. Vanamee to see how she has grown. Smartest little tad in Tulare County, boys. Can recite the whole of 'Snow Bound,' end to end, without skipping or looking at the book. Maybe you don't believe that. Mother, ain't I right—without skipping a line, hey?"

Mrs. Dyke nodded to say that it was so, but explained that Sidney was in Guadalajara. In putting on her new slippers for the first time the morning before, she had found a dime in the toe of one of them and had had the whole house by the ears ever since till she could spend it.

"Was it for licorice to make her licorice water?" inquired Dyke gravely.

"Yes," said Mrs. Dyke. "I made her tell me what she was going to get before she went, and it was licorice."

Dyke, though his mother protested that he was foolish and that Presley and Vanamee had no great interest in "young ones," insisted upon showing the visitors Sidney's copy-books. They were monuments of laborious, elaborate neatness, the trite moralities and ready-made aphorisms of the philanthropists and publicists, repeated from page to page with wearying insistence. "I, too, am an American Citizen. S. D.," "As the Twig is Bent the Tree is Inclined," "Truth Crushed to Earth Will Rise Again," "As for Me, Give Me Liberty or Give Me Death," and last of all, a strange intrusion amongst the mild, well-worn phrases, two legends. "My motto—Public Control of Public Franchises," and "The P. and S. W. is an Enemy of the State."

"I see," commented Presley, "you mean the little tad to understand 'the situation' early."

"I told him he was foolish to give that to Sid to copy," said Mrs. Dyke, with indulgent remonstrance. "What can she understand of public franchises?"

"Never mind," observed Dyke, "she'll remember it when she grows up and when the seminary people have rubbed her up a bit, and then she'll begin to ask questions and understand. And don't you make any mistake, mother," he went on, "about the little tad not knowing who her dad's enemies are. What do you think, boys? Listen, here. Precious little I've ever told her of the railroad or how I was turned off, but the other day I was working down by the fence next the railroad tracks and Sid was there. She'd brought her doll rags down and she was playing house behind a pile of hop poles. Well, along comes a through freight—mixed train from Missouri points and a string of empties from New Orleans,—and when it had passed, what do you suppose the tad did? SHE didn't know I was watching her. She goes to the fence and spits a little spit after the caboose and puts out her little head and, if you'll believe me, HISSES at the train; and mother says she does that same every time she sees a train go by, and never crosses the tracks that she don't spit her little spit on 'em. What do you THINK of THAT?"

"But I correct her every time," protested Mrs. Dyke seriously. "Where she picked up the trick of hissing I don't know. No, it's not funny. It seems dreadful to see a little girl who's as sweet and gentle as can be in every other way, so venomous. She says the other little girls at school and the boys, too, are all the same way. Oh, dear," she sighed, "why will the General Office be so unkind and unjust? Why, I couldn't be happy, with all the money in the world, if I thought that even one little child hated me—hated me so that it would spit and hiss at me. And it's not one child, it's all of them, so Sidney says; and think of all the grown people who hate the road, women and men, the whole county, the whole State, thousands and thousands of people. Don't the managers and the directors of the road ever think of that? Don't they ever think of all the hate that surrounds them, everywhere, everywhere, and the good people that just grit their teeth when the name of the road is mentioned? Why do they want to make the people hate them? No," she murmured, the tears starting to her eyes, "No, I tell you, Mr. Presley, the men who own the railroad are wicked, bad-hearted men who don't care how much the poor people suffer, so long as the road makes its eighteen million a year. They don't care whether the people hate them or love them, just so long as they are afraid of them. It's not right and God will punish them sooner or later."

A little after this the two young men took themselves away, Dyke obligingly carrying them in the wagon as far as the gate that opened into the Quien Sabe ranch. On the way, Presley referred to what Mrs. Dyke had said and led Dyke, himself, to speak of the P. and S. W.

"Well," Dyke said, "it's like this, Mr. Presley. I, personally, haven't got the right to kick. With you wheat-growing people I guess it's different, but hops, you see, don't count for much in the State. It's such a little business that the road don't want to bother themselves to tax it. It's the wheat growers that the road cinches. The rates on hops ARE FAIR. I've got to admit that; I was in to Bonneville a while ago to find out. It's two cents a pound, and Lord love you, that's reasonable enough to suit any man. No," he concluded, "I'm on the way to make money now. The road sacking me as they did was, maybe, a good thing for me, after all. It came just at the right time. I had a bit of money put by and here was the chance to go into hops with the certainty that hops would quadruple and quintuple in price inside the year. No, it was my chance, and though they didn't mean it by a long chalk, the railroad people did me a good turn when they gave me my time—and the tad'll enter the seminary next fall."

About a quarter of an hour after they had said goodbye to the one-time engineer, Presley and Vanamee, tramping briskly along the road that led northward through Quien Sabe, arrived at Annixter's ranch house. At once they were aware of a vast and unwonted bustle that revolved about the place. They stopped a few moments looking on, amused and interested in what was going forward.

The colossal barn was finished. Its freshly white-washed sides glared intolerably in the sun, but its interior was as yet innocent of paint and through the yawning vent of the sliding doors came a delicious odour of new, fresh wood and shavings. A crowd of men—Annixter's farm hands— were swarming all about it. Some were balanced on the topmost rounds of ladders, hanging festoons of Japanese lanterns from tree to tree, and all across the front of the barn itself. Mrs. Tree, her daughter Hilma and another woman were inside the barn cutting into long strips bolt after bolt of red, white and blue cambric and directing how these strips should be draped from the ceiling and on the walls; everywhere resounded the tapping of tack hammers. A farm wagon drove up loaded to overflowing with evergreens and with great bundles of palm leaves, and these were immediately seized upon and affixed as supplementary decorations to the tri-coloured cambric upon the inside walls of the barn. Two of the larger evergreen trees were placed on either side the barn door and their tops bent over to form an arch. In the middle of this arch it was proposed to hang a mammoth pasteboard escutcheon with gold letters, spelling the word WELCOME. Piles of chairs, rented from I.O.O.F. hall in Bonneville, heaped themselves in an apparently hopeless entanglement on the ground; while at the far extremity of the barn a couple of carpenters clattered about the impromptu staging which was to accommodate the band.

There was a strenuous gayety in the air; everybody was in the best of spirits. Notes of laughter continually interrupted the conversation on every hand. At every moment a group of men involved themselves in uproarious horse-play. They passed oblique jokes behind their hands to each other—grossly veiled double-meanings meant for the women—and bellowed with laughter thereat, stamping on the ground. The relations between the sexes grew more intimate, the women and girls pushing the young fellows away from their sides with vigorous thrusts of their elbows. It was passed from group to group that Adela Vacca, a division superintendent's wife, had lost her garter; the daughter of the foreman of the Home ranch was kissed behind the door of the dairy-house.

Annixter, in execrable temper, appeared from time to time, hatless, his stiff yellow hair in wild disorder. He hurried between the barn and the ranch house, carrying now a wickered demijohn, now a case of wine, now a basket of lemons and pineapples. Besides general supervision, he had elected to assume the responsibility of composing the punch—something stiff, by jingo, a punch that would raise you right out of your boots; a regular hairlifter.

The harness room of the barn he had set apart for: himself and intimates. He had brought a long table down from the house and upon it had set out boxes of cigars, bottles of whiskey and of beer and the great china bowls for the punch. It would be no fault of his, he declared, if half the number of his men friends were not uproarious before they left. His barn dance would be the talk of all Tulare County for years to come. For this one day he had resolved to put all thoughts of business out of his head. For the matter of that, things were going well enough. Osterman was back from Los Angeles with a favourable report as to his affair with Disbrow and Darrell. There had been another meeting of the committee. Harran Derrick had attended. Though he had taken no part in the discussion, Annixter was satisfied. The Governor had consented to allow Harran to "come in," if he so desired, and

Harran had pledged himself to share one-sixth of the campaign expenses, providing these did not exceed a certain figure.

As Annixter came to the door of the barn to shout abuse at the distraught Chinese cook who was cutting up lemons in the kitchen, he caught sight of Presley and Vanamee and hailed them.

"Hello, Pres," he called. "Come over here and see how she looks;" he indicated the barn with a movement of his head. "Well, we're getting ready for you tonight," he went on as the two friends came up. "But how we are going to get straightened out by eight o'clock I don't know. Would you believe that pip Caraher is short of lemons—at this last minute and I told him I'd want three cases of 'em as much as a month ago, and here, just when I want a good lively saddle horse to get around on, somebody hikes the buckskin out the corral. STOLE her, by jingo. I'll have the law on that thief if it breaks me—and a sixty-dollar saddle 'n' head-stall gone with her; and only about half the number of Jap lanterns that I ordered have shown up and not candles enough for those. It's enough to make a dog sick. There's nothing done that you don't do yourself, unless you stand over these loafers with a club. I'm sick of the whole business—and I've lost my hat; wish to God I'd never dreamed of givin' this rotten fool dance. Clutter the whole place up with a lot of feemales. I sure did lose my presence of mind when I got THAT idea."

Then, ignoring the fact that it was he, himself, who had called the young men to him, he added:

"Well, this is my busy day. Sorry I can't stop and talk to you longer."

He shouted a last imprecation at the Chinaman and turned back into the barn. Presley and Vanamee went on, but Annixter, as he crossed the floor of the barn, all but collided with Hilma Tree, who came out from one of the stalls, a box of candles in her arms.

Gasping out an apology, Annixter reentered the harness room, closing the door behind him, and forgetting all the responsibility of the moment, lit a cigar and sat down in one of the hired chairs, his hands in his pockets, his feet on the table, frowning thoughtfully through the blue smoke.

Annixter was at last driven to confess to himself that he could not get the thought of Hilma Tree out of his mind. Finally she had "got a hold on him." The thing that of all others he most dreaded had happened. A feemale girl had got a hold on him, and now there was no longer for him any such thing as peace of mind. The idea of the young woman was with him continually. He went to bed with it; he got up with it. At every moment of the day he was pestered with it. It interfered with his work, got mixed up in his business. What a miserable confession for a man to make; a fine way to waste his time. Was it possible that only the other day he had stood in front of the music store in Bonneville and seriously considered making Hilma a present of a music-box? Even now, the very thought of it made him flush with shame, and this after she had told him plainly that she did not like him. He was running after her—he, Annixter! He ripped out a furious oath, striking the table with his boot heel. Again and again he had resolved to put the whole affair from out his mind. Once he had been able to do so, but of late it was becoming harder and harder with every successive day. He had only to close his eyes to see her as plain as if she stood before him; he saw her in a glory of sunlight that set a fine tinted lustre of pale carnation and gold on the silken sheen of her white skin, her hair sparkled with it, her thick, strong neck, sloping to her shoulders with beautiful, full curves, seemed to radiate the light; her eyes, brown, wide, innocent in expression, disclosing the full disc of the pupil upon the slightest provocation, flashed in this sunlight like diamonds.

Annixter was all bewildered. With the exception of the timid little creature in the glove-cleaning establishment in Sacramento, he had had no acquaintance with any woman. His world was harsh, crude, a world of men only—men who were to be combatted, opposed—his hand was against nearly every one of them. Women he distrusted with the instinctive distrust of the overgrown schoolboy. Now, at length, a young woman had come into his life. Promptly he was struck with discomfiture, annoyed almost beyond endurance, harassed, bedevilled, excited, made angry and exasperated. He was suspicious of the woman, yet desired her, totally ignorant of how to approach her, hating the sex, yet drawn to the individual, confusing the two emotions, sometimes even hating Hilma as a result of this confusion, but at all times disturbed, vexed, irritated beyond power of expression.

At length, Annixter cast his cigar from him and plunged again into the work of the day. The afternoon wore to evening, to the accompaniment of wearying and clamorous endeavour. In some unexplained fashion, the labour of putting the great barn in readiness for the dance was accomplished; the last bolt of cambric was hung in place from the rafters. The last evergreen tree was nailed to the joists of the walls; the last lantern hung, the last nail driven into the musicians' platform. The sun set. There was a great scurry to have supper and dress. Annixter, last of all the other workers, left the barn in the dusk of twilight. He was alone; he had a saw under one arm, a bag of tools was in his hand. He was in his shirt sleeves and carried his coat over his shoulder; a hammer was thrust into one of his hip pockets. He was in execrable temper. The day's work had fagged him out. He had not been able to find his hat.

"And the buckskin with sixty dollars' worth of saddle gone, too," he groaned. "Oh, ain't it sweet?"

At his house, Mrs. Tree had set out a cold supper for him, the inevitable dish of prunes serving as dessert. After supper Annixter bathed and dressed. He decided at the last moment to wear his usual town-going suit, a sack suit of black, made by a Bonneville tailor. But his hat was gone. There were other hats he might have worn, but because this particular one was lost he fretted about it all through his dressing and then decided to have one more look around the barn for it.

For over a quarter of an hour he pottered about the barn, going from stall to stall, rummaging the harness room and feed room, all to no purpose. At last he came out again upon the main floor, definitely giving up the search, looking about him to see if everything was in order.

The festoons of Japanese lanterns in and around the barn were not yet lighted, but some half-dozen lamps, with great, tin reflectors, that hung against the walls, were burning low. A dull half light pervaded the vast interior, hollow, echoing, leaving the corners and roof thick with impenetrable black shadows. The barn faced the west and through the open sliding doors was streaming a single bright bar from the after-glow, incongruous and out of all harmony with the dull flare of the kerosene lamps.

As Annixter glanced about him, he saw a figure step briskly out of the shadows of one corner of the building, pause for the fraction of one instant in the bar of light, then, at sight of him, dart back again. There was a sound of hurried footsteps.

Annixter, with recollections of the stolen buckskin in his mind, cried out sharply:

"Who's there?"

There was no answer. In a second his pistol was in his hand.

"Who's there? Quick, speak up or I'll shoot."

"No, no, no, don't shoot," cried an answering voice. "Oh, be careful. It's I—Hilma Tree."

Annixter slid the pistol into his pocket with a great qualm of apprehension. He came forward and met Hilma in the doorway.

"Good Lord," he murmured, "that sure did give me a start. If I HAD shot——"

Hilma stood abashed and confused before him. She was dressed in a white organdie frock of the most rigorous simplicity and wore neither flower nor ornament. The severity of her dress made her look even larger than usual, and even as it was her eyes were on a level with Annixter's. There was a certain fascination in the contradiction of stature and character of Hilma—a great girl, half-child as yet, but tall as a man for all that.

There was a moment's awkward silence, then Hilma explained:

"I—I came back to look for my hat. I thought I left it here this afternoon."

"And I was looking for my hat," cried Annixter. "Funny enough, hey?"

They laughed at this as heartily as children might have done. The constraint of the situation was a little relaxed and Annixter, with sudden directness, glanced sharply at the young woman and demanded:

"Well, Miss Hilma, hate me as much as ever?"

"Oh, no, sir," she answered, "I never said I hated you."

"Well,—dislike me, then; I know you said that."

"I—I disliked what you did—TRIED to do. It made me angry and it hurt me. I shouldn't have said what I did that time, but it was your fault."

"You mean you shouldn't have said you didn't like me?" asked Annixter. "Why?"

"Well, well,—I don't—I don't DISlike anybody," admitted Hilma.

"Then I can take it that you don't dislike ME? Is that it?"

"I don't dislike anybody," persisted Hilma.

"Well, I asked you more than that, didn't I?" queried Annixter uneasily. "I asked you to like me, remember, the other day. I'm asking you that again, now. I want you to like me."

Hilma lifted her eyes inquiringly to his. In her words was an unmistakable ring of absolute sincerity. Innocently she inquired:

"Why?"

Annixter was struck speechless. In the face of such candour, such perfect ingenuousness, he was at a loss for any words.

"Well—well," he stammered, "well—I don't know," he suddenly burst out. "That is," he went on, groping for his wits, "I can't quite say why." The idea of a colossal lie occurred to him, a thing actually royal.

"I like to have the people who are around me like me," he declared. "I—I like to be popular, understand? Yes, that's it," he continued, more reassured. "I don't like the idea of any one disliking me. That's the way I am. It's my nature."

"Oh, then," returned Hilma, "you needn't bother. No, I don't dislike you."

"Well, that's good," declared Annixter judicially. "That's good. But hold on," he interrupted, "I'm forgetting. It's not enough to not dislike me. I want you to like me. How about THAT?"

Hilma paused for a moment, glancing vaguely out of the doorway toward the lighted window of the dairy-house, her head tilted.

"I don't know that I ever thought about that," she said.

"Well, think about it now," insisted Annixter.

"But I never thought about liking anybody particularly," she observed. "It's because I like everybody, don't you see?"

"Well, you've got to like some people more than other people," hazarded Annixter, "and I want to be one of those 'some people,' savvy? Good Lord, I don't know how to say these fool things. I talk like a galoot when I get talking to feemale girls and I can't lay my tongue to anything that sounds right. It isn't my nature. And look here, I lied when I said I liked to have people like me—to be popular. Rot! I don't care a curse about people's opinions of me. But there's a few people that are more to me than most others—that chap Presley, for instance—and those people I DO want to have like me. What they think counts. Pshaw! I know I've got enemies; piles of them. I could name you half a dozen men right now that are naturally itching to take a shot at me. How about this ranch? Don't I know, can't I hear the men growling oaths under their breath after I've gone by? And in business ways, too," he went on, speaking half to himself, "in Bonneville and all over the county there's not a man of them wouldn't howl for joy if they got a chance to down Buck Annixter. Think I care? Why, I LIKE it. I run my ranch to suit myself and I play my game my own way. I'm a 'driver,' I know it, and a 'bully,' too. Oh, I know what they call me—'a brute beast, with a twist in my temper that would rile up a new-born lamb,' and I'm 'crusty' and 'pig-headed' and 'obstinate.' They say all that, but they've got to say, too, that I'm cleverer than any man-jack in the running. There's nobody can get ahead of me." His eyes snapped. "Let 'em grind their teeth. They can't 'down' me. When I shut my fist there's not one of them can open it. No, not with a CHISEL." He turned to Hilma again. "Well, when a man's hated as much as that, it stands to reason, don't it, Miss Hilma, that the few friends he has got he wants to keep? I'm not such an entire swine to the people that know me best—that jackass, Presley, for instance. I'd put my hand in the fire to do him a real service. Sometimes I get kind of lonesome; wonder if you would understand? It's my fault, but there's not a horse about the place that don't lay his ears back when I get on him; there's not a dog don't put his tail between his legs as soon as I come near him. The cayuse isn't foaled yet here on Quien Sabe that can throw me, nor the dog whelped that would dare show his teeth at me. I kick that Irish setter every time I see him—but wonder what I'd do, though, if he didn't slink so much, if he wagged his tail and was glad to see me? So it all comes to this: I'd like to have you—well, sort of feel that I was a good friend of yours and like me because of it."

The flame in the lamp on the wall in front of Hilma stretched upward tall and thin and began to smoke. She went over to where the lamp hung and, standing on tip-toe, lowered the wick. As she reached her hand up, Annixter noted how the sombre, lurid red of the lamp made a warm reflection on her smooth, round arm.

"Do you understand?" he queried.

"Yes, why, yes," she answered, turning around. "It's very good of you to want to be a friend of mine. I didn't think so, though, when you tried to kiss me. But maybe it's all right since you've explained things. You see I'm different from you. I like everybody to like me and I like to like everybody. It makes one so much happier. You wouldn't believe it, but you ought to try it, sir, just to see. It's so good to be good to people and to have people good to you. And everybody has always been so good to me. Mamma and papa, of course, and Billy, the stableman, and Montalegre, the Portugee foreman, and the Chinese cook, even, and Mr. Delaney—only he went away—and Mrs. Vacca and her little——"

"Delaney, hey?" demanded Annixter abruptly. "You and he were pretty good friends, were you?"

"Oh, yes," she answered. "He was just as GOOD to me. Every day in the summer time he used to ride over to the Seed ranch back of the Mission and bring me a great armful of flowers, the prettiest things, and I used to pretend to pay him for them with dollars made of cheese that I cut out of the cheese with a biscuit cutter. It was such fun. We were the best of friends."

"There's another lamp smoking," growled Annixter. "Turn it down, will you?—and see that somebody sweeps this floor here. It's all littered up with pine needles. I've got a lot to do. Good-bye."

"Good-bye, sir."

Annixter returned to the ranch house, his teeth clenched, enraged, his face flushed.

"Ah," he muttered, "Delaney, hey? Throwing it up to me that I fired him." His teeth gripped together more fiercely than ever. "The best of friends, hey? By God, I'll have that girl yet. I'll show that cow-puncher. Ain't I her employer, her boss? I'll show her—and Delaney, too. It would be easy enough—and then Delaney can have her—if he wants her—after me."

An evil light flashing from under his scowl, spread over his face. The male instincts of possession, unreasoned, treacherous, oblique, came twisting to the surface. All the lower nature of the man, ignorant of women, racked at one and the same time with enmity and desire, roused itself like a hideous and abominable beast. And at the same moment, Hilma returned to her house, humming to herself as she walked, her white dress glowing with a shimmer of faint saffron light in the last ray of the after-glow.

A little after half-past seven, the first carry-all, bearing the druggist of Bonneville and his women-folk, arrived in front of the new barn. Immediately afterward an express wagon loaded down with a swarming family of Spanish-Mexicans, gorgeous in red and yellow colours, followed. Billy, the stableman, and his assistant took charge of the teams, unchecking the horses and hitching them to a fence back of the barn. Then Caraher, the saloon-keeper, in "derby" hat, "Prince Albert" coat, pointed yellow shoes and inevitable red necktie, drove into the yard on his buckboard, the delayed box of lemons under the seat. It looked as if the whole array of invited guests was to arrive in one unbroken procession, but for a long half-hour nobody else appeared. Annixter and Caraher withdrew to the harness room and promptly involved themselves in a wrangle as to the make-up of the famous punch. From time to time their voices could be heard uplifted in clamorous argument.

"Two quarts and a half and a cupful of chartreuse."

"Rot, rot, I know better. Champagne straight and a dash of brandy."

The druggist's wife and sister retired to the feed room, where a bureau with a swinging mirror had been placed for the convenience of the women. The druggist stood awkwardly outside the door of the feed room, his coat collar turned up against the draughts that drifted through the barn, his face troubled, debating anxiously as to the propriety of putting on his gloves. The Spanish-Mexican family, a father, mother and five children and sister-in-law, sat rigid on the edges of the hired chairs, silent, constrained, their eyes lowered, their elbows in at their sides, glancing furtively from under their eyebrows at the decorations or watching with intense absorption young Vacca, son of one of the division superintendents, who wore a checked coat and white thread gloves and who paced up and down the length of the barn, frowning, very important, whittling a wax candle over the floor to make it slippery for dancing.

The musicians arrived, the City Band of Bonneville—Annixter having managed to offend the leader of the "Dirigo" Club orchestra, at the very last moment, to such a point that he had refused his services. These members of the City Band repaired at once to their platform in the corner. At every instant they laughed uproariously among themselves, joshing one of their number, a Frenchman, whom they called "Skeezicks." Their hilarity reverberated in a hollow, metallic roll among the rafters overhead. The druggist observed to young Vacca as he passed by that he thought them pretty fresh, just the same.

"I'm busy, I'm very busy," returned the young man, continuing on his way, still frowning and paring the stump of candle.

"Two quarts 'n' a half. Two quarts 'n' a half."

"Ah, yes, in a way, that's so; and then, again, in a way, it ISN'T. I know better."

All along one side of the barn were a row of stalls, fourteen of them, clean as yet, redolent of new cut wood, the sawdust still in the cracks of the flooring. Deliberately the druggist went from one to the other, pausing contemplatively before each. He returned down the line and again took up his position by the door of the feed room, nodding his head judicially, as if satisfied. He decided to put on his gloves.

By now it was quite dark. Outside, between the barn and the ranch houses one could see a group of men on step-ladders lighting the festoons of Japanese lanterns. In the darkness, only their faces appeared here and there, high above the ground, seen in a haze of red, strange, grotesque. Gradually as the multitude of lanterns were lit, the light spread. The grass underfoot looked like green excelsior. Another group of men invaded the barn itself, lighting the lamps and lanterns there. Soon the whole place was gleaming with points of light. Young Vacca, who had disappeared, returned with his pockets full of wax candles. He resumed his whittling, refusing to answer any questions, vociferating that he was busy.

Outside there was a sound of hoofs and voices. More guests had arrived. The druggist, seized with confusion, terrified lest he had put on his gloves too soon, thrust his hands into his pockets. It was Cutter, Magnus Derrick's division superintendent, who came, bringing his wife and her two girl cousins. They had come fifteen miles by the trail from the far distant division house on "Four" of Los Muertos and had ridden on horseback instead of driving. Mrs. Cutter could be heard declaring that she was nearly dead and felt more like going to bed than dancing. The two girl cousins, in dresses of dotted Swiss over blue sateen, were doing their utmost to pacify her. She could be heard protesting from moment to moment. One distinguished the phrases "straight to my bed," "back nearly broken in two," "never wanted to come in the first place." The druggist, observing Cutter take a pair of gloves from Mrs. Cutter's reticule, drew his hands from his pockets.

But abruptly there was an interruption. In the musicians' corner a scuffle broke out. A chair was overturned. There was a noise of imprecations mingled with shouts of derision. Skeezicks, the Frenchman, had turned upon the joshers.

"Ah, no," he was heard to exclaim, "at the end of the end it is too much. Kind of a bad canary — we will go to see about that. Aha, let him close up his face before I demolish it with a good stroke of the fist."

The men who were lighting the lanterns were obliged to intervene before he could be placated.

Hooven and his wife and daughters arrived. Minna was carrying little Hilda, already asleep, in her arms. Minna looked very pretty, striking even, with her black hair, pale face, very red lips and greenish-blue eyes. She was dressed in what had been Mrs. Hooven's wedding gown, a cheap affair of "farmer's satin." Mrs. Hooven had pendent earrings of imitation jet in her ears. Hooven was wearing an old frock coat of Magnus Derrick's, the sleeves too long, the shoulders absurdly too wide. He and Cutter at once entered into an excited conversation as to the ownership of a certain steer.

"Why, the brand——"

"Ach, Gott, der brendt," Hooven clasped his head, "ach, der brendt, dot maks me laugh some laughs. Dot's goot—der brendt—doand I see um—shoor der boole mit der bleck star bei der vore-head in der middle oaf. Any someones you esk tell you dot is mein boole. You esk any someones. Der brendt? To hell mit der brendt. You aindt got some memorie aboudt does ting I guess nodt."

"Please step aside, gentlemen," said young Vacca, who was still making the rounds of the floor.

Hooven whirled about. "Eh? What den," he exclaimed, still excited, willing to be angry at any one for the moment. "Doand you push soh, you. I tink berhapz you doand OWN dose barn, hey?"

"I'm busy, I'm very busy." The young man pushed by with grave preoccupation.

"Two quarts 'n' a half. Two quarts 'n' a half."

"I know better. That's all rot."

But the barn was filling up rapidly. At every moment there was a rattle of a newly arrived vehicle from outside. Guest after guest appeared in the doorway, singly or in couples, or in families, or in garrulous parties of five and six. Now it was Phelps and his mother from Los Muertos, now a foreman from Broderson's with his family, now a gayly apparelled clerk from a Bonneville store, solitary and bewildered, looking for a place to put his hat, now a couple of Spanish-Mexican girls from Guadalajara with coquettish effects of black and yellow about their dress, now a group of Osterman's tenants, Portuguese, swarthy, with plastered hair and curled mustaches, redolent of cheap perfumes. Sarria arrived, his smooth, shiny face glistening with perspiration. He wore a new cassock and carried his broad-brimmed hat under his arm. His appearance made quite a stir. He passed from group to group, urbane, affable, shaking hands right and left; he assumed a set smile of amiability which never left his face the whole evening.

But abruptly there was a veritable sensation. From out the little crowd that persistently huddled about the doorway came Osterman. He wore a dress-suit with a white waistcoat and patent leather pumps—what a wonder! A little qualm of excitement spread around the barn. One exchanged nudges of the elbow with one's neighbour, whispering earnestly behind the hand. What astonishing clothes! Catch on to the coat-tails! It was a masquerade costume, maybe; that goat Osterman was such a josher, one never could tell what he would do next.

The musicians began to tune up. From their corner came a medley of mellow sounds, the subdued chirps of the violins, the dull bourdon of the bass viol, the liquid gurgling of the flageolet and the deep-toned snarl of the big horn, with now and then a rasping stridulating of the snare drum. A sense of gayety began to spread throughout the assembly. At every moment the crowd increased. The aroma of new-sawn timber and sawdust began to be mingled with the feminine odour of sachet and flowers. There was a babel of talk in the air—male baritone and soprano chatter—varied by an occasional note of laughter and the swish of stiffly starched petticoats. On the row of chairs that went around three sides of the wall groups began to settle themselves. For a long time the guests huddled close to the doorway; the lower end of the floor was crowded! the upper end deserted; but by degrees the lines of white muslin and pink and blue sateen extended, dotted with the darker figures of men in black suits. The conversation grew louder as the timidity of the early moments wore off. Groups at a distance called back and forth; conversations were carried on at top voice. Once, even a whole party hurried across the floor from one side of the barn to the other.

Annixter emerged from the harness room, his face red with wrangling. He took a position to the right of the door, shaking hands with newcomers, inviting them over and over again to cut loose and whoop it along. Into the ears of his more intimate male acquaintances he dropped a word as to punch and cigars in the harness room later on, winking with vast intelligence. Ranchers from remoter parts of the country appeared: Garnett, from the Ruby rancho, Keast, from the ranch of the same name, Gethings, of the San Pablo, Chattern, of the Bonanza, and others and still others, a score of them—elderly men, for the most part, bearded, slow of speech, deliberate, dressed in broadcloth. Old Broderson, who entered with his wife on his arm, fell in with this type, and with them came a certain Dabney, of whom nothing but his name was known, a silent old man, who made no friends, whom nobody knew or spoke to, who was seen only upon such occasions as this, coming from no one knew where, going, no one cared to inquire whither.

Between eight and half-past, Magnus Derrick and his family were seen. Magnus's entry caused no little impression. Some said: "There's the Governor," and called their companions' attention to the thin, erect figure, commanding, imposing, dominating all in his immediate neighbourhood. Harran came with him, wearing a cut-away suit of black. He was undeniably handsome, young and fresh looking, his cheeks highly coloured, quite the finest looking of all the younger men; blond, strong, with that certain courtliness of manner that had always made him liked. He took his mother upon his arm and conducted her to a seat by the side of Mrs. Broderson.

Annie Derrick was very pretty that evening. She was dressed in a grey silk gown with a collar of pink velvet. Her light brown hair that yet retained so much of its brightness was transfixed by a high, shell comb, very Spanish. But the look of uneasiness in her large eyes—the eyes of a young girl—was deepening every day. The expression of innocence and inquiry which they so easily assumed, was disturbed by a faint suggestion of aversion, almost of terror. She settled herself in her place, in the corner of the hall, in the rear rank of chairs, a little frightened by the glare of lights, the hum of talk and the shifting crowd, glad to be out of the way, to attract no attention, willing to obliterate herself.

All at once Annixter, who had just shaken hands with Dyke, his mother and the little tad, moved abruptly in his place, drawing in his breath sharply. The crowd around the great, wide-open main door of the barn had somewhat thinned out and in the few groups that still remained there he had suddenly recognised Mr. and Mrs. Tree and Hilma, making their way towards some empty seats near the entrance of the feed room.

In the dusky light of the barn earlier in the evening, Annixter had not been able to see Hilma plainly. Now, however, as she passed before his eyes in the glittering radiance of the lamps and lanterns, he caught his breath in astonishment. Never had she appeared more beautiful in his eyes. It did not seem possible that this was the same girl whom he saw every day in and around the ranch house and dairy, the girl of simple calico frocks and plain shirt waists, who brought him his dinner, who made up his bed. Now he could not take his eyes from her. Hilma, for the first time, was wearing her hair done high upon her head. The thick, sweet-smelling masses, bitumen brown in the shadows, corruscated like golden filaments in the light. Her organdie frock was long, longer than any she had yet worn. It left a little of her neck and breast bare and all of her arm.

Annixter muttered an exclamation. Such arms! How did she manage to keep them hid on ordinary occasions. Big at the shoulder, tapering with delicious modulations to the elbow and wrist, overlaid with a delicate, gleaming lustre. As often as she turned her head the movement sent a slow undulation over her neck and shoulders, the pale amber-tinted shadows under her chin, coming and going over the creamy whiteness of the skin like the changing moire of silk. The pretty rose colour of her cheek had deepened to a pale carnation. Annixter, his hands clasped behind him, stood watching.

In a few moments Hilma was surrounded by a group of young men, clamouring for dances. They came from all corners of the barn, leaving the other girls precipitately, almost rudely. There could be little doubt as to who was to be the belle of the occasion. Hilma's little triumph was immediate, complete. Annixter could hear her voice from time to time, its usual velvety huskiness vibrating to a note of exuberant gayety.

All at once the orchestra swung off into a march—the Grand March. There was a great rush to secure "partners." Young Vacca, still going the rounds, was pushed to one side. The gayly apparelled clerk from the Bonneville store lost his head in the confusion. He could not find his "partner." He roamed wildly about the barn, bewildered, his eyes rolling. He resolved to prepare an elaborate programme card on the back of an old envelope. Rapidly the line was formed, Hilma and Harran Derrick in the lead, Annixter having obstinately refused to engage in either march, set or dance the whole evening. Soon the confused shuffling of feet settled to a measured cadence; the orchestra blared and wailed, the snare drum, rolling at exact intervals, the cornet marking the time. It was half-past eight o'clock.

Annixter drew a long breath:

"Good," he muttered, "the thing is under way at last."

Singularly enough, Osterman also refused to dance. The week before he had returned from Los Angeles, bursting with the importance of his mission. He had been successful. He had Disbrow "in his pocket." He was impatient to pose before the others of the committee as a skilful political agent, a manipulator. He forgot his attitude of the early part of the evening when he had drawn attention to himself with his wonderful clothes. Now his comic actor's face, with its brownish-red cheeks, protuberant ears and horizontal slit of a mouth, was overcast with gravity. His bald forehead was seamed with the wrinkles of responsibility. He drew Annixter into one of the empty stalls and began an elaborate explanation, glib, voluble, interminable, going over again in detail what he had reported to the committee in outline.

"I managed—I schemed—I kept dark—I lay low——"

But Annixter refused to listen.

"Oh, rot your schemes. There's a punch in the harness room that will make the hair grow on the top of your head in the place where the hair ought to grow. Come on, we'll round up some of the boys and walk into it."

They edged their way around the hall outside "The Grand March," toward the harness room, picking up on their way Caraher, Dyke, Hooven and old Broderson. Once in the harness room, Annixter shot the bolt.

"That affair outside," he observed, "will take care of itself, but here's a little orphan child that gets lonesome without company."

Annixter began ladling the punch, filling the glasses.

Osterman proposed a toast to Quien Sabe and the Biggest Barn. Their elbows crooked in silence. Old Broderson set down his glass, wiping his long beard and remarking:

"That—that certainly is very—very agreeable. I remember a punch I drank on Christmas day in '83, or no, it was '84—anyhow, that punch—it was in Ukiah—'TWAS '83—" He wandered on aimlessly, unable to stop his flow of speech, losing himself in details, involving his talk in a hopeless maze of trivialities to which nobody paid any attention.

"I don't drink myself," observed Dyke, "but just a taste of that with a lot of water wouldn't be bad for the little tad. She'd think it was lemonade." He was about to mix a glass for Sidney, but thought better of it at the last moment.

"It's the chartreuse that's lacking," commented Caraher, lowering at Annixter. The other flared up on the instant.

"Rot, rot. I know better. In some punches it goes; and then, again, in others it don't."

But it was left to Hooven to launch the successful phrase:

"Gesundheit," he exclaimed, holding out his second glass. After drinking, he replaced it on the table with a long breath. "Ach Gott!" he cried, "dat poonsch, say I tink dot poonsch mek some demn goot vertilizer, hey?"

Fertiliser! The others roared with laughter.

"Good eye, Bismarck," commented Annixter. The name had a great success. Thereafter throughout the evening the punch was invariably spoken of as the "Fertiliser." Osterman, having spilt the bottom of a glassful on the floor, pretended that he saw shoots of grain coming up on the spot. Suddenly he turned upon old Broderson. "I'm bald, ain't I? Want to know how I lost my hair? Promise you won't ask a single other question and I'll tell you. Promise your word of honour."

"Eh? What—wh—I—I don't understand. Your hair? Yes, I'll promise. How did you lose it?"

"It was bit off."

The other gazed at him stupefied; his jaw dropped. The company shouted, and old Broderson, believing he had somehow accomplished a witticism, chuckled in his beard, wagging his head. But suddenly he fell grave, struck with an idea. He demanded:

"Yes—I know—but—but what bit it off?"

"Ah," vociferated Osterman, "that's JUST what you promised not to ask."

The company doubled up with hilarity. Caraher leaned against the door, holding his sides, but Hooven, all abroad, unable to follow, gazed from face to face with a vacant grin, thinking it was still a question of his famous phrase.

"Vertilizer, hey? Dots some fine joke, hey? You bedt."

What with the noise of their talk and laughter, it was some time before Dyke, first of all, heard a persistent knocking on the bolted door. He called Annixter's attention to the sound. Cursing the intruder, Annixter unbolted and opened the door. But at once his manner changed.

"Hello. It's Presley. Come in, come in, Pres."

There was a shout of welcome from the others. A spirit of effusive cordiality had begun to dominate the gathering. Annixter caught sight of Vanamee back of Presley, and waiving for the moment the distinction of employer and employee, insisted that both the friends should come in.

"Any friend of Pres is my friend," he declared.

But when the two had entered and had exchanged greetings, Presley drew Annixter aside.

"Vanamee and I have just come from Bonneville," he explained. "We saw Delaney there. He's got the buckskin, and he's full of bad whiskey and dago-red. You should see him; he's wearing all his cow-punching outfit, hair trousers, sombrero, spurs and all the rest of it, and he has strapped himself to a big revolver. He says he wasn't invited to your barn dance but that he's coming over to shoot up the place. He says you promised to show him off Quien Sabe at the toe of your boot and that he's going to give you the chance to-night!" "Ah," commented Annixter, nodding his head, "he is, is he?"

Presley was disappointed. Knowing Annixter's irascibility, he had expected to produce a more dramatic effect. He began to explain the danger of the business. Delaney had once knifed a greaser in the Panamint country. He was known as a "bad" man. But Annixter refused to be drawn.

"All right," he said, "that's all right. Don't tell anybody else. You might scare the girls off. Get in and drink."

Outside the dancing was by this time in full swing. The orchestra was playing a polka. Young Vacca, now at his fiftieth wax candle, had brought the floor to the slippery surface of glass. The druggist was dancing with one of the Spanish-Mexican girls with the solemnity of an automaton, turning about and about, always in the same direction, his eyes glassy, his teeth set. Hilma Tree was dancing for the second time with Harran Derrick. She danced with infinite grace. Her cheeks were bright red, her eyes half-closed, and through her parted lips she drew from time to time a long, tremulous breath of pure delight. The music, the weaving colours, the heat of the air, by now a little oppressive, the monotony of repeated sensation, even the pain of physical fatigue had exalted all her senses. She was in a dreamy lethargy of happiness. It was her "first ball." She could have danced without stopping until morning. Minna Hooven and Cutter were "promenading." Mrs. Hooven, with little Hilda already asleep on her knees, never took her eyes from her daughter's gown. As often as Minna passed near her she vented an energetic "pst! pst!" The metal tip of a white draw string was showing from underneath the waist of Minna's dress. Mrs. Hooven was on the point of tears.

The solitary gayly apparelled clerk from Bonneville was in a fever of agitation. He had lost his elaborate programme card. Bewildered, beside himself with trepidation, he hurried about the room, jostled by the dancing couples, tripping over the feet of those who were seated; he peered distressfully under the chairs and about the floor, asking anxious questions.

Magnus Derrick, the centre of a listening circle of ranchers—Garnett from the Ruby rancho, Keast from the ranch of the same name, Gethings and Chattern of the San Pablo and Bonanza—stood near the great open doorway of the barn, discussing the possibility of a shortage in the world's wheat crop for the next year.

Abruptly the orchestra ceased playing with a roll of the snare drum, a flourish of the cornet and a prolonged growl of the bass viol. The dance broke up, the couples hurrying to their seats, leaving the gayly apparelled clerk suddenly isolated in the middle of the floor, rolling his eyes. The druggist released the Spanish-Mexican girl with mechanical precision out amidst the crowd of dancers. He bowed, dropping his chin upon his cravat; throughout the dance neither had hazarded a word. The girl found her way alone to a chair, but the druggist, sick from continually revolving in the same direction, walked unsteadily toward the wall. All at once the barn reeled around him; he fell down. There was a great laugh, but he scrambled to his feet and disappeared abruptly out into the night through the doorway of the barn, deathly pale, his hand upon his stomach.

Dabney, the old man whom nobody knew, approached the group of ranchers around Magnus Derrick and stood, a little removed, listening gravely to what the governor was saying, his chin sunk in his collar, silent, offering no opinions.

But the leader of the orchestra, with a great gesture of his violin bow, cried out:

"All take partners for the lancers and promenade around the hall!"

However, there was a delay. A little crowd formed around the musicians' platform; voices were raised; there was a commotion. Skeezicks, who played the big horn, accused the cornet and the snare-drum of stealing his cold lunch. At intervals he could be heard expostulating:

"Ah, no! at the end of the end! Render me the sausages, you, or less I break your throat! Aha! I know you. You are going to play me there a bad farce. My sausages and the pork sandwich, else I go away from this place!"

He made an exaggerated show of replacing his big horn in its case, but the by-standers raised a great protest. The sandwiches and one sausage were produced; the other had disappeared. In the end Skeezichs allowed himself to be appeased. The dance was resumed.

Half an hour later the gathering in the harness room was considerably reinforced. It was the corner of the barn toward which the male guests naturally gravitated. Harran Derrick, who only cared to dance with Hilma Tree, was admitted. Garnett from the Ruby rancho and Gethings from the San Pablo, came in a little afterwards. A fourth bowl of punch was mixed, Annixter and Caraher clamouring into each other's face as to its ingredients. Cigars were lighted. Soon the air of the room became blue with an acrid haze of smoke. It was very warm. Ranged in their chairs around the side of the room, the guests emptied glass after glass.

Vanamee alone refused to drink. He sat a little to one side, disassociating himself from what was going forward, watching the others calmly, a little contemptuously, a cigarette in his fingers.

Hooven, after drinking his third glass, however, was afflicted with a great sadness; his breast heaved with immense sighs. He asserted that he was "obbressed;" Cutter had taken his steer. He retired to a corner and seated himself in a heap on his chair, his heels on the rungs, wiping the tears from his eyes, refusing to be comforted. Old Broderson startled Annixter, who sat next to him, out of all measure by suddenly winking at him with infinite craftiness.

"When I was a lad in Ukiah," he whispered hoarsely, "I was a devil of a fellow with the girls; but Lordy!" he nudged him slyly, "I wouldn't have it known!"

Of those who were drinking, Annixter alone retained all his wits. Though keeping pace with the others, glass for glass, the punch left him solid upon his feet, clear-headed. The tough, cross-grained fibre of him seemed proof against alcohol. Never in his life had he been drunk. He prided himself upon his power of resistance. It was his nature.

"Say!" exclaimed old Broderson, gravely addressing the company, pulling at his beard uneasily—"say! I—I—listen! I'm a devil of a fellow with the girls." He wagged his head doggedly, shutting his eyes in a knowing fashion. "Yes, sir, I am. There was a young lady in Ukiah—that was when I was a lad of seventeen. We used to meet in the cemetery in the afternoons. I was to go away to school at Sacramento, and the afternoon I left we met in the cemetery and we stayed so long I almost missed the train. Her name was Celestine."

There was a pause. The others waited for the rest of the story.

"And afterwards?" prompted Annixter.

"Afterwards? Nothing afterwards. I never saw her again. Her name was Celestine."

The company raised a chorus of derision, and Osterman cried ironically:

"Say! THAT'S a pretty good one! Tell us another."

The old man laughed with the rest, believing he had made another hit. He called Osterman to him, whispering in his ear:

"Sh! Look here! Some night you and I will go up to San Francisco—hey? We'll go skylarking. We'll be gay. Oh, I'm a—a—a rare old BUCK, I am! I ain't too old. You'll see."

Annixter gave over the making of the fifth bowl of punch to Osterman, who affirmed that he had a recipe for a "fertiliser" from Solotari that would take the plating off the ladle. He left him wrangling with Caraher, who still persisted in adding chartreuse, and stepped out into the dance to see how things were getting on.

It was the interval between two dances. In and around a stall at the farther end of the floor, where lemonade was being served, was a great throng of young men. Others hurried across the floor singly or by twos and threes, gingerly carrying overflowing glasses to their "partners," sitting in long rows of white and blue and pink against the opposite wall, their mothers and older sisters in a second dark-clothed rank behind them. A babel of talk was in the air, mingled with gusts of laughter. Everybody seemed having a good time. In the increasing heat the decorations of evergreen trees and festoons threw off a pungent aroma that suggested a Sunday-school Christmas festival. In the other stalls, lower down the barn, the young men had brought chairs, and in these deep recesses the most desperate love-making was in progress, the young man, his hair neatly parted, leaning with great solicitation over the girl, his "partner" for the moment, fanning her conscientiously, his arm carefully laid along the back of her chair.

By the doorway, Annixter met Sarria, who had stepped out to smoke a fat, black cigar. The set smile of amiability was still fixed on the priest's smooth, shiny face; the cigar ashes had left grey streaks on the front of his cassock. He avoided Annixter, fearing, no doubt, an allusion to his game cocks, and took up his position back of the second rank of chairs by the musicians' stand, beaming encouragingly upon every one who caught his eye.

Annixter was saluted right and left as he slowly went the round of the floor. At every moment he had to pause to shake hands and to listen to congratulations upon the size of his barn and the success of his dance. But he was distrait, his thoughts elsewhere; he did not attempt to hide his impatience when some of the young men tried to engage him in conversation, asking him to be introduced to their sisters, or their friends' sisters. He sent them about their business harshly, abominably rude, leaving a wake of angry disturbance behind him, sowing the seeds of future quarrels and renewed unpopularity. He was looking for Hilma Tree.

When at last he came unexpectedly upon her, standing near where Mrs. Tree was seated, some half-dozen young men hovering uneasily in her neighbourhood, all his audacity was suddenly stricken from him; his gruffness, his overbearing insolence vanished with an abruptness that left him cold. His old-time confusion and embarrassment returned to him. Instead of speaking to her as he intended, he affected not to see her, but passed by, his head in the air, pretending a sudden interest in a Japanese lantern that was about to catch fire.

But he had had a single distinct glimpse of her, definite, precise, and this glimpse was enough. Hilma had changed. The change was subtle, evanescent, hard to define, but not the less unmistakable. The excitement, the enchanting delight, the delicious disturbance of "the first ball," had produced its result. Perhaps there had only been this lacking. It was hard to say, but for that brief instant of time Annixter was looking at Hilma, the woman. She was no longer the young girl upon whom he might look down, to whom he might condescend, whose little, infantile graces were to be considered with amused toleration.

When Annixter returned to the harness room, he let himself into a clamour of masculine hilarity. Osterman had, indeed, made a marvellous "fertiliser," whiskey for the most part, diluted with champagne and lemon juice. The first round of this drink had been welcomed with a salvo of cheers. Hooven, recovering his spirits under its violent stimulation, spoke of "heving ut oudt mit Cudder, bei Gott," while Osterman, standing on a chair at the end of the room, shouted for a "few moments quiet, gentlemen," so that he might tell a certain story he knew. But, abruptly, Annixter discovered that the liquors—the champagne, whiskey, brandy, and the like—were running low. This would never do. He felt that he would stand disgraced if it could be said afterward that he had not provided sufficient drink at his entertainment. He slipped out, unobserved, and, finding two of his ranch hands near the doorway, sent them down to the ranch house to bring up all the cases of "stuff" they found there.

However, when this matter had been attended to, Annixter did not immediately return to the harness room. On the floor of the barn a square dance was under way, the leader of the City Band calling the figures. Young Vacca indefatigably continued the rounds of the barn, paring candle after candle, possessed with this single idea of duty, pushing the dancers out of his way, refusing to admit that the floor was yet sufficiently slippery. The druggist had returned indoors, and leaned dejected and melancholy against the wall near the doorway, unable to dance, his evening's enjoyment spoiled. The gayly apparelled clerk from Bonneville had just involved himself in a deplorable incident. In a search for his handkerchief, which he had lost while trying to find his programme card, he had inadvertently wandered into the feed room, set apart as the ladies' dressing room, at the moment when Mrs. Hooven, having removed the waist of Minna's dress, was relacing her corsets. There was a tremendous scene. The clerk was ejected forcibly, Mrs. Hooven filling all the neighbourhood with shrill expostulation. A young man, Minna's "partner," who stood near the feed room door, waiting for her to come out, had invited the clerk, with elaborate sarcasm, to step outside for a moment; and the clerk, breathless, stupefied, hustled from hand to hand, remained petrified, with staring eyes, turning about and about, looking wildly from face to face, speechless, witless, wondering what had happened.

But the square dance was over. The City Band was just beginning to play a waltz. Annixter assuring himself that everything was going all right, was picking his way across the floor, when he came upon Hilma Tree quite alone, and looking anxiously among the crowd of dancers.

"Having a good time, Miss Hilma?" he demanded, pausing for a moment.

"Oh, am I, JUST!" she exclaimed. "The best time—but I don't know what has become of my partner. See! I'm left all alone—the only time this whole evening," she added proudly. "Have you seen him—my partner, sir? I forget his name. I only met him this evening, and I've met SO many I can't begin to remember half of them. He was a young man from Bonneville—a clerk, I think, because I remember seeing him in a store there, and he wore the prettiest clothes!"

"I guess he got lost in the shuffle," observed Annixter. Suddenly an idea occurred to him. He took his resolution in both hands. He clenched his teeth.

"Say! look here, Miss Hilma. What's the matter with you and I stealing this one for ourselves? I don't mean to dance. I don't propose to make a jumping-jack of myself for some galoot to give me the laugh, but we'll walk around. Will you? What do you say?"

Hilma consented.

"I'm not so VERY sorry I missed my dance with that—that—little clerk," she said guiltily. "I suppose that's very bad of me, isn't it?"

Annixter fulminated a vigorous protest.

"I AM so warm!" murmured Hilma, fanning herself with her handkerchief; "and, oh! SUCH a good time as I have had! I was so afraid that I would be a wall-flower and sit up by mamma and papa the whole evening; and as it is, I have had every single dance, and even some dances I had to split. Oh-h!" she breathed, glancing lovingly around the barn, noting again the festoons of tri-coloured cambric, the Japanese lanterns, flaring lamps, and "decorations" of evergreen; "oh-h! it's all so lovely, just like a fairy story; and to think that it can't last but for one little evening, and that to-morrow morning one must wake up to the every-day things again!"

"Well," observed Annixter doggedly, unwilling that she should forget whom she ought to thank, "I did my best, and my best is as good as another man's, I guess."

Hilma overwhelmed him with a burst of gratitude which he gruffly pretended to deprecate. Oh, that was all right. It hadn't cost him much. He liked to see people having a good time himself, and the crowd did seem to be enjoying themselves. What did SHE think? Did things look lively enough? And how about herself—was she enjoying it?

Stupidly Annixter drove the question home again, at his wits' end as to how to make conversation. Hilma protested volubly she would never forget this night, adding:

"Dance! Oh, you don't know how I love it! I didn't know myself. I could dance all night and never stop once!"

Annixter was smitten with uneasiness. No doubt this "promenading" was not at all to her taste. Wondering what kind of a spectacle he was about to make of himself, he exclaimed:

"Want to dance now?"

"Oh, yes!" she returned.

They paused in their walk, and Hilma, facing him, gave herself into his arms. Annixter shut his teeth, the perspiration starting from his forehead. For five years he had abandoned dancing. Never in his best days had it been one of his accomplishments.

They hesitated a moment, waiting to catch the time from the musicians. Another couple bore down upon them at precisely the wrong moment, jostling them out of step. Annixter swore under his breath. His arm still about the young woman, he pulled her over to one corner.

"Now," he muttered, "we'll try again."

A second time, listening to the one-two-three, one-two-three cadence of the musicians, they endeavoured to get under way. Annixter waited the fraction of a second too long and stepped on Hilma's foot. On the third attempt, having worked out of the corner, a pair of dancers bumped into them once more, and as they were recovering themselves another couple caromed violently against Annixter so that he all but lost his footing. He was in a rage. Hilma, very embarrassed, was trying not to laugh, and thus they found themselves, out in the middle of the floor, continually jostled from their position, holding clumsily to each other, stammering excuses into one another's faces, when Delaney arrived.

He came with the suddenness of an explosion. There was a commotion by the doorway, a rolling burst of oaths, a furious stamping of hoofs, a wild scramble of the dancers to either side of the room, and there he was. He had ridden the buckskin at a gallop straight through the doorway and out into the middle of the floor of the barn.

Once well inside, Delaney hauled up on the cruel spade-bit, at the same time driving home the spurs, and the buckskin, without halting in her gait, rose into the air upon her hind feet, and coming down again with a thunder of iron hoofs upon the hollow floor, lashed out with both heels simultaneously, her back arched, her head between her knees. It was the running buck, and had not Delaney been the hardest buster in the county, would have flung him headlong like a sack of sand. But he eased off the bit, gripping the mare's flanks with his knees, and the buckskin, having long since known her master, came to hand quivering, the bloody spume dripping from the bit upon the slippery floor.

Delaney had arrayed himself with painful elaboration, determined to look the part, bent upon creating the impression, resolved that his appearance at least should justify his reputation of being "bad." Nothing was lacking—neither the campaign hat with upturned brim, nor the dotted blue handkerchief knotted behind the neck, nor the heavy gauntlets stitched with red, nor—this above all—the bear-skin "chaparejos," the hair trousers of the mountain cowboy, the pistol holster low on the thigh. But for the moment this holster was empty, and in his right hand, the hammer at full cock, the chamber loaded, the puncher flourished his teaser, an army Colt's, the lamplight dully reflected in the dark blue steel.

In a second of time the dance was a bedlam. The musicians stopped with a discord, and the middle of the crowded floor bared itself instantly. It was like sand blown from off a rock; the throng of guests, carried by an impulse that was not to be resisted, bore back against the sides of the barn, overturning chairs, tripping upon each other, falling down, scrambling to their feet again, stepping over one another, getting behind each other, diving under chairs, flattening themselves against the wall—a wild, clamouring pell-mell, blind, deaf, panic-stricken; a confused tangle of waving arms, torn muslin, crushed flowers, pale faces, tangled legs, that swept in all directions back from the centre of the floor, leaving Annixter and Hilma, alone, deserted, their arms about each other, face to face with Delaney, mad with alcohol, bursting with remembered insult, bent on evil, reckless of results.

After the first scramble for safety, the crowd fell quiet for the fraction of an instant, glued to the walls, afraid to stir, struck dumb and motionless with surprise and terror, and in the instant's silence that followed Annixter, his eyes on Delaney, muttered rapidly to Hilma:

"Get back, get away to one side. The fool MIGHT shoot."

There was a second's respite afforded while Delaney occupied himself in quieting the buckskin, and in that second of time, at this moment of crisis, the wonderful thing occurred. Hilma, turning from Delaney, her hands clasped on Annixter's arm, her eyes meeting his, exclaimed:

"You, too!"

And that was all; but to Annixter it was a revelation. Never more alive to his surroundings, never more observant, he suddenly understood. For the briefest lapse of time he and Hilma looked deep into each other's eyes, and from that moment on, Annixter knew that Hilma cared.

The whole matter was brief as the snapping of a finger. Two words and a glance and all was done. But as though nothing had occurred, Annixter pushed Hilma from him, repeating harshly:

"Get back, I tell you. Don't you see he's got a gun? Haven't I enough on my hands without you?"

He loosed her clasp and his eyes once more on Delaney, moved diagonally backwards toward the side of the barn, pushing Hilma from him. In the end he thrust her away so sharply that she gave back with a long stagger; somebody caught her arm and drew her in, leaving Annixter alone once more in the middle of the floor, his hands in his coat pockets, watchful, alert, facing his enemy.

But the cow-puncher was not ready to come to grapples yet. Fearless, his wits gambolling under the lash of the alcohol, he wished to make the most of the occasion, maintaining the suspense, playing for the gallery. By touches of the hand and knee he kept the buckskin in continual, nervous movement, her hoofs clattering, snorting, tossing her head, while he, himself, addressing himself to Annixter, poured out a torrent of invective.

"Well, strike me blind if it ain't old Buck Annixter! He was going to show me off Quien Sabe at the toe of his boot, was he? Well, here's your chance,—with the ladies to see you do it. Gives a dance, does he, high-falutin' hoe-down in his barn and forgets to invite his old broncho-bustin' friend. But his friend don't forget him; no, he don't. He remembers little things, does his broncho-bustin' friend. Likes to see a dance hisself on occasion, his friend does. Comes anyhow, trustin' his welcome will be hearty; just to see old Buck Annixter dance, just to show Buck Annixter's friends how Buck can dance—dance all by hisself, a little hen-on-a-hot-plate dance when his broncho-bustin' friend asks him so polite. A little dance for the ladies, Buck. This feature of the entertainment is alone worth the price of admission. Tune up, Buck. Attention now! I'll give you the key."

He "fanned" his revolver, spinning it about his index finger by the trigger-guard with incredible swiftness, the twirling weapon a mere blur of blue steel in his hand. Suddenly and without any apparent cessation of the movement, he fired, and a little splinter of wood flipped into the air at Annixter's feet.

"Time!" he shouted, while the buckskin reared to the report. "Hold on—wait a minute. This place is too light to suit. That big light yonder is in my eyes. Look out, I'm going to throw lead."

A second shot put out the lamp over the musicians' stand. The assembled guests shrieked, a frantic, shrinking quiver ran through the crowd like the huddling of frightened rabbits in their pen.

Annixter hardly moved. He stood some thirty paces from the buster, his hands still in his coat pockets, his eyes glistening, watchful. Excitable and turbulent in trifling matters, when actual bodily danger threatened he was of an abnormal quiet.

"I'm watching you," cried the other. "Don't make any mistake about that. Keep your hands in your COAT pockets, if you'd like to live a little longer, understand? And don't let me see you make a move toward your hip or your friends will be asked to identify you at the morgue to-morrow morning. When I'm bad, I'm called the Undertaker's Friend, so I am, and I'm that bad to-night that I'm scared of myself. They'll have to revise the census returns before I'm done with this place. Come on, now, I'm getting tired waiting. I come to see a dance."

"Hand over that horse, Delaney," said Annixter, without raising his voice, "and clear out."

The other affected to be overwhelmed with infinite astonishment, his eyes staring. He peered down from the saddle.

"Wh-a-a-t!" he exclaimed; "wh-a-a-t did you say? Why, I guess you must be looking for trouble; that's what I guess."

"There's where you're wrong, m'son," muttered Annixter, partly to Delaney, partly to himself. "If I was looking for trouble there wouldn't be any guess-work about it."

With the words he began firing. Delaney had hardly entered the barn before Annixter's plan had been formed. Long since his revolver was in the pocket of his coat, and he fired now through the coat itself, without withdrawing his hands.

Until that moment Annixter had not been sure of himself. There was no doubt that for the first few moments of the affair he would have welcomed with joy any reasonable excuse for getting out of the situation. But the sound of his own revolver gave him confidence. He whipped it from his pocket and fired again.

Abruptly the duel began, report following report, spurts of pale blue smoke jetting like the darts of short spears between the two men, expanding to a haze and drifting overhead in wavering strata. It was quite probable that no thought of killing each other suggested itself to either Annixter or Delaney. Both fired without aiming very deliberately. To empty their revolvers and avoid being hit was the desire common to both. They no longer vituperated each other. The revolvers spoke for them.

Long after, Annixter could recall this moment. For years he could with but little effort reconstruct the scene—the densely packed crowd flattened against the sides of the barn, the festoons of lanterns, the mingled smell of evergreens, new wood, sachets, and powder smoke; the vague clamour of distress and terror that rose from the throng of guests, the squealing of the buckskin, the uneven explosions of the revolvers, the reverberation of trampling hoofs, a brief glimpse of Harran Derrick's excited face at the door of the harness room, and in the open space in the centre of the floor, himself and Delaney, manoeuvring swiftly in a cloud of smoke.

Annixter's revolver contained but six cartridges. Already it seemed to him as if he had fired twenty times. Without doubt the next shot was his last. Then what? He peered through the blue haze that with every discharge thickened between him and the buster. For his own safety he must "place" at least one shot. Delaney's chest and shoulders rose suddenly above the smoke close upon him as the distraught buckskin reared again. Annixter, for the first time during the fight, took definite aim, but before he could draw the trigger there was a great shout and he was aware of the buckskin, the bridle trailing, the saddle empty, plunging headlong across the floor, crashing into the line of chairs. Delaney was scrambling off the floor. There was blood on the buster's wrist and he no longer carried his revolver. Suddenly he turned and ran. The crowd parted right and left before him as he made toward the doorway. He disappeared.

Twenty men promptly sprang to the buckskin's head, but she broke away, and wild with terror, bewildered, blind, insensate, charged into the corner of the barn by the musicians' stand. She brought up against the wall with cruel force and with impact of a sack of stones; her head was cut. She turned and charged again, bull-like, the blood streaming from her forehead.

The crowd, shrieking, melted before her rush. An old man was thrown down and trampled. The buckskin trod upon the dragging bridle, somersaulted into a confusion of chairs in one corner, and came down with a terrific clatter in a wild disorder of kicking hoofs and splintered wood. But a crowd of men fell upon her, tugging at the bit, sitting on her head, shouting, gesticulating. For five minutes she struggled and fought; then, by degrees, she recovered herself, drawing great sobbing breaths at long intervals that all but burst the girths, rolling her eyes in bewildered, supplicating fashion, trembling in every muscle, and starting and shrinking now and then like a young girl in hysterics. At last she lay quiet. The men allowed her to struggle to her feet. The saddle was removed and she was led to one of the empty stalls, where she remained the rest of the evening, her head low, her pasterns quivering, turning her head apprehensively from time to time, showing the white of one eye and at long intervals heaving a single prolonged sigh.

And an hour later the dance was progressing as evenly as though nothing in the least extraordinary had occurred. The incident was closed — that abrupt swoop of terror and impending death dropping down there from out the darkness, cutting abruptly athwart the gayety of the moment, come and gone with the swiftness of a thunderclap. Many of the women had gone home, taking their men with them; but the great bulk of the crowd still remained, seeing no reason why the episode should interfere with the evening's enjoyment, resolved to hold the ground for mere bravado, if for nothing else. Delaney would not come back, of that everybody was persuaded, and in case he should, there was not found wanting fully half a hundred young men who would give him a dressing down, by jingo! They had been too surprised to act when Delaney had first appeared, and before they knew where they were at, the buster had cleared out. In another minute, just another second, they would have shown him—yes, sir, by jingo!—ah, you bet!

On all sides the reminiscences began to circulate. At least one man in every three had been involved in a gun fight at some time of his life. "Ah, you ought to have seen in Yuba County one time—" "Why, in Butte County in the early days—" "Pshaw! this to-night wasn't anything! Why, once in a saloon in Arizona when I was there—" and so on, over and over again. Osterman solemnly asserted that he had seen a greaser sawn in two in a Nevada sawmill. Old Broderson had witnessed a Vigilante lynching in '55 on California Street in San Francisco. Dyke recalled how once in his engineering days he had run over a drunk at a street crossing. Gethings of the San Pablo had taken a shot at a highwayman. Hooven had bayonetted a French Chasseur at Sedan. An old Spanish-Mexican, a centenarian from Guadalajara, remembered Fremont's stand on a mountain top in San Benito County. The druggist had fired at a burglar trying to break into his store one New Year's eve. Young Vacca had seen a dog shot in Guadalajara. Father Sarria had more than once administered the sacraments to Portuguese desperadoes dying of gunshot wounds. Even the women recalled terrible scenes. Mrs. Cutter recounted to an interested group how she had seen a claim jumped in Placer County in 1851, when three men were shot, falling in a fusillade of rifle shots, and expiring later upon the floor of her kitchen while she looked on. Mrs. Dyke had been in a stage hold-up, when the shotgun messenger was murdered. Stories by the hundreds went the round of the company. The air was surcharged with blood, dying groans, the reek of powder smoke, the crack of rifles. All the legends of '49, the violent, wild life of the early days, were recalled to view, defiling before them there in an endless procession under the glare of paper lanterns and kerosene lamps.

But the affair had aroused a combative spirit amongst the men of the assembly. Instantly a spirit of aggression, of truculence, swelled up underneath waistcoats and starched shirt bosoms. More than one offender was promptly asked to "step outside." It was like young bucks excited by an encounter of stags, lowering their horns upon the slightest provocation, showing off before the does and fawns. Old quarrels were remembered. One sought laboriously for slights and insults, veiled in ordinary conversation. The sense of personal honour became refined to a delicate, fine point. Upon the slightest pretext there was a haughty drawing up of the figure, a twisting of the lips into a smile of scorn. Caraher spoke of shooting S. Behrman on sight before the end of the week. Twice it became necessary to separate Hooven and Cutter, renewing their quarrel as to the ownership of the steer. All at once Minna Hooven's "partner" fell upon the gayly apparelled clerk from Bonneville, pummelling him with his fists, hustling him out of the hall, vociferating that Miss Hooven had been grossly insulted. It took three men to extricate the clerk from his clutches, dazed, gasping, his collar unfastened and sticking up into his face, his eyes staring wildly into the faces of the crowd.

But Annixter, bursting with pride, his chest thrown out, his chin in the air, reigned enthroned in a circle of adulation. He was the Hero. To shake him by the hand was an honour to be struggled for. One clapped him on the back with solemn nods of approval. "There's the BOY for you;" "There was nerve for you;" "What's the matter with Annixter?" "How about THAT for sand, and how was THAT for a SHOT?" "Why, Apache Kid couldn't have bettered that." "Cool enough." "Took a steady eye and a sure hand to make a shot like that." "There was a shot that would be told about in Tulare County fifty years to come."

Annixter had refrained from replying, all ears to this conversation, wondering just what had happened. He knew only that Delaney had run, leaving his revolver and a spatter of blood behind him. By degrees, however, he ascertained that his last shot but one had struck Delaney's pistol hand, shattering it and knocking the revolver from his grip. He was overwhelmed with astonishment. Why, after the shooting began he had not so much as seen Delaney with any degree of plainness. The whole affair was a whirl.

"Well, where did YOU learn to shoot THAT way?" some one in the crowd demanded. Annixter moved his shoulders with a gesture of vast unconcern.

"Oh," he observed carelessly, "it's not my SHOOTING that ever worried ME, m'son."

The crowd gaped with delight. There was a great wagging of heads.

"Well, I guess not."

"No, sir, not much."

"Ah, no, you bet not."

When the women pressed around him, shaking his hands, declaring that he had saved their daughters' lives, Annixter assumed a pose of superb deprecation, the modest self-obliteration of the chevalier. He delivered himself of a remembered phrase, very elegant, refined. It was Lancelot after the tournament, Bayard receiving felicitations after the battle.

"Oh, don't say anything about it," he murmured. "I only did what any man would have done in my place."

To restore completely the equanimity of the company, he announced supper. This he had calculated as a tremendous surprise. It was to have been served at mid-night, but the irruption of Delaney had dislocated the order of events, and the tables were brought in an hour ahead of time. They were arranged around three sides of the barn and were loaded down with cold roasts of beef, cold chickens and cold ducks, mountains of sandwiches, pitchers of milk and lemonade, entire cheeses, bowls of olives, plates of oranges and nuts. The advent of this supper was received with a volley of applause. The musicians played a quick step. The company threw themselves upon the food with a great scraping of chairs and a vast rustle of muslins, tarletans, and organdies; soon the clatter of dishes was a veritable uproar. The tables were taken by assault. One ate whatever was nearest at hand, some even beginning with oranges and nuts and ending with beef and chicken. At the end the paper caps were brought on, together with the ice cream. All up and down the tables the pulled "crackers" snapped continually like the discharge of innumerable tiny rifles.

The caps of tissue paper were put on—"Phrygian Bonnets," "Magicians' Caps," "Liberty Caps;" the young girls looked across the table at their vis-a-vis with bursts of laughter and vigorous clapping of the hands.

The harness room crowd had a table to themselves, at the head of which sat Annixter and at the foot Harran. The gun fight had sobered Presley thoroughly. He sat by the side of Vanamee, who ate but little, preferring rather to watch the scene with calm observation, a little contemptuous when the uproar around the table was too boisterous, savouring of intoxication. Osterman rolled bullets of bread and shot them with astonishing force up and down the table, but the others—Dyke, old Broderson, Caraher, Harran Derrick, Hooven, Cutter, Garnett of the Ruby rancho, Keast from the ranch of the same name, Gethings of the San Pablo, and Chattern of the Bonanza— occupied themselves with eating as much as they could before the supper gave out. At a corner of the table, speechless, unobserved, ignored, sat Dabney, of whom nothing was known but his name, the silent old man who made no friends. He ate and drank quietly, dipping his sandwich in his lemonade.

Osterman ate all the olives he could lay his hands on, a score of them, fifty of them, a hundred of them. He touched no crumb of anything else. Old Broderson stared at him, his jaw fallen. Osterman declared he had once eaten a thousand on a bet. The men called each others' attention to him. Delighted to create a sensation, Osterman persevered. The contents of an entire bowl disappeared in his huge, reptilian slit of a mouth. His cheeks of brownish red were extended, his bald forehead glistened. Colics seized upon him. His stomach revolted. It was all one with him. He was satisfied, contented. He was astonishing the people.

"Once I swallowed a tree toad." he told old Broderson, "by mistake. I was eating grapes, and the beggar lived in me three weeks. In rainy weather he would sing. You don't believe that," he vociferated. "Haven't I got the toad at home now in a bottle of alcohol."

And the old man, never doubting, his eyes starting, wagged his head in amazement.

"Oh, yes," cried Caraher, the length of the table, "that's a pretty good one. Tell us another."

"That reminds me of a story," hazarded old Broderson uncertainly; "once when I was a lad in Ukiah, fifty years."

"Oh, yes," cried half a dozen voices, "THAT'S a pretty good one. Tell us another."

"Eh—wh—what?" murmured Broderson, looking about him. "I—I don't know. It was Ukiah. You—you—you mix me all up."

As soon as supper was over, the floor was cleared again. The guests clamoured for a Virginia reel. The last quarter of the evening, the time of the most riotous fun, was beginning. The young men caught the girls who sat next to them. The orchestra dashed off into a rollicking movement. The two lines were formed. In a second of time the dance was under way again; the guests still wearing the Phrygian bonnets and liberty caps of pink and blue tissue paper.

But the group of men once more adjourned to the harness room. Fresh boxes of cigars were opened; the seventh bowl of fertiliser was mixed. Osterman poured the dregs of a glass of it upon his bald head, declaring that he could feel the hair beginning to grow.

But suddenly old Broderson rose to his feet.

"Aha," he cackled, "I'M going to have a dance, I am. Think I'm too old? I'll show you young fellows. I'm a regular old ROOSTER when I get started."

He marched out into the barn, the others following, holding their sides. He found an aged Mexican woman by the door and hustled her, all confused and giggling, into the Virginia reel, then at its height. Every one crowded around to see. Old Broderson stepped off with the alacrity of a colt, snapping his fingers, slapping his thigh, his mouth widening in an excited grin. The entire company of the guests shouted. The City Band redoubled their efforts; and the old man, losing his head, breathless, gasping, dislocated his stiff joints in his efforts. He became possessed, bowing, scraping, advancing, retreating, wagging his beard, cutting pigeons' wings, distraught with the music, the clamour, the applause, the effects of the fertiliser.

Annixter shouted:

"Nice eye, Santa Claus."

But Annixter's attention wandered. He searched for Hilma Tree, having still in mind the look in her eyes at that swift moment of danger. He had not seen her since then. At last he caught sight of her. She was not dancing, but, instead, was sitting with her "partner" at the end of the barn near her father and mother, her eyes wide, a serious expression on her face, her thoughts, no doubt, elsewhere. Annixter was about to go to her when he was interrupted by a cry.

Old Broderson, in the midst of a double shuffle, had clapped his hand to his side with a gasp, which he followed by a whoop of anguish. He had got a stitch or had started a twinge somewhere. With a gesture of resignation, he drew himself laboriously out of the dance, limping abominably, one leg dragging. He was heard asking for his wife. Old Mrs. Broderson took him in charge. She jawed him for making an exhibition of himself, scolding as though he were a ten-year-old.

"Well, I want to know!" she exclaimed, as he hobbled off, dejected and melancholy, leaning upon her arm, "thought he had to dance, indeed! What next? A gay old grandpa, this. He'd better be thinking of his coffin."

It was almost midnight. The dance drew towards its close in a storm of jubilation. The perspiring musicians toiled like galley slaves; the guests singing as they danced.

The group of men reassembled in the harness room. Even Magnus Derrick condescended to enter and drink a toast. Presley and Vanamee, still holding themselves aloof, looked on, Vanamee more and more disgusted. Dabney, standing to one side, overlooked and forgotten, continued to sip steadily at his glass, solemn, reserved. Garnett of the Ruby rancho, Keast from the ranch of the same name, Gethings of the San Pablo, and Chattern of the Bonanza, leaned back in their chairs, their waist-coats unbuttoned, their legs spread wide, laughing—they could not tell why. Other ranchers, men whom Annixter had never seen, appeared in the room, wheat growers from places as far distant as Goshen and Pixley; young men and old, proprietors of veritable principalities, hundreds of thousands of acres of wheat lands, a dozen of them, a score of them; men who were strangers to each other, but who made it a point to shake hands with Magnus Derrick, the "prominent man" of the valley. Old Broderson, whom every one had believed had gone home, returned, though much sobered, and took his place, refusing, however, to drink another spoonful.

Soon the entire number of Annixter's guests found themselves in two companies, the dancers on the floor of the barn, frolicking through the last figures of the Virginia reel and the boisterous gathering of men in the harness room, downing the last quarts of fertiliser. Both assemblies had been increased. Even the older people had joined in the dance, while nearly every one of the men who did not dance had found their way into the harness room. The two groups rivalled each other in their noise. Out on the floor of the barn was a very whirlwind of gayety, a tempest of laughter, hand-clapping and cries of amusement. In the harness room the confused shouting and singing, the stamping of heavy feet, set a quivering reverberation in the oil of the kerosene lamps, the flame of the candles in the Japanese lanterns flaring and swaying in the gusts of hilarity. At intervals, between the two, one heard the music, the wailing of the violins, the vigorous snarling of the cornet, and the harsh, incessant rasping of the snare drum.

And at times all these various sounds mingled in a single vague note, huge, clamorous, that rose up into the night from the colossal, reverberating compass of the barn and sent its echoes far off across the unbroken levels of the surrounding ranches, stretching out to infinity under the clouded sky, calm, mysterious, still.

Annixter, the punch bowl clasped in his arms, was pouring out the last spoonful of liquor into Caraher's glass when he was aware that some one was pulling at the sleeve of his coat. He set down the punch bowl.

"Well, where did YOU come from?" he demanded.

It was a messenger from Bonneville, the uniformed boy that the telephone company employed to carry messages. He had just arrived from town on his bicycle, out of breath and panting.

"Message for you, sir. Will you sign?"

He held the book to Annixter, who signed the receipt, wondering.

The boy departed, leaving a thick envelope of yellow paper in Annixter's hands, the address typewritten, the word "Urgent" written in blue pencil in one corner.

Annixter tore it open. The envelope contained other sealed envelopes, some eight or ten of them, addressed to Magnus Derrick, Osterman, Broderson, Garnett, Keast, Gethings, Chattern, Dabney, and to Annixter himself.

Still puzzled, Annixter distributed the envelopes, muttering to himself:

"What's up now?"

The incident had attracted attention. A comparative quiet followed, the guests following the letters with their eyes as they were passed around the table. They fancied that Annixter had arranged a surprise.

Magnus Derrick, who sat next to Annixter, was the first to receive his letter. With a word of excuse he opened it.

"Read it, read it, Governor," shouted a half-dozen voices. "No secrets, you know. Everything above board here to-night."

Magnus cast a glance at the contents of the letter, then rose to his feet and read:

> *Magnus Derrick,*
>
> *Bonneville, Tulare Co., Cal.*
>
> *Dear Sir:*
>
> *By regrade of October 1st, the value of the railroad land you occupy, included in your ranch of Los Muertos, has been fixed at $27.00 per acre. The land is now for sale at that price to any one.*
>
> *Yours, etc.,*
>
> *CYRUS BLAKELEE RUGGLES,*
>
> *Land Agent, P. and S. W. R. R.*
>
> *S. BEHRMAN,*
>
> *Local Agent, P. and S. W. R. R.*

In the midst of the profound silence that followed, Osterman was heard to exclaim grimly:

"THAT'S a pretty good one. Tell us another."

But for a long moment this was the only remark.

The silence widened, broken only by the sound of torn paper as Annixter, Osterman, old Broderson, Garnett, Keast, Gethings, Chattern, and Dabney opened and read their letters. They were all to the same effect, almost word for word like the Governor's. Only the figures and the proper names varied. In some cases the price per acre was twenty-two dollars. In Annixter's case it was thirty.

"And—and the company promised to sell to me, to—to all of us," gasped old Broderson, "at TWO DOLLARS AND A HALF an acre."

It was not alone the ranchers immediately around Bonneville who would be plundered by this move on the part of the Railroad. The "alternate section" system applied throughout all the San Joaquin. By striking at the Bonneville ranchers a terrible precedent was established. Of the crowd of guests in the harness room alone, nearly every man was affected, every man menaced with ruin. All of a million acres was suddenly involved.

Then suddenly the tempest burst. A dozen men were on their feet in an instant, their teeth set, their fists clenched, their faces purple with rage. Oaths, curses, maledictions exploded like the firing of successive mines. Voices quivered with wrath, hands flung upward, the fingers hooked, prehensile, trembled with anger. The sense of wrongs, the injustices, the oppression, extortion, and pillage of twenty years suddenly culminated and found voice in a raucous howl of execration. For a second there was nothing articulate in that cry of savage exasperation, nothing even intelligent. It was the human animal hounded to its corner, exploited, harried to its last stand, at bay, ferocious, terrible, turning at last with bared teeth and upraised claws to meet the death grapple. It was the hideous squealing of the tormented brute, its back to the wall, defending its lair, its mate and its whelps, ready to bite, to rend, to trample, to batter out the life of The Enemy in a primeval, bestial welter of blood and fury.

The roar subsided to intermittent clamour, in the pauses of which the sounds of music and dancing made themselves audible once more.

"S. Behrman again," vociferated Harran Derrick.

"Chose his moment well," muttered Annixter. "Hits his hardest when we're all rounded up having a good time."

"Gentlemen, this is ruin."

"What's to be done now?"

"FIGHT! My God! do you think we are going to stand this? Do you think we CAN?"

The uproar swelled again. The clearer the assembly of ranchers understood the significance of this move on the part of the Railroad, the more terrible it appeared, the more flagrant, the more intolerable. Was it possible, was it within the bounds of imagination that this tyranny should be contemplated? But they knew—past years had driven home the lesson—the implacable, iron monster with whom they had to deal, and again and again the sense of outrage and oppression lashed them to their feet, their mouths wide with curses, their fists clenched tight, their throats hoarse with shouting.

"Fight! How fight? What ARE you going to do?"

"If there's a law in this land"

"If there is, it is in Shelgrim's pocket. Who owns the courts in California? Ain't it Shelgrim?"

"God damn him."

"Well, how long are you going to stand it? How long before you'll settle up accounts with six inches of plugged gas-pipe?"

"And our contracts, the solemn pledges of the corporation to sell to us first of all——"

"And now the land is for sale to anybody."

"Why, it is a question of my home. Am I to be turned out? Why, I have put eight thousand dollars into improving this land."

"And I six thousand, and now that I have, the Railroad grabs it."

"And the system of irrigating ditches that Derrick and I have been laying out. There's thousands of dollars in that!"

"I'll fight this out till I've spent every cent of my money."

"Where? In the courts that the company owns?"

"Think I am going to give in to this? Think I am to get off my land? By God, gentlemen, law or no law, railroad or no railroad, I—WILL—NOT."

"Nor I."

"Nor I."

"Nor I."

"This is the last. Legal means first; if those fail—the shotgun."

"They can kill me. They can shoot me down, but I'll die—die fighting for my home—before I'll give in to this."

At length Annixter made himself heard:

"All out of the room but the ranch owners," he shouted. "Hooven, Caraher, Dyke, you'll have to clear out. This is a family affair. Presley, you and your friend can remain."

Reluctantly the others filed through the door. There remained in the harness room—besides Vanamee and Presley—Magnus Derrick, Annixter, old Broderson Harran, Garnett from the Ruby rancho, Keast from the ranch of the same name, Gethings of the San Pablo, Chattern of the Bonanza, about a score of others, ranchers from various parts of the county, and, last of all, Dabney, ignored, silent, to whom nobody spoke and who, as yet, had not uttered a word. But the men who had been asked to leave the harness room spread the news throughout the barn. It was repeated from lip to lip. One by one the guests dropped out of the dance. Groups were formed. By swift degrees the gayety lapsed away. The Virginia reel broke up. The musicians ceased playing, and in the place of the noisy, effervescent revelry of the previous half hour, a subdued murmur filled all the barn, a mingling of whispers, lowered voices, the coming and going of light footsteps, the uneasy shifting of positions, while from behind the closed doors of the harness room came a prolonged, sullen hum of anger and strenuous debate. The dance came to an abrupt end. The guests, unwilling to go as yet, stunned, distressed, stood clumsily about, their eyes vague, their hands swinging at their sides, looking stupidly into each others' faces. A sense of impending calamity, oppressive, foreboding, gloomy, passed through the air overhead in the night, a long shiver of anguish and of terror, mysterious, despairing.

In the harness room, however, the excitement continued unchecked. One rancher after another delivered himself of a torrent of furious words. There was no order, merely the frenzied outcry of blind fury. One spirit alone was common to all—resistance at whatever cost and to whatever lengths.

Suddenly Osterman leaped to his feet, his bald head gleaming in the lamp-light, his red ears distended, a flood of words filling his great, horizontal slit of a mouth, his comic actor's face flaming. Like the hero of a melodrama, he took stage with a great sweeping gesture.

"ORGANISATION," he shouted, "that must be our watch-word. The curse of the ranchers is that they fritter away their strength. Now, we must stand together, now, NOW. Here's the crisis, here's the moment. Shall we meet it? I CALL FOR THE LEAGUE. Not next week, not to-morrow, not in the morning, but now, now, now, this very moment, before we go out of that door. Every one of us here to join it, to form the beginnings of a vast organisation, banded together to death, if needs be, for the protection of our rights and homes. Are you ready? Is it now or never? I call for the League."

Instantly there was a shout. With an actor's instinct, Osterman had spoken at the precise psychological moment. He carried the others off their feet, glib, dexterous, voluble. Just what was meant by the League the others did not know, but it was something, a vague engine, a machine with which to fight. Osterman had not done speaking before the room rang with outcries, the crowd of men shouting, for what they did not know.

"The League! The League!"

"Now, to-night, this moment; sign our names before we leave."

"He's right. Organisation! The League!"

"We have a committee at work already," Osterman vociferated. "I am a member, and also Mr. Broderson, Mr. Annixter, and Mr. Harran Derrick. What our aims are we will explain to you later. Let this committee be the nucleus of the League—temporarily, at least. Trust us. We are working for you and with you. Let this committee be merged into the larger committee of the League, and for President of the League"—he paused the fraction of a second—"for President there can be but one name mentioned, one man to whom we all must look as leader—Magnus Derrick."

The Governor's name was received with a storm of cheers. The harness room reechoed with shouts of:

"Derrick! Derrick!"

"Magnus for President!"

"Derrick, our natural leader."

"Derrick, Derrick, Derrick for President."

Magnus rose to his feet. He made no gesture. Erect as a cavalry officer, tall, thin, commanding, he dominated the crowd in an instant. There was a moment's hush. "Gentlemen," he said, "if organisation is a good word, moderation is a better one. The matter is too grave for haste. I would suggest that we each and severally return to our respective homes for the night, sleep over what has happened, and convene again to-morrow, when we are calmer and can approach this affair in a more judicious mood. As for the honour with which you would inform me, I must affirm that that, too, is a matter for grave deliberation. This League is but a name as yet. To accept control of an organisation whose principles are not yet fixed is a heavy responsibility. I shrink from it—"

But he was allowed to proceed no farther. A storm of protest developed. There were shouts of:

"No, no. The League to-night and Derrick for President."

"We have been moderate too long."

"The League first, principles afterward."

"We can't wait," declared Osterman. "Many of us cannot attend a meeting to-morrow. Our business affairs would prevent it. Now we are all together. I propose a temporary chairman and secretary be named and a ballot be taken. But first the League. Let us draw up a set of resolutions to stand together, for the defence of our homes, to death, if needs be, and each man present affix his signature thereto."

He subsided amidst vigorous applause. The next quarter of an hour was a vague confusion, every one talking at once, conversations going on in low tones in various corners of the room. Ink, pens, and a sheaf of foolscap were brought from the ranch house. A set of resolutions was draughted, having the force of a pledge, organising the League of Defence. Annixter was the first to sign. Others followed, only a few holding back, refusing to join till they had thought the matter over. The roll grew; the paper circulated about the table; each signature was welcomed by a salvo of cheers. At length, it reached Harran Derrick, who signed amid tremendous uproar. He released the pen only to shake a score of hands.

"Now, Magnus Derrick."

"Gentlemen," began the Governor, once more rising, "I beg of you to allow me further consideration. Gentlemen—"

He was interrupted by renewed shouting.

"No, no, now or never. Sign, join the League."

"Don't leave us. We look to you to help."

But presently the excited throng that turned their faces towards the Governor were aware of a new face at his elbow. The door of the harness room had been left unbolted and Mrs. Derrick, unable to endure the heart-breaking suspense of waiting outside, had gathered up all her courage and had come into the room. Trembling, she clung to Magnus's arm, her pretty light-brown hair in disarray, her large young girl's eyes wide with terror and distrust. What was about to happen she did not understand, but these men were clamouring for Magnus to pledge himself to something, to some terrible course of action, some ruthless, unscrupulous battle to the death with the iron-hearted monster of steel and steam. Nerved with a coward's intrepidity, she, who so easily obliterated herself, had found her way into the midst of this frantic crowd, into this hot, close room, reeking of alcohol and tobacco smoke, into this atmosphere surcharged with hatred and curses. She seized her husband's arm imploring, distraught with terror.

"No, no," she murmured; "no, don't sign."

She was the feather caught in the whirlwind. En masse, the crowd surged toward the erect figure of the Governor, the pen in one hand, his wife's fingers in the other, the roll of signatures before him. The clamour was deafening; the excitement culminated brusquely. Half a hundred hands stretched toward him; thirty voices, at top pitch, implored, expostulated, urged, almost commanded. The reverberation of the shouting was as the plunge of a cataract.

It was the uprising of The People; the thunder of the outbreak of revolt; the mob demanding to be led, aroused at last, imperious, resistless, overwhelming. It was the blind fury of insurrection, the brute, many-tongued, red-eyed, bellowing for guidance, baring its teeth, unsheathing its claws, imposing its will with the abrupt, resistless pressure of the relaxed piston, inexorable, knowing no pity.

"No, no," implored Annie Derrick. "No, Magnus, don't sign."

"He must," declared Harran, shouting in her ear to make himself heard, "he must. Don't you understand?"

Again the crowd surged forward, roaring. Mrs. Derrick was swept back, pushed to one side. Her husband no longer belonged to her. She paid the penalty for being the wife of a great man. The world, like a colossal iron wedge, crushed itself between. She was thrust to the wall. The throng of men, stamping, surrounded Magnus; she could no longer see him, but, terror-struck, she listened. There was a moment's lull, then a vast thunder of savage jubilation. Magnus had signed.

Harran found his mother leaning against the wall, her hands shut over her ears; her eyes, dilated with fear, brimming with tears. He led her from the harness room to the outer room, where Mrs. Tree and Hilma took charge of her, and then, impatient, refusing to answer the hundreds of anxious questions that assailed him, hurried back to the harness room. Already the balloting was in progress, Osterman acting as temporary chairman on the very first ballot he was made secretary of the League pro tem., and Magnus unanimously chosen for its President. An executive committee was formed, which was to meet the next day at the Los Muertos ranch house.

It was half-past one o'clock. In the barn outside the greater number of the guests had departed. Long since the musicians had disappeared. There only remained the families of the ranch owners involved in the meeting in the harness room. These huddled in isolated groups in corners of the garish, echoing barn, the women in their wraps, the young men with their coat collars turned up against the draughts that once more made themselves felt.

For a long half hour the loud hum of eager conversation continued to issue from behind the door of the harness room. Then, at length, there was a prolonged scraping of chairs. The session was over. The men came out in groups, searching for their families.

At once the homeward movement began. Every one was worn out. Some of the ranchers' daughters had gone to sleep against their mothers' shoulders.

Billy, the stableman, and his assistant were awakened, and the teams were hitched up. The stable yard was full of a maze of swinging lanterns and buggy lamps. The horses fretted, champing the bits; the carry-alls creaked with the straining of leather and springs as they received their loads. At every instant one heard the rattle of wheels as vehicle after vehicle disappeared in the night.

A fine, drizzling rain was falling, and the lamps began to show dim in a vague haze of orange light.

Magnus Derrick was the last to go. At the doorway of the barn he found Annixter, the roll of names—which it had been decided he was to keep in his safe for the moment—under his arm. Silently the two shook hands. Magnus departed. The grind of the wheels of his carry-all grated sharply on the gravel of the driveway in front of the ranch house, then, with a hollow roll across a little plank bridge, gained the roadway. For a moment the beat of the horses' hoofs made itself heard on the roadway. It ceased. Suddenly there was a great silence.

Annixter, in the doorway of the great barn, stood looking about him for a moment, alone, thoughtful. The barn was empty. That astonishing evening had come to an end. The whirl of things and people, the crowd of dancers, Delaney, the gun fight, Hilma Tree, her eyes fixed on him in mute confession, the rabble in the harness room, the news of the regrade, the fierce outburst of wrath, the hasty organising of the League, all went spinning confusedly through his recollection. But he was exhausted. Time enough in the morning to think it all over. By now it was raining sharply. He put the roll of names into his inside pocket, threw a sack over his head and shoulders, and went down to the ranch house.

But in the harness room, lighted by the glittering lanterns and flaring lamps, in the midst of overturned chairs, spilled liquor, cigar stumps, and broken glasses, Vanamee and Presley still remained talking, talking. At length, they rose, and came out upon the floor of the barn and stood for a moment looking about them.

Billy, the stableman, was going the rounds of the walls, putting out light after light. By degrees, the vast interior was growing dim. Upon the roof overhead the rain drummed incessantly, the eaves dripping. The floor was littered with pine needles, bits of orange peel, ends and fragments of torn organdies and muslins and bits of tissue paper from the "Phrygian Bonnets" and "Liberty Caps." The buckskin mare in the stall, dozing on three legs, changed position with a long sigh. The sweat stiffening the hair upon her back and loins, as it dried, gave off a penetrating, ammoniacal odour that mingled with the stale perfume of sachet and wilted flowers.

Presley and Vanamee stood looking at the deserted barn. There was a long silence. Then Presley said:

"Well... what do you think of it all?"

"I think," answered Vanamee slowly, "I think that there was a dance in Brussels the night before Waterloo."